The
Baddest
Chick
Part 5

On the Run

Buy

for Melodrama

JAN 2018

SF

The
Baddest
Chick
Part 5

On
the Run

NISA
SANTIAGO

This is a work of fiction. All of the characters, organizations, and events portrayed in this novel are
either products of the author's imagination or are
used fictitiously.

www. melodramapublishing.com

Library of Congress Control Number: 2015912277
ISBN-13: 978-1620780688
ISBN-10: 1620780682
Mass Market Edition: January 2017

Editor: Brian Sandy
Model Photo:  Marion Designs
Model: Vanessa

# ALSO BY NISA SANTIAGO

# ONE

The black Maybach slowly drove up to the large secluded mansion cradled in the luscious landscape and vast countryside with acres and acres of manicured lawns, trees, and secondary homes. The entire area was pure paradise stretching for miles—overflowing with greenery, rolling hills, and continuing warm weather. Under a clear blue sky, the SUV slowly came to a stop at the front entrance where four large pillars stretched high, making it look like the entrance to the White House in DC. This place was no White House, but it was made for a lord—a drug lord.

The chauffeur got out and hurried to open the passenger door behind him. He stood erect and quiet as Kola took her time exiting the black chariot. Holding her hand and exiting too was her nicely dressed niece, Peaches, smiling and excited to be home. Now five years old, she looked beautiful with her long, black hair flowing down to her small shoulders, her eyes framed by long lashes.

She was a precious little girl. When she laughed, the room would laugh with her. And if she wept, everyone wanted to comfort her. Kola had fallen in love with Peaches and treated her like she was her own daughter.

It was early evening now, and Kola had had a long day. She wanted to get some rest and enjoy a nice meal prepared by one of her top chefs in the home.

"Call the maids," an unsmiling Kola told the chauffeur. "Tell them to get my bags out of the trunk, take them up to my room. And I want the chef to prepare our lunch on the outside patio."

The chauffeur nodded. "Yes, Ms. Kola, they'll get right on it," he replied, jumping to her command.

She marched forward, Peaches' hand still clasped inside hers.

It seemed like the older Kola was lovelier and more exotic. Her eyes were bright with long lashes, her hair was raven-black dark, and her body was a man's dream come true—firm ass, slim waist that curved both up and down to beautiful thighs and breasts, high cheekbones, and sensual lips.

She'd just come from shopping. In the trunk of the Maybach was over a dozen shopping bags from various stores, all expensive and high quality.

Kola strutted inside the mansion, where the head butler stood in the large foyer to greet her. A tall, well-mannered man, Edward was there, like the other servants, to respond to her every beck and call.

"Welcome home, madam," he said civilly.

"Thank you, Edward," she replied quickly, walking by him. "Is Eduardo home?"

"Not yet, madam."

Kola sighed. Eduardo was never home, presumably always away on business. She had grown tired of his constant absence. Living a very comfortable life in Colombia, Kola had everything a woman could dream of—a niece she loved dearly, a beautiful home, power, and respect. The sex with Eduardo was still great, but there were times she felt lonely. Except for Peaches, she had no family left, since Apple and Nichols were dead, and her father and mother were gone.

She and Peaches went up to the second floor, into the master bedroom. Her bags from shopping were already placed inside the room.

Peaches went into her bedroom to play. Inside the cozy, pink room, the little girl had everything she wanted, including her own nanny. She had so many things to keep her busy. It looked like Toys "R" Us had exploded inside her room. There were teddy bears of all sizes, games, outfits, and expensive dolls. Some of the gifts came from Kola, but most of the toys were from Eduardo, who took to loving Peaches and raising her like she was his own daughter.

Kola undressed and walked toward the large mirror. She sighed. She gazed at herself for a moment, remaining silent, looking pensive. She was beginning to miss home, but she was a wanted woman in the States. She'd had to escape her old life and thrust herself into a whole new world. Colombia had been her home for quite some time. She'd gotten used to hearing their language, and knowing their ways. She barely spoke any Spanish, knowing only a few words or sentences. But Peaches spoke Spanish and English fluently, so she became Kola's translator.

Everything was different abroad. It took some time to get used to, but she still felt like she didn't belong sometimes.

Apple popped into her head. She missed her twin sister. It was hard to swallow that she was dead, murdered violently in a Miami fire; most likely by the cartel she went to war with. They'd been through a lot together, and she remembered at one time warring with Apple herself. It was stupid. She felt foolish. They were blood.

Then she started to think about Nichols. It'd been a long time since they'd buried their younger sister. Every soul responsible for Nichols' death paid with their life. Now with Apple dead too, Kola truly felt alone. She wished there was some way she could have kept Apple in Colombia. Maybe begged her to stay and work things out. But her sister was a rebellious woman. Apple wasn't happy in Colombia, and Kola couldn't force her to stay.

Kola began removing her items from the shopping bags—shoes, dresses, jewelry, and a few nice accessories. Nothing she'd bought was necessary, and she had more than she could ever wear.

First, she tried on a few evening dresses with the shoes to match. Every dress looked perfect on her. The pricey shoes she'd bought were remarkable—red bottoms and high heels, but her favorite was a pair of leather Gucci ankle-strap sandals costing nine hundred American dollars.

She twirled in front of the mirror and smiled at what she had on. "Perfect," she purred.

Kola admired herself in the red V-neck dress. As she inspected the dress, she heard the doorbell ring incessantly.

Then she heard a ruckus coming from downstairs, two women shouting in Spanish. "What the fuck!" she uttered to herself.

Kola spun around in her heels and exited the bedroom to find out why there was loud fussing and arguing going on inside her home. She hurried toward the first floor, moving down the spiral staircase and into the large, stylish foyer. There, she was stunned and stupefied by two familiar faces suddenly barging into her home— Maria and Marisol. The two sisters were once Eduardo's concubines when she was dealing with Cross.

"¡*Estúpida*!" Maria shouted. "Bitch!"

Kola didn't know what she said, but she recognized the word *bitch*, and knew Maria had nothing nice to say to her.

The butler was having a hard time containing them. He grabbed both ladies simultaneously, but they charged farther into the home, going after Kola. Kola had no idea what they were enraged about, but she wasn't about to be bullied and intimidated in her own home.

Kola was shocked at everyone's reaction. The staff stood around watching the entire incident. Even her armed driver stood aside, looking lost. Everyone in the house looked momentarily frozen.

"¡*Te odio!*" Marisol shouted.

What brought these two sisters to her home suddenly? Did they forget whose home they were in? Did they want to die?

Kola couldn't understand them, since they were screaming in Spanish. Maria looked to be about five months pregnant. The incident brought Peaches running out of her room.

"Go back upstairs!" Kola screamed at her niece.

Peaches quickly obeyed and scurried back into her bedroom, where her nanny was there to comfort her.

With a hit to his face, and a knee in his ribs, the butler was losing the battle with the two women in the room. He kept his composure, not wanting to strike back. Maybe it was fear; they too were Eduardo's women. Or maybe he didn't want to hit a woman at all, especially with Maria being pregnant.

Maria and Marisol continued yelling in Spanish, their rage aimed at Kola.

Kola gave a stern look to her armed driver, and he quickly involved himself in the melee, helping the butler to usher the sisters out of the house, but they continued to be defiant. Behind the sisters, Kola noticed the small children, a boy and a girl, who suddenly appeared out of nowhere. They both looked to be around five years old. They somberly stood behind the sisters, not saying a word, their eyes moist with tears, fear, and uneasiness.

The sisters refused to leave. Kola noticed that both men weren't using any brute force to remove the women. Her driver, known to be violent, was carrying a pistol, but he chose to use his hands. Both men were speaking nicely to them in Spanish, but the two sisters were still screaming, acting out erratically, and tussling with the men.

Although she was told to stay in her room, Peaches was back out, her nanny by her side, and the two children behind the sisters looked scared, as the melee grew louder. Kola could see a likeness of Eduardo in their innocent faces.

The driver finally grabbed Marisol in a chokehold, while the butler was still trying to restrain Maria. The two children moved back toward the door from the scuffling adults.

"Mama!" Peaches hollered. She ran toward Kola, looking afraid.

Kola scooped Peaches into her arms. The two of them looked at the struggle from a short distance.

The butler and the driver were finally bringing things under control, ushering the ladies out of the house, but the sisters continued yelling and screaming at Kola, who didn't understand them.

Kola turned to Peaches and asked her, "What are they saying?"

Peaches looked at her aunt. "They mad at you."

"About what?"

Peaches went on to explain the issue they had with Kola. They both loved Eduardo and were shocked to see

Kola riding around in his Maybach. They didn't want to share him. The sisters came across Kola and Peaches while they were shopping in the city, recognized Kola and decided to follow them back to Eduardo's compound.

Both of the sisters' kids—Eduardo Jr. and Sophia— were Eduardo's. Maria and Marisol accepted that they would share Eduardo between each other, but they didn't plan on sharing the man they both loved with anyone else. They had been convinced there wasn't anyone else. When they saw Peaches, who was five years old too, and looked like she was a mixed child, they assumed that Peaches was Eduardo's child and wanted to tear Kola apart.

Maria screamed at Kola, "¡*Usted maldito puta!*"

"What did she say?"

"Mama, she called you a whore," Peaches answered.

Kola had heard enough. She was ready to show them how a bitch from Harlem got down. She handed Peaches over to her nanny and charged at the sisters like a bull seeing red. It was two against one, but she didn't care.

She swung first, striking Marisol in the stomach with a closed fist. Flesh met flesh, and Marisol folded over like a chair, an "*Oomph!*" coming from her lips, a blast of air shooting out of her mouth.

Maria tried to defend her sister. Though pregnant, she attacked Kola, grabbing for her long hair. Kola quickly spun around and punched her in the face repeatedly, and Maria stumbled backwards, falling like a drunken hobo, confused and unaware.

Marisol came at Kola screaming in Spanish. She grabbed Kola physically by her new, expensive dress, tearing it by the seams and spitting in Kola's face.

"Nasty bitch!"

Kola went off. She hit Marisol in her face so hard she folded once again, blood spewing from her lips, and she fell to the ground. Kola attacked her with her new shoes, making her bleed.

Maria struggled to her feet and limped very slowly in Kola's direction. She jumped on Kola from behind, her fists and nails digging into her skin. Marisol jumped up too, aiding her sister.

It was a nasty brawl between the three of them. They rolled around on the floor, fighting and tearing into each other. Kola was on top of Marisol, punching her in the face, while Maria was digging her fingernails into Kola's face and trying to pull her off her sister.

Suddenly, a hand finally pulled Kola out of the fray, quickly and roughly breaking up the fight in the foyer. Eduardo had just returned from one of his business trips. He looked disgusted by what was happening.

All three women started to yell and curse at one another, in Spanish and English, their kids screaming and crying.

Eduardo quickly silenced the room. "What is going on here?" he yelled in Spanish, glaring at the sisters.

They replied to him in Spanish, leaving Kola lost.

"English! Speak fuckin' English!" Kola screamed out heatedly, looking at Eduardo. "I fuckin' live here too!"

Eduardo cut his eyes at Kola. "What is going on here?" he gently asked her.

"I want these bitches out of my house!" she yelled. Her new dress was ruined, her hair was in disarray, and her lip was bleeding.

"Them your fuckin' kids, Eduardo?" Kola asked roughly, eyeing Eduardo Jr. and Sophia standing in silence by the doorway.

Eduardo turned and looked at the kids behind the sisters. He didn't say a word, his expression stoic. His silence was proof enough.

Eduardo had been living a double life. Kola couldn't understand how she could have been so stupid. She felt like a fool, his fool. Of course, he was cheating on her, fucking other women. He was a powerful man. He owned this town and could have anything he wanted, including numerous women, while his prized woman remained at home, unaware of his cheating ways.

His business trips were merely about going across town to live with his other family, where the sisters lived with his kids in a huge mansion just as opulent as Kola's. He was making babies and had lied to her face years ago when he told her that he'd had them murdered— supposedly shot in the back of their heads and dumped in the jungle—for stealing money from him. They were supposed to be dead.

Kola felt hurt. In all the years she had been with Eduardo, she never had gotten pregnant by him. And although he treated Peaches like she was his own child, she wasn't. Now, he had two children of his own and apparently another on the way.

# TWO

Baltimore, Maryland—a place where you can drive less than five minutes and find something to do. It has a cultural scene that rivals New York's, from live bands to high art. But B-more, as some affectionately call it, is also a place where driving could become a battle for your life. And if you happen to stop at a red light, at least one crackhead or prostitute could approach you. Some say it is the roughest city in the nation.

Baltimore had been Apple's home for almost a year. After escaping death in Miami, she quickly fled back north. She wanted to stay away from the major cities like New York, Philadelphia, and DC. Baltimore was quaint in her eyes. It was a different place to live. No one knew her, so she was able to keep a low profile. Her face blended in with the crowd; she was just another young black female struggling like the others.

Apple, surprisingly, tried to put her past behind her. There were no more megalomania moments or obsessions with money and power. In her time, when she was a boss bitch, she left behind so many dead, so many ruined lives, and so many families torn apart, including her own. Her road to perdition had begun years earlier, with the summer jam concert she yearned to attend, which led to her young sister's murder.

Nichols had always been a sweet and smart girl with a bright future. Now she was gone. She was truly missed. Apple always felt guilty about her sister's death. Supreme and his goons had pulled the trigger, but Apple felt she'd loaded the gun. Supreme had brainwashed her. She'd fallen victim to his charm and money, becoming a mental hostage in Supreme's organization. Soon she started to express empathy and sympathy for him—the man who'd murdered her sister and captured her mind.

Thinking about the past disgusted Apple. She was lucky to still be alive after everything she had been through. She thought about old friends, Ayesha, who she had killed, and Meesha. She thought about Cross and Guy Tony. Everyone from her past was either dead or had gone missing.

All the murders, the drug dealing, being kidnapped and taken to Mexico and becoming a whore for Shawn, it all tired her out. Her soul felt burnt out, and her mind twisted with mental issues. She'd had too many close calls with death.

Apple was now focusing her attention on going and staying legit. She wanted the life she had before meeting Supreme.

Back then, Kola was the only corrupt one, always the bad ass in the family. Apple was always in her sister's shadow. For a long time, the streets belonged to Kola. The only thing Apple wanted was Cross, to be held in his arms and loved by him.

During the day, Apple worked for a debt collector, a job she'd found online, and at nights, she bartended for a local nightclub on East Baltimore Street. Both jobs were mundane, but for now, it was paying her bills and keeping her busy.

Miami had been a wake-up call for her. Everyone thought she was dead. She wanted to stay dead; it was the safest way. Being dead was how she survived this long. She, Cartier, and Citi had raised hell in Miami. They went to war with the Gonzales Cartel, drowning the city in bloodshed. All three ladies were deep in shit from an intense federal investigation to the criminal organizations with high-paying contracts out on their heads. It had gotten too hot in Miami, and the Gonzales Cartel was closing in on them, and they all feared they wouldn't live much longer. So Apple, Cartier, and Citi all decided to live on the run.

Cartier came up with the idea to fake their deaths by paying off a coroner. They all liquidated their assets and had it stored in a storage unit on the outskirts of town to make a clean getaway. But Citi double-crossed them both. The unit was cleaned out, and she was long gone like the wind.

Broke and on the run, Apple and Cartier decided to go their separate ways. Apple went to Maryland, and

Cartier went to Seattle, Washington to escape her former life and get her mind right.

The music blared inside the downtown Baltimore club. Apple was busy behind the bar mixing drinks and serving them to thirsty customers. She had to get used to listening to club music, a blend of hip-hop and chopped, staccato house music created in Baltimore. The customers inside the nightclub loved it, and the place was filled to capacity each night.

Clad in a tight skirt and halter-top, Apple was one of two bartenders serving everyone inside. She'd been bartending for three months.

"You lookin' good today, Sassy," one of the clubbers said to Apple.

Apple smiled. "Thank you. What you drinking tonight, Billy?"

"Vodka, straight."

Apple removed a Smirnoff bottle from the shelf behind the bar, poured the vodka into a shot glass, and handed it to Billy.

Billy downed it down his throat like it was water. "Another!" he quickly said, slamming the shot glass on the countertop and ready to get buzz before the night's end.

Apple told him, "Slow it down tonight, Billy. You don't want a repeat of last week."

"We only live once, right?" Billy said, cheerful and energetic. "Yolo!"

She chuckled. "You're right . . . you only live once."

She poured him another shot, and Billy downed it like the first. The tall, handsome, clean-shaven white male continued to smile Apple's way. He stood six feet with a lean body and a narrow face and was a heavy drinker and chain smoker.

It was obvious he had a crush on Apple. He was always lingering by the bar, trying to make conversation with her. His eyes showed he had a fondness for black women.

"Where you from, Sassy?" he asked, his attention directed toward Apple.

"Out of town," she simply replied.

"I know you're from out of town. You're definitely not from here, I can tell."

"Oh really? You can tell? How?"

"Simple—you're too beautiful to be born anywhere in Baltimore."

"Aaaah, you're so sweet."

His comment was flattering. Apple kept herself busy serving others while keeping Billy entertained.

"You like white boys, Sassy?" he asked.

"I don't discriminate."

Billy smiled. "Me either." He leaned forward, his elbows on the lengthy countertop, his hands clasped. His eyes didn't avert from Apple for one moment. He had swag, dressed nicely in fitted jeans and a trendy collared shirt, his dark hair cropped.

"You look like you're from the South, maybe Atlanta, or Charlotte," he said.

"Not even close."

"Give me a hint."

"You gonna have to work for it," she said.

"I do, huh? Well, I'm a hard-working man."

"You know nothing worth having comes cheap."

"I'll drink to that." Billy downed his third glass.

Apple smiled his way again, and he matched her smile. She didn't mind flirting with him, and he played right along.

The bar was swamped with people; the alcohol was flowing into glasses nonstop. Apple busied herself behind the bar, mixing drink after drink. The music got louder, the lights were dimmed, and the strobe lights bounced off the walls, floors, and ceiling. The dance floor was crowded with bodies tangled together. With the music blaring loud, the bass made the room shake, glow stick jewelry dancing to the beat.

One particular partyer stood out, dancing like a gorilla on fire. It was obvious he was on something—ecstasy, bath salts. Whatever it was, he was having the time of his life.

Billy continued to talk Apple's head off. Sometimes she listened, sometimes she didn't. It was what he did every night. When he got alcohol in his system, his mouth ran like diarrhea. Most times, it was just shit coming out.

Apple was mixing rum and coke for someone when she noticed Twin, one of Baltimore's heavyweights come striding into the club with his crew. *Drug dealer* was written all over each one of them. Their demeanor was hardcore with heavy jewelry, name-brand jeans riding off their asses, and exposed tattoos.

Apple watched them go up the stairs to the balcony with booths to sit and chill, overlooking the dance floor. They always sat in VIP. For a moment, she began to reminisce. Twin reminded her of Cross somewhat, the first guy she had a crush on. But that life didn't work out for her, and she met Chico.

From behind the bar, she could see Twin socializing with his peoples and popping bottles. All the ladies in the place wanted to fuck him.

"Hey, you can go on your break now," the manager said to Apple.

He didn't have to tell her twice. Apple finished making one more drink for a customer and hurried from behind the bar. She needed her nicotine. She pushed her way through the crowd, receiving a few polite looks from men interested in her. The skirt she wore did her body justice.

She stepped out the front entrance where security was holding down the fort. Thomas and Gene both looked like giants standing outside the club, both six two, with a combined weight of five hundred pounds. They could be cool as ice, or nothing nice to play with when you pissed them off. Apple had seen them in action a few times, and they'd never lost a fight.

Gene had a crush on Apple. "You good, Sassy?" he asked her.

"Yeah, I'm good, on my break right now," she said, pulling out a cigarette.

She lit up the cancer stick and took a much-needed drag. She exhaled and looked around. It was a nice night; clear sky, lots of activity in the area, police regularly patrolling.

Despite what you might have heard about Baltimore, most times, things were calm and tranquil downtown. On occasion, someone who'd had too much to drink could become a pest to others and security. They'd exchange rough words, and a fight would ensue, but it would be quickly broken up. Sometimes the police were called, and sometimes not.

Apple lingered outside, standing on the corner from her job, enjoying a little solitude. It was two a.m. Her break was fifteen minutes. She finished off her cigarette and took a deep breath. So much was on her mind. She started to think about her daughter Peaches. She felt bad that she'd given up on looking for her. No mother should ever give up looking for their child. But, honestly, it was too dangerous.

Going from having wealth, power, and respect, to suddenly living a menial life, paycheck to paycheck, was tear-jerking. But keeping a low profile was imperative. The Gonzales Cartel had people everywhere. If they got a whiff that she was still alive, they would come hunting for her and would kill her.

Apple thought about Kola in Colombia. She couldn't reach out to her sister because everyone assumed she was dead, and because Eduardo had threatened her.

"Never come back!" he'd said.

She knew he was a man of his word, and if she tried to go back to Colombia and look for her sister, she would be executed at first sight.

They had a deal, Eduardo and Apple, and she planned on keeping up her end of it.

She flicked away the cigarette, and as she was about to walk back inside, she saw a black Benz sitting on 18-inch chrome rims turning the corner, rap music blaring and two black men inside. She recognized the car and the driver. His name was Pug. She was having a fling with him.

Pug stopped the car where she stood. He gazed at her from his reclined leather seat and asked, "You miss me, baby?"

Actually, she didn't. She didn't really care for Pug. He was just something to do, or someone to do. Apple smiled halfheartedly. "You miss me?"

"You know I do. You off work?"

"On break."

"How long?" he asked.

"I go back in ten."

"So you wanna play for five?"

She sighed. "Why not?"

Pug kicked his passenger out the car.

Apple slid into his seat, and Pug drove off. He parked on a side street where there were fewer cars and less traffic. Pug was already unzipping his jeans, ready to fuck, and Apple was hiking up her skirt, ready to get pleased.

Pug had tattoos up and down his tank-topped arms; he flashed teeth filled with played-out gold and silver.

Though he was only in his late twenties, stress had him balding.

Apple had met him on a humble, outside of the club after closing three weeks ago. Like every hustler, Pug lingered outside the nightclub blasting his music, looking to holler at some sexy chicks. He quickly focused his attention on Apple, remembering her from the bar. The two talked, and she fucked him the next night.

During her time in Baltimore, Apple had some flings with other hustlers who came to the nightclub, but nothing serious. No one took her seriously because she had issues that they couldn't put their finger on. Pug was the one who wanted to stick around. He became the one taking her out to dinner and buying her things. She didn't care for him. He was ugly, but he had an okay dick and a couple of okay sex moves.

Pug slid the condom on. She straddled him while he sat in the driver seat. He shoved his cock into her.

Apple moaned. Knowing Pug, it wouldn't be too long. He was almost a minute-man. He had the machinery but lacked the skills to work it.

Pug continued to stroke his dick feverishly into her. He gripped her ass with his wide hands as his eyes rolled into the back of his head. "You feel so good, ma," he cooed, grunting afterwards.

Apple didn't reply. She simply fucked him because she was bored, and he came with the best weed in the city. In her heyday, she wouldn't have given him a second look or thought. But she had issues. Her time in Mexico had made her addicted to something nasty. Her scare in Miami made her humble herself somewhat. Apple couldn't pinpoint what she wanted exactly, but she felt a void like a gaping hole in her heart.

She grinded her hips into Pug's lap. He cupped her tits and sucked on her nipples. Her break would be over in a few minutes.

Pug kissed her neck, being a little passionate. She didn't care for his kisses, she just wanted him to finish. And he did with delight, three minutes after entering her.

Apple climbed off his lap and sat back in the passenger seat, pulling down her skirt and throwing her panties back on.

Like predicted, Pug pulled out an already rolled blunt and was ready to light up. It's what Apple needed. She was ready to smoke with him before she went back to work. Pug sparked the blunt and took a few pulls. He then passed it to Apple.

"I really like you, ma," he said. "You cool peoples."

Apple didn't respond. Her only interest was smoking and getting lifted.

After she got high, Pug dropped her off at the front entrance to the club. She was ten minutes over her break. Apple climbed out of the car and hurried inside.

As she was entering, Twin was exiting with his crew. Apple looked his way but didn't smile. He looked back at her, and they locked eyes briefly. Twin initiated the first smile between them, and Apple smiled back.

It was back to work.

# THREE

Kola sat in her bedroom drying her tears. She couldn't stop crying. The shades were drawn, making the room dark, and it was quiet. She didn't want to be disturbed by anyone, and she threatened the staff that there would be consequences. Her heart was broken. She sat at the edge of the bed, clad in her panties and bra, a cigarette burning between her fingers. What was she going to do? The previous night was still heavy on her mind.

After Eduardo pulled her apart from the sisters and screamed at them, calling her and the sisters savages, he had the audacity to say to them, "You can either take my way of living, or you can leave."

He'd said it in Spanish and in English, so Kola and the sisters could both understand him. Then he had each woman stand next to each other. Eduardo abruptly slapped Maria so hard, she dropped to the floor. He didn't care that she was pregnant. Marisol was next. She got hit and stood there scowling.

When Eduardo struck Kola, she swung back. No man was ever going to lay their hands on her without her doing something about it. She'd punched Eduardo squarely in his jaw.

Eduardo clenched his fists. He could have beaten Kola to a pulp, but he didn't.

Kola continued to go berserk. Eduardo had his driver restrain her. He glared at her but didn't say anything. He walked out of the room and went into his private den.

This left all three women seething.

The fact that Kola wasn't beaten or, worse, murdered didn't go unnoticed by the sisters. Maria and Marisol soon realized that they had overstepped their boundaries barging into Eduardo's home. They knew they could possibly be murdered for violating Eduardo and what everyone called his "*negra* whore." The sisters thought they were the only ones Eduardo truly loved, but seeing what had transpired between Eduardo and Kola had them rethinking their arrangement.

Kola continued to sit quietly in the bedroom, crying and drying her tears. *How could he?* she kept thinking. *How could I be so foolish?* She was upset with herself.

In her mind, she was better than the sisters and their perverted setup. They definitely did things differently in Colombia. She and Apple would have never gone for sharing a man. She actually thought she and Eduardo had something special, especially after he went to hell and back to find Peaches for her, and also gave her and Apple new identities because the United States had warrants out for their arrest. He'd also allowed Apple to leave the compound and let her flee back to the States with money, but all along he was living a double life.

On so many levels, Kola was crushed. She was upset with the whole staff. It bothered her that they did nothing when the sisters attacked her. Kola was mostly disappointed with her driver, who was responsible for her life on a daily basis. He did nothing but stare like an idiot. He sickened her.

In fact, everything about Colombia suddenly started to sicken Kola. She started to feel like a hostage in Colombia. Apple had seen this coming years ago when she had said they didn't belong in Colombia. It wasn't their country; it wasn't their culture. They would always be guests, no matter whose home they lived in. Maybe Apple was right.

Kola stood up and walked out onto the balcony on the clear, warm evening. The mansion was quiet. The sprawling property was absent of staff and company. Standing on the balcony, Kola watched the sun sink lower in the sky, the light of day draining away and giving way to the velvety dark night. Her heart was sinking like the sun.

She looked to be in a trance as she gripped the railing tightly. The crickets were chirping. The day was almost gone. She felt like an outsider, she missed home, and she missed her sister.

The sun dipped lower in the sky until the trees that lined the long driveway stood as silhouettes against the darkening sky, slowly their shadows melting away into the blackness of night. Kola observed Eduardo exiting the mansion with his henchmen right behind him. He walked toward the idling black Escalade where his driver already had the passenger door open for him. Kola frowned, her eyes fixed on him.

Before Eduardo climbed inside, he peered up and saw Kola watching him from the balcony. She didn't avert her attention from his cold stare. Eduardo didn't say a word. He got into the truck, his men got in with him, and they drove away.

She sighed deeply. She thought about the bastard babies Eduardo had. She should have left Colombia when Apple left. She hated to admit it, but perhaps Apple would've still been alive if they'd left together.

Kola stared at the back of the Escalade driving away from the mansion. Her tears started to fall again. She stormed back into her room. She was so upset, she couldn't control herself. She screamed like a madwoman as she trashed her bedroom. Pictures went flying off the wall, the silk sheets were ripped away from the bed, and the television went smashing into the floor.

After trashing the bedroom, Kola fell to her knees, her legs feeling like jelly, her eyes stained with tears. She wanted to kill someone.

"Mama," Peaches called out.

Kola quickly looked up and saw Peaches standing in the doorway, her soft, young eyes fixated on her auntie. The little girl looked worried. She looked past her aunt and noticed the room torn apart.

"Mama, you okay?" she asked.

Kola didn't want her niece to see her in this condition. "Go back into your room, Peaches."

As on cue, Peaches' nanny, Esmeralda, came into view.

"I'm so sorry," Esmeralda said quickly, ready to snatch Peaches out of her aunt's sight. "I didn't see her leave the room."

"What did I fuckin' say, Esmeralda? I don't want anybody coming into this room and disturbing me."

"My apologies," Esmeralda meekly replied.

Esmeralda grabbed Peaches by her arm and pulled her from the room so fast, she almost lifted her off her feet and dislocated her arm. Esmeralda said something to the child in Spanish, and it definitely wasn't polite. Kola was too wrapped up in her pain to see the minor abuse.

The second Esmeralda and her niece were out of her sight, Kola took a deep breath and stood up. For the umpteenth time, she dried her tears. She had to stay strong, though her heart had been shattered like the items in the room. She stepped back out onto the balcony. She wanted to leave Colombia, but her heart wouldn't let her. With Apple dead, no family back in New York, no home, and Peaches in her life, she couldn't just pick up and leave.

No, Kola wasn't a stupid bitch. A natural-born hustler, she had learned a long time ago to never depend entirely on any man and set something aside for rainy days. The way things were looking, there was going to be a lot of rainy days coming her way.

Kola's driver pulled into the hilltop cemetery and came to a stop before the numerous headstones that stretched in every direction. She stepped out and told her driver to stay seated and that she wasn't going to be long. He was curious about why they were in a cemetery, but he was in no position to question her.

Alone, she strutted into the massive, well-kept cemetery, the scent of freshly mown grass and flowers permeating the air, and the white and gray granite tombstones reflecting the sunlight. The gravesites were lovingly cared for.

She walked where she was out of sight from the driver. She wasn't there to see a particular grave; she didn't know any of the dead. Kola was there for one reason only, to continue what she'd been doing for years—burying her money.

In her Marc Jacobs bag, she had over a hundred thousand dollars. She walked to a shaded area under a large tree, which for her was the perfect landmark in the huge, desolate cemetery. Throughout the years, she had hidden large lump sums of money there.

Kola kept a shovel, overalls, gloves, and sneakers in a hidden large black duffle bag. She took off her expensive high heels, put on her protective clothing and she started to dig. An hour later, she was done. She made sure that the ground didn't look disturbed.

She strutted back to the truck, got inside, and said, "Take me back home."

Kola sat back and sighed. The money she was burying was a safety net—a security deposit. Her previous experience, from the streets to the sheets, taught her that nothing lasts forever.

The minute Kola walked into the mansion, Peaches came running to her with open arms. "Mama," Peaches said excitedly.

Kola smiled and scooped her niece into her arms and hugged her lovingly.

"I miss you, Mama. Where did you go?"

"I had to take care of a little business. You okay?"

Peaches was quiet for a moment, looking at her aunt with her innocence. She nodded.

"You hungry?"

Peaches nodded.

"Esmeralda didn't feed you?"

"No."

"Why not?"

Peaches shrugged. "I think she was busy, Mama."

"The only thing she should be busy with is taking care of you," Kola said, becoming upset. "Where is she?"

Peaches shrugged again.

On cue, Esmeralda entered the foyer. She locked eyes with the woman of the house.

"You're home, *señorita*," Esmeralda said, looking surprised.

"Yes, I'm home. Is that a problem?"

"No, is not."

"And why isn't Peaches fed?" Kola said sharply. "It's after one."

"She said she wasn't hungry."

"She's hungry, Esmeralda. My child is not a liar, and she should never go hungry. Do you understand me?"

Esmeralda shrugged, which irritated Kola.

"Do your fuckin' job!" Kola shouted.

"Yes, *señorita*."

"Now go in there and make her something to fuckin' eat."

Esmeralda quickly pivoted and left out of the room like it was on fire.

Kola put her niece down, gently held her by her shoulders, and said, "I'm sorry about the cursing and my loudness, Peaches. I've been going through a lot lately, and some people been making your mommy upset."

Peaches nodded. "Why are they making you upset?"

"Because some people are not nice. They do not care about other people's feelings. They are selfish and ignorant. Don't ever become selfish when it comes to family, Peaches. I'm the only family you have left."

"Is Papá my family too?"

Peaches called Eduardo "Papá." He'd been in her life for a long time, and his love toward her was endless. He treated her like his own daughter, and she became his little

38

princess. It was one of the reasons why Kola loved him so much.

Kola sighed heavily. She couldn't tell her the truth. "Yes, he is your family too. But I want you to know one thing—You are everything to me. You are my shining star, my beautiful little pony."

Peaches smiled. "I like ponies."

"I know you do." Kola hugged her niece. She would do anything for the little girl. Peaches was smart and beautiful. Apple would have been proud. It was a shame her mother was dead. Kola had to become her mother, but one day, she would have to tell her niece the truth about her biological mother.

"Go in the kitchen and get you something to eat. I'll be in my bedroom." She kissed Peaches on the forehead.

Peaches smiled and went running into the kitchen.

While walking to her bedroom, in passing Kola asked one of the maids in the home if Eduardo was home. He wasn't. She wasn't surprised. Since the incident with Marisol and Maria, he had made himself scarce. Their relationship has become estranged. They were sleeping in separate bedrooms on opposite sides of his compound.

It was the start of another beautiful day with the spreading sunrise. Powerful sunrays flooded over the landscape, lighting up every blade of grass. Though it was an impeccable morning in Colombia, trouble was still in

Kola's heart. She'd slept alone again the night before. She didn't get much sleep. She continued to have bad dreams.

She arose from her large canopy bed and looked around her bedroom, which was filled with luxury items but felt so empty. She donned her short, silk robe and stepped out onto the balcony.

The compound was busy with activity. Andre was doing some landscaping in the garden below her balcony. Kola set her eyes on him. He was six one, shirtless, and sweaty, with dark skin and darker hair. He was one of Colombia's finest men. The female staff adored him, and the men envied him. The man was humble and hard-working, and he had a green thumb. Day after day, he tended to his plants like they were his children.

Kola stared at Andre and smiled. She wanted his attention. He didn't speak English, but she had no need in communicating with him verbally. She watched his every move intently. When Andre finally looked her way, their eyes locked. Now it was time for her to put on a small show. Slowly, she slid the robe off her shoulders, and it fell down to her feet and meshed around her ankles, exposing her nakedness.

Andre stood in the garden transfixed by Kola's sudden nakedness—her dark nipples, her perky breasts, her curvy hips, her shaved pussy.

It was risky. Eduardo had made it clear to everyone, mostly the men on his compound, that anyone caught staring at Kola too hard would have their eyes cut out. If they dared touch her in any way, he would personally castrate them and then kill them with his bare hands. Kola knew what she was doing out in the open could get them both killed.

Eduardo was fond of Andre, who had been growing his food and maintaining the land in the area for ten years. Andre was like family to him.

Andre couldn't turn his attention away. His eyes stayed glued to Kola's naked frame.

Kola wanted her revenge someway, somehow. Eduardo could be out there gallivanting with his whores, indulging himself in pleasures and drowning himself in debauchery, but she had to remain loyal and faithful to him. She wanted the same love and respect she'd always shown him.

Kola touched her breasts softly and gently, a strong sexual gleam in her eyes. "You wanna fuck me, Andre?" she asked.

Andre had no idea what she was saying, but her body language spoke clearly to him.

*Why can't I have him?* Kola said to herself. *I'm entitled to some payback.*

If Eduardo ever found out she'd fucked another man, it would drive him crazy, and there was no telling how far his rage would go. Andre was so much fun to gawk at, but she couldn't have him. She could only fantasize, and he the same.

The bedroom doors burst open, and Eduardo came into the room. His abrupt presence startled Kola. He came in alone, dressed in cargo shorts, a white silk shirt, and sandals. He saw Kola standing naked on the balcony and immediately became suspicious. He marched onto the balcony and looked over the railing. He frowned, searching for the culprit that dared to see his woman naked. But he didn't see anyone below, just his garden and the gentle breeze. Andre was gone.

"Why are you out here standing naked?" he asked her.

"Can a girl enjoy a beautiful morning in her birthday suit and catch some sun?" she replied coolly.

"No." Eduardo snatched the robe off the ground and thrust it into her arms. "Put some clothes on."

Kola took her robe and did what she was told. She tied it closed by her waist. Eduardo looked at her, and for good measure, he peered off the balcony again. Still, no one.

"You have fun with your two whores?" Kola spat at him with sarcasm.

Eduardo quickly slapped her, snapping her face to the left. She glared at him, fighting hard to keep her composure.

"I'm tired of your mouth," he said.

"And you know what I'm tired of," Kola quickly shot back, but she stopped herself short from completing her sentence.

"Get dressed," he told her.

"Why?"

The look he gave Kola said she was pushing her limits. He didn't have time to tolerate her attitude. Kola humbled herself.

"Meet me in my den in twenty minutes." He pivoted on his sandals and made his exit from the bedroom.

*The audacity of him,* Kola screamed to herself. She was his woman, not his slave or some concubine.

It had been a week since the catfight, and they were still sleeping in different rooms. She could count on one hand how many times she'd seen him. So, what was up with him now?

Clad in a simple white T and short shorts, Kola walked out the bedroom barefoot. Peaches was still asleep in her bedroom. She walked down the stairway. The door to Eduardo's den was ajar. Kola pushed in the door and walked into the room. He was standing by the window, looking outside, puffing on a cigar.

He turned her way and immediately smiled at her. "You're beautiful," he proclaimed out of the blue.

*Why the change of attitude?*

Eduardo moved closer to Kola as she stood in the center of his den. He had an assortment of guns displayed on his walls. Some of his collection went as far back as the seventh century.

"I have a surprise for you," he said.

Kola wasn't in the mood for surprises. She was still upset with him. Not too long ago, he'd slapped the shit out of her and threatened her. *Why is he playing nice now?*

Eduardo went into his desk and removed a long, rectangular jewelry case. He handed it to Kola, who reluctantly took it.

"Open it. I know you're going to like it."

She opened it. Her eyes widened to what was inside. "Oh my God!"

"A jewel for my jewel."

The stunning platinum and diamond necklace had a price tag of just under a million dollars.

"You like it?"

Kola was speechless. It was the most expensive piece of jewelry he'd ever bought her. It was his way of making up with her.

"I love it," Kola softly replied.

"Try it on." Eduardo removed the necklace from the case. He stood behind her and gently clamped it around her slim neck.

Kola went to the nearest mirror and stared at it. She immediately fell in love with the reflection. The necklace gleamed beautifully, and could make any bitch jealous.

"I'm sorry about everything. Let me make it up to you the right way. I promised you nothing but the best in my country, and I always keep my promises."

He wrapped his arms around her, as she continued to look in the mirror. Kola couldn't take her eyes off the necklace.

"They mean nothing to me," Eduardo said. "You are the love of my life, and you will always be most important to me." He whispered something in Spanish in her ear.

She didn't know what he said, but it sounded romantic and sweet. His accent, the way his tongue rolled with his words, turned her on.

She wanted to stay angry at him, but his gift and his charm made it difficult.

Eduardo slid his hand into her T-shirt and cupped her right tit. Gently, he pinched her nipple. His touch always made her weak. His sweet words broke her down into a temperate chill. Before she knew it, her clothes were peeling away from her skin, and she had Eduardo's hard dick in her hand, jerking him off.

Subsequently, Kola was on her back with her legs spread and Eduardo between them, thrusting himself inside of her, her manicured nails digging into his back. She closed her eyes, and they enjoyed each other.

He'd cheated on her. How many times, she didn't know, and right now, she didn't care. Between the expensive necklace and the good dick, Kola caught Alzheimer's.

"I love you," she said in his ear.

"I know you do. *Te amo, mi amor.*" He continued to thrust his dick inside of her.

Fifteen minutes after their lovemaking started, Kola was putting her clothes back on. Her pussy had been scratched nicely. Eduardo always knew where her itch was. He knew the right words to say, the right things to do, what gifts to buy for her to forget about his infractions.

"That was nice," she said.

"My golden negro," he said to her in Spanish. "I will do anything for you," he then said in English.

"I just want you to love me, and only me," she said.

He didn't reply.

His silence to her most important statement prompted her to turn and leave the den, but Eduardo said, "I have one more gift for you."

It was another jewelry box, a velvet ring box. He held it toward her in the palm of her hand. Kola didn't know what to think. Was he proposing to her?

"Open it. I'm sure you'll like this one too." Eduardo looked at her deadpan.

Kola took the box, smiling. She took a deep breath and opened it. She was shocked by what was inside; it wasn't what she expected. In fact, she was appalled by his second gift. Why would he give her this? It was someone's severed eye. It was slimy and gross.

"You love it?" Eduardo asked with a twisted smile.

"What is this, some kind of joke?"

"No joke. If he ever looks at you again, then I'll take his other eye. And then I will kill him," he said calmly, his tone serious.

Kola immediately knew who the eye belonged to. But how did he know? Their flirting was brief, and on the down low.

"You look surprised. I know and I see everything. Andre worked for me for a long time. It still didn't matter. Only you matter to me. Never show your naked body to another man again. . ." he told her with an intense look, ". . . unless you want that man's blood on your hands."

Kola didn't know what to say. She felt honored to hear him say that, but there was a part of her that felt fearful.

# FOUR

Apple woke up early in the morning to get ready for another hard day of work. She wasn't used to living like this—having a nine-to-five and then bartending at night. Her job at the debt collection agency was tedious. She hated the work, she hated her supervisors, and she didn't like her nosy, judgmental coworkers. Some of them could be very offensive. Two years earlier, she would have had them slaughtered.

Apple wasn't a people person. She simply wanted to do her job and mind her business. It wasn't a job she planned on doing long; just something to pay her bills and keep her distracted. She needed to become a different person, and working in an office was that something different.

The sun was high in the sky when she removed herself from her bed, quickly showered, got dressed, and jumped into her small hooptie to travel to work. She was running late. The morning traffic in Baltimore was nothing like

New York. It had its moments, but the streets weren't as congested during rush hour like in the Big Apple.

She made a quick stop to the local mart for a breakfast sandwich, coffee, and the local paper before heading to work. Apple felt like she was in the Witness Protection Program, with her new nondescript life and run-down apartment in East Baltimore.

She sat in her small cubicle at work in front of a computer screen with the phone glued to her ear and talking to strangers, trying to get them to pay their debts. She worked for National Credit Collectors. For most of her day, she made phone call after phone call from a list of names. She knew nothing about these people and wasn't interested in their lives at all. They made a purchase or attained a service, then the bill needed to be paid. Nobody wanted to pay their debt.

Calling was never easy. Man or woman, it didn't matter. She was constantly getting into disputes with the debtors. They had an attitude; she had an attitude too.

A National Credit Collectors employee received rigorous training before joining the call center, including instructions on all legal requirements for debt collection and, above all else, that all customers are to be treated with courtesy and respect.

Apple knew she was on thin ice with her job. She was late for work, and she always had some friction with her supervisor. She saw Ms. Cass, a single white dyke, as a dumb bitch. Her skin was pale and pasty, and she was overweight with bad hair and bad breath. She always looked like she was having a bad day.

Some days, while at work, Apple felt like she should have taken her chances with the Gonzalez Cartel. A nine-to-five was just as treacherous, since most days she felt like putting a gun to her head and pulling the trigger. Better yet, point the pistol at her supervisor and squeeze. Put that old bitch out of her misery.

"This is an attempt to collect a debt by a debt collector. Any information obtained will be used for this purpose." It was what she was trained to say.

National Credit Collectors had a company motto to focus not only on the recovery of lost revenue, but on the retention of customers. It was bullshit. The entire country was in debt.

Her lunch hour was at one. She always ate alone, and she never frequented the same place. She didn't have any interest in making friends and didn't trust anyone.

After lunch, it was back to work, back on the phones and watching the clock wind down to when it was time to go home.

How long would she last? She cursed Citi for taking off with her money, which was enough to live off for a long time. If she ever saw Citi again, she wouldn't hesitate to shoot to kill.

After five o clock, it was back home. It was TV dinners or fast food then a quick nap for a few hours, and then it was time for her second job at the nightclub.

East Baltimore felt like one of the most unsafe places in America. Known for drugs, murder, and violence, the place is swamped with drug users and drug dealers, impoverished families, and dilapidated row houses.

Apple climbed out of her Ford Escort, fortunate to find parking right outside her building. Lingering on the block and corners were the local fiends desperately trying to find a way to support their addiction, either by panhandling or committing a crime. Apple ignored them and went into her building, climbing the pissy stairway to her second-floor place. Inside, the place was sparsely furnished with secondhand furniture. She barely had any food in her fridge or any of the amenities to call it home sweet home.

First thing inside, Apple locked her doors, inspected her small place, and went into her bedroom. In her room, she was armed to the teeth, with guns and ammunition hidden under her bed just in case someone wanted to be stupid enough to break inside. It would be their last mistake. Even with a change of hair color, a new address, and a new life, she didn't know who could be watching and plotting.

Before her shift started at the nightclub, Apple took another shower and ordered Chinese food. The warm evening brought out everyone in East Baltimore. From her bedroom window, she could hear the neighborhood coming alive like it always did when sunset loomed. Cars driving by with their blaring music, and the drug fiends moved up and down the block on a mission to get their next high. The neighbors and children were trying to enjoy what was left of the day and sunlight, knowing that at night, their neighborhood became an even deadlier place.

In her bedroom watching regular TV, Apple heard knocking at her door. Assuming it was her Chinese food being delivered, she still wasn't about to take any chances. She grabbed her gun and went to the door. The area was known for the stickup kids, home invasions, and burglaries.

"Who?"

"You ordered Chinese?"

"Yeah."

She slowly opened the door, being cautious. The gun was already cocked back and ready. She opened the door slightly, grabbed her food, paid the deliveryman hurriedly, and he went on his merry way.

Apple had four hours until her shift started at the nightclub. She got the job because of luck, and she was cute. She went out alone one night and met the owner at the store nearby by chance. He wanted her number, and she needed a job. Apple picked him apart, was able to read him from a mile. He was a flashy guy who liked pussy a lot. So, she used what she had to get what she wanted, or needed.

He was a weak fuck, but her pussy got her the job.

Working in the club wasn't low profile, but it was extra income, and it was a whole lot better than her daytime gig. Working the bar, she got closer and more acquainted with the local hustlers. It came with its perks: she got to drink for free, made extra tips, and she got to take her work home some nights—if they were cute enough. Apple may have been a fugitive, supposedly dead to world, but she still had needs. She was still a woman.

"She Will," by Drake and Lil Wayne, blared throughout the packed nightclub.

Tonight, instead of being behind the bar serving drinks, she became one of the bottle girls. They received bigger tips and got cooler with the ballers and shot-callers.

The manager saw that she had the body and looks, and when one of his regular girls called in sick for the night, he asked Apple if she could fill in, and she didn't hesitate.

Dressed in a pair of white skimpy shorts, heels, and a revealing halter-top, Apple made her way through the thick crowd carrying a bucket with two bottles of Cristal on ice, Voss waters, and one bottle of Remy. She was on her way to the VIP area where Twin and his cronies were. The party upstairs was in full swing.

She placed the bottles in front of Twin and smiled his way. He was seated amongst his wolves, and had a big chested, scantily clad groupie sitting on his lap. Once again, they locked eyes. He smiled back and nodded.

*God! He looks like Cross,* she said to herself.

He was six two and handsome with low waves, caramel skin, and muscles. He was half Trinidadian and half Dominican. His wardrobe was urban—fresh Timberland boots, a baseball cap, a rose gold link chain with a diamond cross, and a pocket full of money.

"Keep 'em comin', ma," Twin said. "We celebratin' tonight."

"Celebratin' what?" Apple asked.

"My nigga's twenty-fifth birthday."

"Happy birthday to him," Apple said coolly.

"Yo, ma, have a drink with us," Twin said.

"I'm working."

"Yo, I know the owner. He ain't gonna fire you. When you wit' us, you wit' us."

The woman sitting on his lap scowled Apple's way and said smugly, "Ain't the help not supposed to fraternize with the guests? I mean, that's rude. Bitches need to stay in their lane."

"Bitch?"

"Yes, bitch! Why are you still standing here lookin' all retarded?"

Apple shot a hard look at the bimbo. "Excuse me?"

"You heard me, bitch!"

Apple was ready to snatch that bitch off Twin's lap and fuck her up. She had no idea who she was fucking with.

"Y'all ladies, play nice," Twin joked.

"Tell your cum-collector groupie that she don't fuckin' know me, and if she keeps coming out of her mouth sideways, then I'll shut that bitch up permanently," Apple said through clenched teeth.

"What, bitch?" The girl was about to remove herself from Twin's lap and confront Apple.

Twin grabbed her by her arm and held her tight. "Don't ruin my homie's birthday party," he told her.

"You gonna let her disrespect me like that, Twin?"

"She holdin' her own—that's what up, ma." Twin looked at Apple and winked.

The girl frowned heavily.

Apple was ready to remove herself from the area. She didn't want to lose her job. As she walked away, Twin kept his eyes on her and nodded slightly.

The girl on Twin's lap didn't like the look he gave Apple at all. But she wasn't about to disrespect him. The only thing she could do was keep silent and continue to frown.

"Bitch is so lucky I didn't snatch her fuckin' eyes out," Apple said to Tina, a co-worker in the back room.

"Who you talkin' about?"

"That bitch in VIP sitting on Twin's lap. She done pissed me the fuck off. That bitch don't know me."

"Yeah, that bitch don't." Tina barely knew Apple herself, but she was a ghetto girl who loved a fight, no matter where it came from.

"I need a fuckin' cigarette."

"I smoked my last one."

Apple asked everybody in the back room, "Anybody got a cigarette?"

No luck. Everyone was out, or they didn't smoke.

Apple needed her nicotine break. The night was still young, and the club was at full throttle. Every employee was extremely busy, with the DJ pumping out jam after jam. Apple couldn't take her mind off the rude bitch in VIP. She wanted to teach her a lesson.

The duration of the night went on with Apple serving expensive bottles to the paying customers, and still stuck on the incident earlier.

Apple saw her moment of revenge when she noticed the girl exiting the upstairs area to use the bathroom. She fixated her eyes on the girl and pushed her way through the thick party crowd with an attitude.

"Tina, I need you to do me a favor," she said.

"What you need, girl?"

"I need you to come with me to the bathroom and watch my back."

"No problem."

Apple and Tina followed the girl to the bathroom. They were right behind her, their eyes on her like a hawk. Her being alone was going to cost her. It was going to be a mistake that bitch would regret.

Tina went in first, while Apple lingered outside the door. Luckily for her, the traffic flow was sparse.

A short moment later, Tina came out and said, "That thot is alone. Go get her."

"Watch the door," Apple said.

Tina nodded.

Apple went inside. The bathroom was pristine white with mirrors everywhere. The girl was in one of the stalls.

While waiting patiently near the stall, Apple cracked her knuckles. She couldn't wait to pound her fist into the groupie.

The toilet flushed, and the door to the bathroom stall opened.

The second the young girl stepped out, Apple shouted, "What now, bitch!" and lunged for her like a gust of wind. She grabbed a handful of her long weave and slammed her into the wall.

The girl yelped and collapsed to the floor. Apple repeatedly threw her fists into her face while the girl attempted to fight back.

"Don't you ever disrespect me again!"

She had all the privacy she needed. Tina was doing her job at the door.

In shock, the girl stared at Apple wide-eyed. She spat blood, paralyzed by the sudden attack.

Apple dragged her across the bathroom floor by her weave. The girl's hair was in disarray, her outfit soiled and torn. The punishment continued—a kick into her ribs, a smack in the face. Apple thrust her clenched right fist into her jaw and temple.

"I want you to remember me, bitch!" she shouted.

Tina stood coolly outside the door. She could hear the commotion going on. She smirked. She wanted a piece of that bitch too, despite not knowing the girl.

Five minutes later, Apple walked out the bathroom cool and calm, not a scratch or bruise on her.

"That bitch knows now not to fuck with me," she said.

Apple strutted off, and Tina followed behind her. Apple left the girl a bloody and dazed hot mess for someone to find in the bathroom.

On her way to the employees' room, Apple could see Twin coming her way, parting his way through the tight crowd, his eyes looking everywhere, probably looking for his groupie chick.

"Hey, ma. What's good?" he said to her.

"You looking for your goon?"

He chuckled. "Fuck that bitch. We don't rock like that."

"So you do have taste."

He laughed. "I like your style, shorty."

The way he towered over Apple with the height of an athlete was such a turn-on. His dark, brown eyes locked into hers. He was a thug, it was easy to tell, but there was a charm and swag that he was also working with.

"What do you want?" she asked. She did have a crush on him, but she wasn't about to throw herself all over him like the other bitches in the club. She had to humble herself because of her predicament, but she was still a pit bull in a skirt.

"I just want to chat with you for a moment. You have a problem with that?"

"No, I don't have a problem. I do have a job, though. I don't get paid enough to lounge around VIP like you."

"Well, how much for your time?" Twin asked, pulling out a wad of hundred-dollar bills.

Apple snickered. "Seriously?"

"Yeah, seriously. Like I told you before, me and the owner are cool."

"Well, tell your homie to give me a raise."

Twin laughed. "Yo, I really like you."

"I'm sure you like all the pretty girls."

"There's something different about you, ma."

Right then, some commotion stirred up. Security went rushing toward the women's bathroom.

Apple didn't look worried. She looked at Twin and simply said, "Someone is having a bad night."

Twin observed security carry a beaten girl out of the bathroom in the threshold. She was in bad shape. He didn't look upset about it. "That's your handiwork?"

"Like I said, someone is just having a bad day."

"Yeah, you are something different. What's your name?"

"Sassy."

"I'm Twin, but I think you already know that." He extended his hand, like a gentleman.

Apple shook it. She didn't smile.

# FIVE

Y o, I'm outside," Twin said to Apple, calling from his
cell phone.

"I'll be out in five minutes," she replied.

"Okay. Don't keep me waiting too long, shorty."

"I won't."

Apple hung up. She scurried around her small
apartment, putting the finishing touches on her outfit
and her makeup. She was excited about her first date with
Twin. He was definitely a step up from dating Pug.

The night was young and the weather perfect. She
was becoming Sassy all the way—thinking different and
being different. But sometimes, like the fight at the club,
her old self would slip back. The hardest thing she had to
change was her attitude and her behavior.

Clad in tight-fitting jeans, a lace shirt, and heels, she
walked out of her apartment and approached Twin in his
black E-Class Benz. He was reclined in his seat, smoking
a cigarette and on his cell phone.

When he saw Apple coming his way, he curtailed the call and focused on her. "Nice," he said to himself, smiling.

Apple climbed into his Benz, and though she had been in many nice cars before, she acted like she was brand-new to his luxury vehicle. "Ooh, this is so nice. I like this." She passed her hands along the leather seats and then across the dashboard.

"You like my ride, huh?"

"I love it."

"You ever been in a Benz like this before?"

"No," she lied.

"You know, this is how I roll. Every day all day like Fifty Tyson."

Apple chuckled at his joke about the social media phenomenon.

"But you look good, Sassy. You wearing them jeans."

"I'm glad you like what you see."

"I do. Definitely would like to see how you would look without them," he teased. But Twin wasn't joking. He had sex on his mind.

"Ain't you blunt and up front?"

"I like what I see."

"I bet you do."

"You hungry?"

"Yeah, I am," Apple said.

"I know the perfect spot. You gonna love it."

"The ball's in your court."

Twin put the car in drive and pulled away from the curb. Apple sat back and was feeling ready to enjoy a good night with him. He turned up the Meek Mill he had playing. It wasn't loud, but his lyrics were crystal clear.

Twin nodded to "Young & Gettin' It" while driving. "This is me right here," he said to Apple. He rhymed along with the track and bounced around in his seat like he was performing on stage as he drove.

Apple thought it was cute. Twin was a goon, but he seemed like a cool guy; someone she could have fun with.

"I love Meek Mill—he be talking that truth," Twin said.

"He ayyite," she said dryly.

Twin looked at Apple like she'd said something about his mother. "What! He ayyite? Shorty, you crazy! Meek Mill is the fuckin' truth. He's one of the best rappers in the game right now."

"Everybody has their opinion."

"What you know about rap? I only listen to thorough and real niggas. Niggas that know the game, and been in the streets, real talk."

Apple replied coolly, "I respect that."

"You respect that." He laughed. "Who your favorite rapper?"

"I really don't have a favorite rapper."

"Then who you listen to? They say that who or what you listen to tells you a lot about that person."

"Oh, really?"

Twin nodded.

"Like me, I'm a Meek Mill and 50 Cent fan, real talk. I ain't on these niggas' dick, because I get mines out here too. Plenty. Ask around about me—I'm a young, rough nigga gettin' plenty of that paper."

"You ever thought about becoming a rapper too?"

"Yeah, at one time. But I ain't got the patience to be dealing wit' all these fake-ass niggas in the industry. These studio rappers and shit. I'm the real thing, ma. Niggas try to war wit' me on wax or in the streets, and I'm gonna put three in 'em, true story. I'll lay a nigga down fast."

He was a beast. Apple definitely liked him. She could have used a nigga like him in her crew when she was in charge of things. He was energetic and looked ruthless. She wouldn't be surprised if he carried at least two pistols on him.

Their conversation continued flowing like a waterfall. Twin traveled on E North Avenue, moving through one of the roughest places in the neighborhood. He sat coolly at a red light. His Benz stood out, sitting on 20-inch chrome rims and dark tints.

He lit up another cigarette. "You smoke?" he asked.

"I do."

"My bad. Here, take one," he offered, handing Apple his pack of Newport.

Apple took two out the pack. She lit up and took a deep drag. Twin continued driving, heading toward Jones Falls Expressway. The city was quiet, for once. However, the fiends were everywhere in the city, like usual, searching desperately for their next high, yearning for their fixes.

It was a sad sight, but Apple didn't care about them or their addiction. If they were stupid enough to use drugs, it was on them. In her days of hustling, she stayed away from using. Her only high was getting money and gaining power.

"Where you from?" Twin asked.

Apple didn't want to be truthful to him, so she lied. "Atlanta."

"Atlanta?" His left eyebrow arched. His look said he didn't believe her. "You don't look like you from Atlanta. I know plenty of bitches from Atlanta. You look like an up north girl, Philly, New York, maybe Boston."

"I may look like a lot of things, but that doesn't make it true."

"I feel you."

Apple didn't want to get into where she was from. She wanted to forget about where she was from. She wanted to enjoy a simple evening with a handsome thug.

"You know, you ain't gotta be scared of me, ma. I'm not the bogeyman."

*Afraid?* Apple stopped herself from laughing in his face.

Apple wasn't intimidated by him, or afraid. She found him amusing, though. If he only knew about her pedigree, would he be the afraid one. Apple was once a vicious queenpin who went to war with some of the most ruthless men New York had ever seen, and she still came up on top.

Twin may have been a killer, but she'd seen worse.

He pulled up to Captain James Landing on Boston Street, a popular restaurant in the harbor that was shaped like a ship. You couldn't miss the place. It was a totally private venue known for its extraordinary cuisine, warm and casual elegance, and friendly, professional service.

"You like seafood?" he asked.

"I love it."

"My kind of woman."

Twin stepped out the Benz, and Apple followed.

Baltimore's Inner Harbor was a hub of activity. Traffic was heavy. People were everywhere. The warm evening brought out everybody. A calm breeze blew off the water as the sun slowly set behind the horizon.

Twin wasn't afraid to take Apple by her hand and escort her inside the seafood restaurant. He was a territorial man. He definitely had an affectionate side to him. Once inside, they were seated right away. Twin had made reservations. He didn't like to wait. Wherever he went, he expected the VIP treatment, even if he had to pay a little extra for it.

Twin wasn't what most would consider a spendthrift. In fact, he hated to splurge. He had money to burn, but he hated for his pockets to feel burnt. However, splurge was exactly what he always did when chasing new pussy.

Inside the restaurant, the ambience was nice. The interior felt like being in a ship. There were even copper sinks in the bathroom. There was a small band playing, and the music was surprisingly a really good mix.

Twin and Apple sat at their table. They ordered their drinks right away—Twin got Grey Goose, and Apple got her Cîroc Peach with Sprite. Their waitress was an affable white female with a huge smile and warm personality.

Before they ordered their food, Apple looked at Twin and asked, "So, why do they call you Twin?"

He chuckled. "Because, I have two personalities. I can be cool as fuck or your worst nightmare."

Apple downed her drink, not knowing how to take his response. She could describe herself the same way, but was having two personalities a good thing? There was a thin line between calculated killer and cuckoo crazy. She hoped he wasn't the latter.

Twin's cell phone rang. He answered. It was business, obviously. She didn't mind it. She ordered another drink and glanced around the room then focused on the band of three white boys. They were young, talented, and vocal. Two were on guitars, and one on the keyboard. They filled the restaurant with Outkast's song, "The Way You Move."

For white boys, they all had soul and rhythm.

Twin excused himself from the table. "This is important," he said, pushing his chair back. He walked toward the exit.

Apple was now alone. The crab cakes came in a small basket. They were huge and had a good amount of crab in them. She didn't hesitate to bite into one. She truly loved seafood, and so far, Captain James Landing was receiving an A in her book.

She started to munch on another one. She ate the second one quickly. If Twin didn't hurry back, she was about to eat the whole basket. She listened to the band and observed other patrons in the place. They were mostly white, looking affluent. Everything seemed relaxed.

"I had to take care of some business," Twin said, coming back to the table. "You don't mind, right?"

"No, it's cool."

Their waiter came back to take their orders. Apple ordered first, choosing a dozen oysters that came with lemon, horseradish, and cocktail sauce. She also ordered cream of crab soup. Twin ordered a crab cake sandwich, minus the bread, and some crabs. Baltimore was known for its crabs.

"How you liking the place so far?"

"It's nice."

"You fuck wit' me, I give you the best."

*Cute,* she thought.

He was trying to impress her. The men in Baltimore were a different breed than Harlem niggas, and their accent—the Baltimore dialect, also known as Baltimorese, an accent of Mid-Atlantic American English—originated among the white blue-collar residents of the southern region of Baltimore. At times it sort of sounded like a Philly twang. Twin didn't carry their accent, though. Apple found it strange.

"Let me ask you a question," Twin said.

"Go for it."

"You really beat down that girl in the bathroom?"

"I plead the fifth."

He smirked. "I ain't no snitch."

"I believe that, but why should I snitch on myself?"

Twin smiled. "You're smart, ma. I respect that. You don't tell on yourself, no matter who you think you can trust. There's something about you that I can't put my finger on, but you ain't from no Atlanta."

"We on this again?" she spat back.

"Nah, I'm off it." He smiled.

She didn't.

While waiting for their orders, Twin signaled for their waitress to come their way. "Yo, let me get a bottle of Moët," he told the waitress. "I don't care about the cost."

She nodded.

"Bottle service wherever you go, huh?"

"It's the way I live. There ain't no other way."

Their food came, and everything was delicious. The oysters seemed to melt in Apple's mouth, especially with the lemon. Twin downed his Moët. He showed little etiquette at the table, drinking straight from the bottle and then tearing into his crabs like he was a hungry, homeless man who hadn't eaten for days. He didn't care who was watching him. His appearance always spoke shadiness, with his long, gold, diamond link chain with a TEC-9 pendant, a big-face diamond watch, and both his ears pierced with diamond stud earrings. The only thing he was missing was a platinum or gold hip-hop grill.

While they ate, Twin stared at Apple's face. "If you don't mind me asking, how did you get that faint scar across your face?"

"I mind you asking."

"Don't get me wrong, I like it. It gives you character. You're still a beautiful woman."

"I don't want to talk about it," she bluntly told him.

"It's that personal, huh?"

"It is."

"Ayyite, shorty, I ain't gonna push it."

Apple didn't want to talk about anything from her past. Not Kola, her mother, Denise, Nichols, or Peaches. In her mind, Apple was really dead. She was now Sassy.

Their dinner continued. After seafood, they had dessert. After dessert, and an almost four-hundred-dollar bill, they went for a walk around the harbor. The sun had set. The night was young, and the area beautiful. It was a far cry from the harshness of East Baltimore.

After hanging out in the Inner Harbor and downtown Baltimore, Apple rode with Twin into the west side of town. They came to a stop at the projects/low-rises on Druid Hill Avenue. While Apple remained seated in the passenger seat, Twin stepped out of his E-Class. Across the street were a group of thuggish-looking drug dealers. Twin walked their way without any concern, like he owned the place.

From the passenger seat, Apple observed Twin greet the group of men. She saw the respect they had for him. A serious conversation ensued between two of the men from the group. Twin was in their faces, scolding them about something. The other men stayed away from the discussion.

Suddenly, a pistol was in Twin's hand, and he abruptly smashed it across the young hustler's face, instantly breaking his nose. His blood spewed out. He collapsed to his knees, crying out from the pain. Twin was all over him, pistol-whipping him and shouting, "Nigga, I told you—don't be fuckin' wit' my money!"

His cronies didn't dare try to interrupt Twin's assault. From zero to a hundred, Twin had transformed into a violent brute. He repeatedly pistol-whipped the young thug. When he was done, the boy's face was coated in blood.

Twin pointed the gun at his partner and dared him to react, but each one of them stood frozen. "Yeah, I thought so," he barked. He pivoted from them and coolly walked back to his car.

He climbed into the driver's seat and said, "I'm sorry you had to see that, baby, but that's how I get down. I ain't playin' wit' these niggas out here about my fuckin' bread. I told you, I'm a fuckin' beast on these streets." He drove off, tires screeching, seat reclined wayyyy back.

His antics were no longer cute or entertaining in Apple's eyes. She had seen worse, and she'd done worse. Eduardo, Cross, Chico, Two-Face—now those were savages and psychopaths. Twin was trying too hard, and Apple wasn't impressed.

However Apple was drawn to him. He reminded her of Cross, a man she never got to have. She wanted to keep his company a little while longer. If his dick was wack then she would dead him. Not literally, of course . . . unless she had to.

# SIX

Kola was supposed to be in the city shopping, but she came back early. It was raining heavily. The rain battered the roof of the black SUV she was in like a hail of bullets, hammering down everywhere. The rain fell without break all through the day, leaving the roads like shallow rivers.

She refused to go shopping in such harsh weather. There was no way she was going to tread through it with shopping bags in her hands and mess up her new shoes. Hopefully, tomorrow would be a better day.

The truck pulled in front of the mansion. The driver hurried out the vehicle carrying an umbrella and opened the door for Kola. He tried his best to shield her from the downpour as he escorted her into the home.

She didn't say thank you to him, as he was still on her "eat a dick" list. Besides, he was doing his job, what he was being paid to do—Drive her around and make sure all her needs were taken care of.

The second she stepped inside, the butler and maid were there to serve her needs, but Kola waved them away. She had no need for them now. She wanted to find Peaches. The only thing she wanted to do was spend some quality time with her niece.

She went up the stairway and headed toward Peaches' bedroom. The door was ajar. Before she could step inside, she heard the nanny say something harsh in Spanish.

"*¡Pequena perra!*" Esmeralda exclaimed to Peaches, meaning in English, "You little bitch!"

Kola didn't understand what she was saying, but from the nanny's tone, she was sure it wasn't anything nice. She stood by the door silently, listening to Esmeralda speak very nasty to her niece. Kola observed Esmeralda crouch down in front of Peaches. She held her niece firmly by her young, slim arms and glared into the child's face. She exclaimed something harshly in Spanish.

Esmeralda yanked Peaches by her arm and exclaimed, "*¡Te voy a salir a la luz!*" She then pinched Peaches so hard on her arm, Peaches howled and burst into tears.

Kola charged into the bedroom. Esmeralda was shocked to see her home. She immediately stood up. Before Esmeralda could speak, Kola slapped her so hard, she spun around and fell backwards. But it wasn't about to end there.

"You put your fuckin' hands on my child?!" she yelled.

Esmeralda held the right side of her face, staring up wide-eyed at Kola. The tears in her eyes were already building.

"Peaches, step outside for a moment," Kola said. "I need to talk to your nanny."

Peaches hurried out of the room, and Kola closed the bedroom door, leaving her and Esmeralda alone in the room. The look on Esmeralda's face was one of pure panic.

"You put your fuckin' hands on my niece?" Kola growled, approaching closer.

"Ms. *Senorita*, it was a misunderstanding," Esmeralda pleaded.

Kola wasn't trying to hear any explanations. "I saw you, bitch!" She backed Esmeralda into a corner, clenched her fists, and swung. Her fist met the left side of Esmeralda's face, spinning her around before she hit the floor.

Esmeralda cried out. She struggled to stand up. When she was standing on her feet again, Kola rushed her and slammed her foot into her stomach.

The nanny folded over, a strong "Oomph!" escaping from her lips, and fell to the floor.

Kola didn't give her time to shake off the effects of her attack. She rushed in, kicking the nanny in the face with her shoes. Her blood spewed. Kola's shoe once again slammed into the fallen woman's jaw, lifting her six inches off the floor before she fell back. The only sound beyond the crack of her skull on the ground was the soft exhalation that escaped her lips again then a tiny whimper.

Kola was all over her like stink on shit. She buried her fists into the woman's face. She wrapped the nanny's long hair around her fist and nearly yanked every strand of hair she had from its roots.

"Don't you ever touch her again!" Kola yelled, slamming her fist repeatedly into Esmeralda's eye socket and cheek.

Esmeralda screamed loudly, but no one came into the bedroom to help her. If they heard the assault, they were too afraid to interfere.

While Kola was beating the bitch down, she wondered how long this had been happening.

Kola didn't realize she was beating the nanny in the head with a blunt object. She had blacked out. Her hands were coated with blood. It took two of Eduardo's men to finally stop her. They stormed into the bedroom and grabbed her from behind. They almost slipped in Esmeralda's blood that was pooling on the floor.

They had to pick her up off the floor. She was barely moving. They dragged her out the room. Esmeralda was conscious, but she was in really bad shape from extreme head wounds.

Kola regained her composure and then went into her bedroom where Peaches was sitting quietly on her bed. She looked at her niece and said, "You will never have to worry about her hurting you again. I promise."

Peaches didn't say a word.

Kola hugged her niece, ashamed that she hadn't protected her from that sick bitch.

Eduardo heard what'd happened at his home, and he was very upset. He had to rush home early. He stormed inside and immediately looked for Kola. He charged into the bedroom and found her standing outside on the balcony alone. The balcony was becoming one of her favorite places to be.

In Spanish, he screamed, "Are you fuckin' crazy?" Then, in English, he exclaimed, "You attacked Esmeralda, for what reason?"

Kola spun around, matching Eduardo's hard scowl. "She's been abusing Peaches."

"Nonsense," he spat back. "Esmeralda would never do such a thing. She takes care of Peaches. She loves her just the same."

"I want her gone!" Kola said. "In fact, I want her dead."

"She would never lay a hand on that child."

"She has, Eduardo. I've witnessed it with my own fuckin' eyes. I want her dead!"

"You are losing your mind."

"No, I'm not."

"She would never disrespect me by laying hands on that beautiful girl."

"She has disrespected you. She has disrespected us."

Kola was fuming. *Why is he defending her? Why is he going against my word, the word of the woman he loves, for a bitch who simply works for him?*

Unbeknownst to Kola, Eduardo was fucking Esmeralda as well. The two were having a six-month affair. Esmeralda resented Kola and Peaches, the black

Americans, or the *negros*, she would call them. She strongly felt that Eduardo should be with his own kind, but she was in no position to speak up. Eduardo was her boss. She did what she was told. Others in his household felt the same way, but they kept their feelings and opinions to themselves.

"Why do you take her side?" Kola shouted, tears trickling down her face. Once again, Eduardo had hurt her deeply. Did he really love her?

"I'm not taking anyone's side."

"Why am I here, Eduardo? Do you love me? Do you love Peaches like you say you do?"

"I love that little girl more than anything. Since she came into my life, I treated her like she was my own daughter. She *is* my daughter."

"Then you need to protect her, and believe me, I have no reason to fuckin' lie to you. That bitch has been putting hands on her," Kola screamed out.

"You need to calm down."

"Don't fuckin' tell me to calm down, when this bitch is still in this fuckin' house!"

Eduardo glared at her, his look intense. She was becoming loud and disrespectful to him. He coolly closed the bedroom door, giving them extra privacy.

Kola continued to glare at him. She wasn't about to become afraid of him. She understood his power and his reputation, but she refused to become a docile bitch and a prisoner in her own home—the home he promised her, the life he guaranteed for her. Yes, her life in Colombia was lovely. She had money and many fine things, but today, Kola would give it all away just to be happy again. She wanted to feel secure and loved by Eduardo.

"Are you fuckin' that bitch?" she asked out of the blue, words spewing from her mouth before she had time to process them.

"If you want to keep living like this, I caution you to watch your tongue and choose your next words carefully," he evenly said to her. "You can stay, or you can go."

Kola's eyes were flooded with tears. She was overwhelmed with grief. She locked eyes with Eduardo. His eyes were on fire, but her eyes were fading fast. She wanted to go, but how, and where? It was all too much for her to handle.

"If you don't believe me, then you need to believe her," Kola said. She charged past Eduardo and stormed out of the bedroom. She ran to get Peaches.

The little girl was in her bedroom playing with her dolls. Kola rushed inside and scooped Peaches up into her arms. As she was making her way back to her bedroom, she said to Peaches, "I want you to tell *Papá* what happened to you today, and what's been happening."

Peaches nodded.

Kola went back into the bedroom with Peaches in her arms.

The minute Eduardo saw her, he smiled at her and said in Spanish, "Hello, my little princess."

Peaches smiled back and replied to him in Spanish, "*Hola, Papá.*"

They both were delighted to see each other. Kola placed her niece down on the floor, near Eduardo.

Eduardo looked at Peaches. He continued to smile. Her presence always made him happy. She would never see the evil that he did, because he protected her from any cruelty or harshness. He felt it was his duty. He only wanted the little girl to see the beauty of his world, not the ugliness of it. To many people, Eduardo was a brutal, psychopath drug kingpin. To Peaches, he was merely *Papá*.

Eduardo crouched toward Peaches and then decided to rest on his knees. She would be the only thing that got him on his knees. He was the same eye level with her. His expression was still even-tempered. He looked at her and simply said, "Princess, talk to *Papá*, and I want you to be truthful with me, okay?"

Peaches nodded.

Kola stood in the background with her arms crossed over her chest. She looked at her man with an attitude. She was waiting for some results. And she was still angry that it had to come to this. Her word should have been enough.

Eduardo asked, "Has anyone in this house been hurting you?"

Peaches hesitated for a quick moment, staring at Eduardo innocently, and then she nodded. "Yes."

Hearing her say yes, already, he could feel his blood boiling. "Yes. Who?"

Peaches looked at Kola. She was somewhat afraid. She didn't want to answer. She didn't want to get into trouble, or have someone else get into trouble.

"Tell him the truth, Peaches," Kola said. "We're here to help you, because we love you." Peaches nodded. Her eyes went back to Eduardo, who was no longer smiling.

"Tell us who, Peaches," he said.

"Esmeralda," she blurted out.

"Esmeralda? She's the one that has been mistreating you?"

Peaches nodded. "Yes."

"I told you."

"Hush!" Eduardo barked out.

Kola didn't say another word.

"Princess, continue on. What has she been doing to you? Talk to me. You won't get into any trouble. I promise you."

"Okay, Papá. She's mean to me and tells me I'm ugly and that I'm nobody's baby. She says my hair is not Colombian and my face . . . my face, Papá, is not like your face. She pinches me, and sometimes slaps me," Peaches said. "And when I cry, she tells me I'm a bad girl and if I keep crying that God will kill my parents in their sleep."

Kola clenched her fists. She started to seethe with rage. She wanted to finish what she'd started. She wasn't alone. Eduardo started to get stirred up with anger by what he was hearing.

"I want that bitch taken care of," Kola said.

"Let her continue to talk," Eduardo said through clenched teeth.

Peaches said, "She calls me names—orphan, ugly black child, and smelly. She pulls my hair all the time and when I say, 'Ouch,' she says, 'Shut up!'"

Eduardo had heard enough. He stood up abruptly.

Kola noticed the rage and anger on his face.

Peaches looked up at him worriedly.

He looked at her and said, "She'll never hurt you again, Princess. I promise." He walked out the bedroom.

Kola went over to her niece and hugged her tightly. She hoped Eduardo would do what needed to be done. Nobody should be able to put their hands on her or her niece and not suffer the consequences.

# SEVEN

Eduardo sat behind his desk in his office, puffing on a thick cigar. He couldn't calm down after what Peaches had told him earlier. He was seething with so much rage that he could take on the Incredible Hulk and probably win. Anyone who hurt or abused children would pay heavily, especially when that child was Peaches.

They didn't take Esmeralda to any hospital. He had a doctor on call, on his payroll. He came and treated Esmeralda in her room. She was still in bad shape, but his doctor was the best.

Ten minutes after Peaches told him what happened, Esmeralda was escorted into Eduardo's office by one of his goons. Before the door could shut, Kola and Peaches walked in. Kola had Peaches' hand in hers. She glared at the badly battered and bruised Esmeralda.

"I should cut your fuckin' head off," Kola said.

Esmeralda looked afraid. She stood timidly in the center of Eduardo's office. She tried to look innocent, like she was the victim. Her eyes shifted from Eduardo to Kola, down to Peaches.

Eduardo stood up and removed himself from around his desk. He positioned himself directly in front of Esmeralda, puffing on his cigar. He looked at her and said in Spanish, "I want the truth. What happened?"

Esmeralda looked despondent. *"¿Qué?"* she asked, looking at her boss with a baffled gaze.

"Don't act stupid with me, Esmeralda. Why are you here?"

*"Para servirle,"* she responded, meaning, "to serve you."

Eduardo narrowed his eyes. "I've heard bad things about you, Esmeralda, from my little princess over there." His voice was harsh, and his stare was deadly. "Things that I will not tolerate in my home."

"Whatever it is, she's lying!" Esmeralda exclaimed in Spanish.

"Are you calling her a liar?"

"I love Peaches."

"Are you calling her a liar?" Eduardo asked sternly.

Esmeralda didn't know what to say or do. She was in the lion's den. She became extremely nervous.

Kola continued to glare at her. Esmeralda's face looked like a bumpy road. Her right eye was swollen shut, her upper lip had bubbled up, and she had bruises and cuts everywhere.

"Princess, tell me what she has done to you again," Eduardo said, looking at Peaches kindly.

Once again, while Esmeralda was standing in the same room, Peaches went on to explain the abuse and mistreatment she suffered when alone with her nanny.

Esmeralda looked in shock by the accusations against her. She tried to lie over and over again, plead her case, and make it look like the little girl had a wild imagination.

Eduardo's face was stone. He didn't want to hear any more. He forgot Peaches was still in the room when he slapped Esmeralda so hard that she toppled over the chair she stood next to.

Esmeralda cried out to him in Spanish, pleading for her lover to have some compassion and mercy on her.

Eduardo walked toward his desk, got on his phone, and made a call.

Esmeralda stood up. She was clearly shaken up by the blow. She staggered toward his desk, her eyes in tears. Didn't he remember all the nights they'd secretly made love and he called out her name? Didn't those moments count for something? Leniency perhaps?

Two goons in black suits looking as serious as Ebola entered Eduardo's office. It didn't take a rocket scientist to know what the men were there for. They were part of Eduardo's hit squad.

The nanny ran toward Eduardo, falling to her knees, throwing herself at his feet. "Eduardo, please, don't do this to me. I love you!" she pleaded to him in Spanish. "I love you! I meant no harm. I'm sorry! I'm so sorry!"

Eduardo scowled down at the quivering bitch and kicked her away. "I want no part of you," he said in Spanish.

As his men in black approached, Esmeralda screamed out, refusing to go. But she didn't have a choice. They reached down and roughly pulled her away from their boss.

"I thought you loved me! How can you kill me, Eduardo? I thought you loved me! I gave you me, my body. Everything!" Esmeralda screamed to him in Spanish. *"¡Haceré cualquiera cosa!"*

Kola smirked at it all. She had a sixth sense they were going to kill her, and seemed very pleased about it.

Peaches stood behind her, observing and listening to everything. They'd forgotten that she was still in the room.

As the two goons in black dragged a screaming and kicking Esmeralda out the room, the third goon simply opened the door. She continued to fight. She was feisty, but it was like a fly trying to attack a cat. She didn't even leave a scratch on them.

Kola followed behind the goons, exiting the office and moving into the hallway, still smirking. For once, Eduardo did something right—something that was in her favor. He showed that he was on her side and that he loved Peaches like his own daughter.

The whole staff stood around watching the spectacle. In their hearts, they all knew they would never see Esmeralda again. Some even looked at Kola with disgust, but their unflattering looks toward the drug kingpin's woman were subtle. They dared not to allow their ugly looks to linger in the wrong direction long enough for Eduardo to see.

The American Negro was the boss. She was taking over.

Kola wanted to know everything that had been said in Eduardo's office. Her gut feeling told her that Eduardo and the nanny had something going on. She saw Esmeralda's reaction, and it showed a woman hurt like her, a woman's heart torn apart.

She took Peaches up to her bedroom and sat her on the bed. "Peaches, I need you to do me a favor. Can you do that for me?"

Peaches nodded.

"Okay. I want to know, what was Esmeralda saying to your papá?"

Peaches looked her aunt in the eye. She then said, "She told Papá that she loved him."

Kola could feel her insides churning with anger. "She did, huh?"

Peaches nodded.

"What else did she say to him?"

Peaches went on to translate their entire conversation.

When Peaches was done, Kola felt like she was on fire. He was fucking the nanny too. He couldn't keep his dick in his pants.

"Go play," she told Peaches.

Peaches hopped off the bed and ran out.

Kola stood there fuming in the bedroom. She was sick and tired of Eduardo's shit.

Eduardo, clad in his suit jacket and walking toward the front door with his men, didn't expect to have a large vase thrown at his head. It went smashing against the wall, barely missing him. His armed men spun around quickly, their guns drawn, and aimed their weapons at a fuming Kola. They were relieved it was her, though, and not a rival of Eduardo.

"You fuckin' bastard!" Kola screamed at him.

Eduardo smirked. He had been expecting the outburst from her. He read her like a book. He knew Kola would ask Peaches to translate what was said in his office, and that she would find out that he was fucking the nanny. He was ready to leave so she could cool down. But he was a little too late.

"You were fuckin' that bitch!"

"Walk away." Eduardo's face tightened.

"Fuck you!"

Kola rushed his way, but his men stopped her, putting up a wall between Eduardo and her.

Right under her nose, he was fucking the nanny, and she felt disgusted by it.

He glared at Kola and said, "If you don't like it, you can leave. Leave with no money, no clothes, and no Peaches."

"No Peaches? Are you crazy?" she exclaimed.

Eduardo's steadfast look gave Kola her answer.

Kola stared at him, protected behind his security, though he didn't need protection from her.

He smirked.

"Did you ever love me?" she asked, point-blank.

He didn't answer right away. Looking her in the eyes, he said, "I could live without you. Now, if you excuse me, I have some business to take care of." He turned and made his exit.

Kola stood there, feeling crushed by his remark, and almost hopeless.

# EIGHT

The morning sun percolated through the open window, shining brightly on Apple as she lay naked against Twin. She looked up and exhaled. Gold and pale, the sunbeams filled the entire room with a warm sensation that almost made her smile. Last night with Twin was amazing. The sex was breathtaking, and she'd needed some good dick.

She removed herself from his hold and walked toward the open window. It was another beautiful day. The sun was giving a new light to Baltimore's dull landscape. Twin was still sleeping, knocked out cold like he'd received an upper cut from Mike Tyson. His body was priceless—a six-pack, nice chest, and well-defined arms, along with a big dick and strong legs.

Last night was the best sex she'd had in a long time. They didn't hesitate to get at each other. They'd gotten naked hurriedly, and he pushed her legs back and had a three-course meal eating her pussy out. The heat was intense. They both were intoxicated with lust. She was ready to fuck him.

Next he took careful aim. He strapped up and had pushed the head in, and they both let out a guttural noise. She acclimated to his size without any pain whatsoever. It helped that she was turned on, ready to achieve her orgasm. Inch by inch, Twin pushed himself deeper into Apple, until she felt like she couldn't breathe anymore.

The pleasure was indescribable. They were two partners ready to experience that mind-blowing, heart-stopping sensation. He was fully inside her, groaning and moaning, cupping her tits, and enjoying her glorious insides.

Apple wrapped herself around him completely. *Fuck Pug, fuck Saint, and the owner of the club!* Twin had the dick she needed.

Twin withdrew himself almost completely and then thrust himself inside her again. He was rhythmic and refined, moving his dick in and out, in and out, in and out.

Apple wrapped her legs around him and pulled him closer. "Aaaah, fuck me," she groaned.

Twin's dick had her open like a good book. His strokes were deep and dynamic. His kisses were passionate.

When they both had reached their peak, they collapsed onto each other, breathless. Apple comforted him with sweet, soft kisses on his face and lips.

They were now lovers. It'd been two weeks since they met, subsequently going out on their first date. Spending time with Twin was fun. He was charismatic and sexual, also intriguing. Being with him helped Apple take her mind off certain things.

Apple stood by the window, gazing out at a wretched East Baltimore. She would be late for work again, but she didn't care. She was having a good time, enjoying her male company. She and Twin—they were living for today, partying, drinking, fucking their brains out. She missed a few days of work. She didn't care.

It was almost afternoon. Twin hadn't moved her bed. It was obvious he wasn't a morning person.

Apple donned a long, white T-shirt and left the bedroom. She went into the kitchen to make a fresh pot of coffee. With the coffee brewing, she sat at the table and lit a cigarette. Taking a deep drag, and then exhaling, Apple looked pensive.

Peaches abruptly flooded her mind. Not knowing if her daughter was dead or alive was a haunting feeling. Too many years had gone by thinking about her torturous time in Mexico, the men who raped her, and what Shawn had done to her. It was a memory she would never share with anyone.

What she knew about Twin was that he lived in DC, but he always was out of town for drug distribution, networking, and doing business in Maryland, Newark, New York, and Philadelphia. Baltimore became his second home. Something about the city captivated him.

The coffeemaker sounded, and Apple stood up and removed two coffee cups from the cupboard. As she was about to pour the coffee, she heard someone knocking at her door. She wasn't expecting any company. She already had company in her bedroom.

Not wanting to take any chances, she grabbed her pistol, cocked it back, and went to see who was at the door. She cautiously looked through the peephole and was surprised and annoyed to see Pug. He continued knocking hard.

Apple sighed. She lowered her weapon and slowly opened the door halfway.

Pug smiled at her, eager to see her. He said, "I missed you, yo. I came by to get some of that good loving."

Apple frowned. She regretted bringing him back to her place.

"You gonna let me in?"

"Why are you here?"

"I told you, I missed you."

"Now is not a good time, Pug. In fact, there will no longer be a good time for you to come by here unannounced."

"Well, I'm here now, so let's take advantage of it. I brought that good weed too." He smiled.

Apple frowned. "You need to leave," she told him.

His smile started to transform. "Fuck you mean, I need to leave?" he growled. "What? You fuckin' someone else?"

"In fact, I am."

He frowned heavily. Though they weren't a couple, Pug had grown feelings for her. He pushed open the door and forced his way inside.

"Nigga, is you fuckin' crazy?"

"I'm crazy for you, Sassy."

Apple raised her pistol at his head. "Get the fuck out!"

He chuckled. "What? You gonna shoot me now?" He figured her to be a simple bitch that was new in town. "Yo, I ain't here to hurt you."

"You need to leave," she said once more through clenched teeth.

"You gonna do me like that?" He stepped forward.

Apple was tempted to put a bullet in his head.

Suddenly, Twin said, "You heard the lady. You need to leave." Twin was shirtless and aiming a .9mm at Pug's head.

Pug shot a hard look at Twin.

"She won't shoot you," Twin said. "But I will, nigga."

"Wow! So it's like that, huh?"

"Yeah, nigga, it is," Twin replied with an intense stare. He approached Pug, making the barrel of his pistol seem larger to him.

Pug took a few steps backwards, moving closer to the door.

"You know what?" Pug said. "Y'all got this one!"

"Got this one," Twin said, incredulously. "You know who the fuck I am? I got all ones!"

"I don't give a fuck, nigga! When we see each other again, I guarantee it's gonna be a different outcome."

Twin was tempted to blow his brains out, but he didn't want the heat at Apple's place. "I'm a nightmare, nigga. You don't want it."

"Ayyite, bruh, enjoy that bitch."

Pug nodded his head, scowling like he'd sucked on a sour lemon. He left the apartment without creating an incident.

Twin slammed the door and looked at Apple. "He your ex?"

"No, just a stupid nigga that was a mistake."

"Well, you ain't gotta worry about him anymore. I got your back." He glanced down at the revolver in Apple's hand. He grinned. "I see you strap. You know how to work that thing, shorty?"

Apple rolled her eyes. "If you looking for a weak bitch, you won't find her here."

"I see that."

She made him a cup of coffee and they sat at the kitchen table and talked.

Apple's job at National Credit Collectors was no more. She had been fired. She was late repeatedly and missed too many days of work. Most of her time went to Twin, and she had to rely on her night job and tips to pay her bills. Losing her job was a gift and a curse. She no longer had to worry about getting up early and juggling two jobs, but she now had less income and more stress.

She hadn't asked Twin for any support, which was shocking to her. But what was more shocking was that Twin was a baller, yet he never offered to help her out with her financial situation. He was aware that she'd lost her job. They were sexing each other crazily, but when it came to his help with money, the muthafucka happened to be stingy. He easily splurged money in the clubs and on the streets, but he was Mr. Scrooge at home.

Apple had a problem with that. She would joke about his stinginess. Sometimes she was blunt and harsh.

"You know, most niggas would pay for this good pussy," she had joked to Twin.

"I ain't most niggas," he would joke back.

Now she had to work extra hard for tips at the club. She steadily cracked on Twin for her rent, a new car, and help with her utilities, and reluctantly, after making many excuses, he gave her a few hundred dollars for her bills and some pocket change. She was turned off by his cheapness, but not enough to drop him. She was in too deep; feelings had developed, and she liked having him around.

The club was extra lively on Saturday night. The bar was swamped. Apple was behind the bar serving customers drinks. With the blaring music and the dancing lights, it was hard to think inside. She tried working extra hard to receive bigger tips, which meant flirting with a few male customers and women too, and smiling repeatedly.

Twin walked in with his crew, and like usual, they were ushered into the VIP section of the club. In passing, he smiled and winked Apple's way.

But what was shocking was that Twin had a girl under his arm. They looked too cozy together. She was pretty and petite, with long, silky, black hair, and tinted eyebrows. Her extra-large ass cheeks were hanging out of her teeny weeny booty shorts, and her double D fake boobs were suffocating in her extra tight T-shirt. She had *hoochie* and *trashy* written all over her.

*Who is this bitch?* Apple thought. Twin never spoke of a girlfriend. She thought they were developing something special. But there was Twin with his arm around this strange woman, showing her off like she was some trophy wife. He seemed very comfortable with her.

Twin's gaze lingered on Apple. While he smiled her way, she frowned back. At the moment, she couldn't question him about it. The bar was too busy, and her break wasn't for another two hours.

The girl noticed Twin's attention on Apple. Immediately, Apple received a weighty scowl from her. They didn't have to say a word to each other, but already there was tension between them.

Apple watched the two walk into VIP like they were Beyoncé and Jay-Z. Twin had the audacity to bring a bitch to the club, knowing how she felt about him. She huffed and puffed faintly. She tried not to let it get to her, but seeing the girl sitting on Twin's lap made her want to act a fool. But she was working.

She'd chanced her job before, beating a bitch's ass in the bathroom, and had gotten away with it. She probably wouldn't be so lucky a second time. So it behooved her to continue keeping a low profile and not think about it. Apple was sour, but she did her best to try and ignore it. Her job was important. She only had one left.

Occasionally, she would look up at VIP and see Twin popping bottles, dancing, and mingling with the girl. A few times, the girl would catch Apple staring up at her.

"You okay?" Apple's coworker asked.

"Yeah, I'm okay. Just a little tired," Apple said.

Every hour, the bar became busier and busier. Little by little, the bottles of Hennessy, E&J, Cîroc, and Grey Goose were being drained.

Apple glanced at VIP once again. The long haired brunette was no longer with Twin. He was alone. She wasn't too concerned, but when she noticed the bitch coming her way, Apple took a deep breath and kept busy.

"Excuse me, let me get a Cîroc and Coke," one customer asked.

"I need two shots of vodka."

"Bartender, over here, I need a Corona and a Heineken," another shouted.

The orders kept on coming and coming.

After Apple was done fulfilling two orders, the girl Twin was with stood at the bar, just a few feet from her. She was frowning and looked upset.

Everything in Apple's gut told her to ignore the girl, but it was hard to do. Inevitably, the two locked eyes and were face to face, the wide bar counter separating them.

"Excuse me, do you know my man?" the girl asked.

"Do you?" Apple snapped back.

"Bitch, I would appreciate if you stop fuckin' eyeballing us. Do you understand me?"

Apple wanted to calm the situation. "Please don't call me a bitch again."

"Bitch! You heard me." The female was bobbing her head from side to side and making aggressive hand movements when she spoke. "I don't fuckin' need to repeat myself. It's rude, and I don't fuckin' like it!"

Apple scowled back and exclaimed, "Cunt! I don't give a fuck what you like—And yes, I'm fuckin' him too."

It came unexpectedly, the drink thrown in Apple's face.

Her reaction was swift. Apple leaped over the bar like a superhero springing into action and attacked. The first punch connected with the girl's chin and sent her staggering backwards. Apple lunged forward, and the crowd around them seemed to part like a zipper opening. The second punch doubled the girl over and expelled the last of choked air from her stomach. Like a wild animal, Apple went for the girl's face. She grabbed her hair with brute force and dragged her down to the floor.

The girl tried to fight back; kicking, pouncing, and screaming. "Get off me, bitch!" she yelled. She moved her legs wildly Apple's way, like she was pedaling an invisible bicycle. Her high heels went flying upwards, trying to strike Apple in her face. Her shirt lifted above her chest while on the club floor, revealing she didn't have a bra on. All her business was shown to people—her ballooned, stiff breasts and all.

Apple repeatedly struck the girl in her face, bloodying her forehead. She went for the body, her fist slamming into the girl's ribs. "I told you don't fuck with me!" Apple shouted.

"Get the fuck off me!"

Three more punches landed, crippling the girl. By the time security pulled Apple off the girl, she was a bloody mess.

Twin came running from VIP in time to see two beefy security guards trying to keep Apple away from the girl.

When a few bystanders tried helping the petite girl to her feet, she staggered and fell into their arms.

"Damn!" someone said. "She fucked her up!"

Another yelled, "That bitch got bodied."

Apple shouted, "Nah let me go! Fuck that bitch! She wanna come at me and throw drinks in my face. Fuck that bitch! Let me go! Let me the fuck go!"

Security had her tightly restrained.

Twin and Apple looked at each other. She screamed, "Fuck you, Twin! Fuck you!"

He had no words. He knew he was wrong. He looked at his girlfriend and shook his head. This was the second bitch Apple done beat down in the club. In a twisted way, it turned him on. There was something about a bitch who could truly handle herself, and fight the way Apple did. That gangster shit made his dick hard. Though she was cursing him out and acting a fool, he wanted her right then and there.

The manager came to inspect the melee. Instantly, Apple was sent to his office. He didn't tolerate his employees fighting with his customers; he didn't care who was right or wrong. Ultimately, she was fired.

Apple stormed out of the club fuming.

When she left the building, Twin followed her out. "Sassy, let me talk to you," he said.

"Fuck you!" she yelled, as she kept walking away from him. "Bitch-ass nothing nigga!"

He hurried her way. "Listen, let me explain."

"Eat my ass, trick!"

He jogged to catch up, and when he did, he forcefully grabbed her by her arm and turned her around.

"I lost my fuckin' job!"

"Look, I'm sorry. I'll get it back for you."

"Fuck your apologies!" Apple shook her head. "You're dumb and too immature to handle a bad bitch like me."

"I'll admit what I did was stupid, but let me make it up to you, shorty."

"You disrespected me, Twin. You got me mixed up with the airheads you fuck with. I ain't that bitch."

"Let me talk."

"Fuck you!"

Twin got in Apple's face, cementing his position, and said, "It was a mistake bringing her to the club. I don't want her. I want you, Sassy. Fuck that bitch inside the club."

"Why you bring her? To embarrass me?"

"No."

"Is she your girlfriend?"

"It's complicated."

"Complicated? It's either a yes or no answer."

"She's my ex, but I don't fuck with her like that."

"You could have fooled me, nigga."

"Look, let's go somewhere and talk."

"I don't want to go anywhere and talk with you, Twin. I lost my job because of that bitch. In fact, I lost my job because of you bringing that bitch. You just don't know, nigga, you just don't know who the fuck I"—Apple had to stop herself from revealing anything that had to do with her past.

Apple was seething. Her eyes were cloudy with tears. She couldn't believe she had caught feelings for Twin, and that she had settled into a new life that was a far cry from her past. This mundane life, working a regular job, having to humble herself to muthafuckas she would deem inferior to her, was sickening.

Twin grabbed her in a bear hug.

"Get off me, Twin," she said.

"I just want us to talk."

Apple screamed out of sheer frustration. "Go talk with that skank bitch in the club!"

"I don't want her, Sassy. I want you and only you. Please baby, please forgive me. Whatever you need me to do, I'll do. I just want your attention. I want you to calm down."

She'd never seen Twin like this, almost looking desperate. Here was a handsome thug who could have any bitch within miles, and he was vying for a little bit of her time, almost begging for her forgiveness.

"Yo, let me make it up to you, ayyite? Whatever you want, you got. You want a new car? Done. New wardrobe? I got you! Those red bottoms? Yours, baby. Just please don't shut me out."

Apple's eyes were softening. Although she was enraged by him, she couldn't let him go so easily. She didn't want him to walk away. In a way, she needed him.

"You better make it up to me, Twin. I swear, because I'm not that bitch to allow you to keep fucking with my heart."

"I know. I see that."

"You gonna get me my job back?"

"You really need that job?"

"I need something," she said. "And you know the owner, right?"

"I'll see what I can do for you, okay?"

It wasn't okay. But it was better than nothing.

"C'mon, let's go back to your place and talk," he said, his voice cooler and a little demanding.

Apple knew what was going to happen if they went back to her place. Despite how mad she was, she couldn't stay mad at him. It was at that moment that she realized she had fallen in love with him.

# NINE

K ola cried her eyes out night after night. Eduardo had become distanced from her. He was constantly gone, either for business or pleasure. She didn't have his undivided attention, or his love. She was still in love with him, but now, she felt he didn't feel the same. She was a prisoner of love. She felt uncomfortable in his home. It was almost the same feeling and situation with Cross years earlier, when he got that Brooklyn bitch pregnant. It was déjà vu all over again.

She wasn't about to suffer through the same thing again in a different country. She thought she'd found love and that Colombia would be her home permanently, but it was starting to feel like hell. Kola noticed herself turning into *that* woman. She was always angry, insecure, and now turning into a full-blown stalker.

Secretly, from her bedroom window she stared at Eduardo climbing into the backseat of his black SUV, his henchmen accompanying him. It was almost midnight.

Eduardo was dressed nicely in a black suit and polished shoes, looking impeccable. It turned Kola's stomach to think that he might be going to see another woman and have sex with her.

The other night, Kola had noticed a woman coming to visit the estate in the middle of the night. From her window, Kola watched the SUV pull up to the entrance, the driver stepping out and opening the door. Stepping out from the backseat of the truck was a beautiful young woman. She was escorted inside and disappeared somewhere inside the mansion. Kola got up and ran throughout the whole house looking and calling for Eduardo. Neither he, nor the woman was found. When she got to one of the twelve en-suites, she was prevented entry by two of Eduardo's henchmen. She knew they were in there, alone. Kola kicked, screamed, scratched at the bodyguards but was unable to penetrate their protective barrier.

As the weeks labored on, more women showed up. Eduardo would have them chauffeured from their home to his estate. There was no way she was going to keep living with him under those circumstances.

She felt the time was right. He was away, so now was her chance. She hurried out her bedroom. Clad in sweats and a T-shirt, she trotted down to his private office. Most of his men were gone, the staff either to their own homes, or sleeping somewhere in the bedrooms in the house. The house was still and dark.

She reached his office door. It was locked, as she predicted. Kola wasn't a stranger to picking locks. Her criminal background was always resourceful to her. Using a flat-sided hairpin to open the turn-style knob lock, she inserted it into the hole on the front knob and turned. She was able to push the little metal bar in, bypassing the lock, and opening the door.

She was inside Eduardo's dark office alone. She didn't want to turn on the lights and attract unwanted attention, so she used the flashlight app on her cell to look around. She went straight to his desk. She picked open the bottom drawer. Inside were Peaches' and her passports, some cash, and a pistol.

Eduardo had paid handsomely for their passports, for when they would travel together as a family. But they hadn't been put to use yet. They simply stayed locked away in his office.

Kola grabbed the passports, the cash, and the pistol. Though Eduardo wasn't home, he still had eyes and ears everywhere. She hurried back to her bedroom, her heart beating fast.

She opened Peaches' bedroom door. Her niece was sound asleep, looking peaceful. It was a shame she had to disturb the little girl from her rest. She plopped down on the bed and began to stir her awake. "Peaches, get up. We have to go. C'mon, you need to get up." She continued shaking the little girl.

Seconds later, Peaches opened her eyes. She was still drowsy. She gazed at Kola and asked, "Is it daytime yet?"

"No, baby, but we have to go."

"Where?"

"Just get dressed. It's important."

Kola hurried Peaches into her clothing. She too hurriedly got dressed. The mansion remained still, the hallways dark or dimmed. Kola's plan was to leave with the clothes on their backs, steal one of Eduardo's numerous cars, and go collect her money from the cemetery.

She carried Peaches in her arms and rushed down the stairway. She jogged through the manor and made her way toward the garage that had a collection of expensive cars. Each step was nerve-wracking for Kola. Her eyes darted everywhere. She held her niece tightly in her arms.

Peaches looked at her aunt baffled. "Where's Papá?"

"Papá's not here, baby. He had to go take care of some business. It's just you and me," Kola said in a low monotone.

Kola looked for car keys and came across a set of keys to one of Eduardo's new toys, a black Bentley Continental GT. Eduardo had a thing for black, from his cars to his clothes to even his women.

Kola placed Peaches into the backseat and strapped her in. She climbed behind the wheel, took a deep breath, and started the ignition. The car purred to life. She opened the garage door, put the Bentley in drive, and eased out.

Sunset was a few hours away. Kola wanted to escape into the darkness. She wanted to reach the nearest airport and escape back to America.

She maneuvered the Bentley off the sprawling property, speeding toward the exit down the hill. So far, so good.

She continued onto the winding road. It was dark, the road winding, and a little bumpy for a half a mile. Peaches was very alert. It was them and the unpaved road. She didn't know the roads of Colombia, but she was going to find her way, especially to the cemetery where her money was buried. How was she going to smuggle five million out of the country? She planned on crossing that bridge when she got to it, but her first thought was to ship it back to the states via FedEx international. It wasn't drugs so it shouldn't be flagged.

Kola made a sharp left on the winding dirt road, maneuvering the Bentley the best she could and approaching a long, paved stretch of road.

Several miles from the house, Kola suddenly noticed a pair of bright headlights in her rearview mirror. The car behind her was moving fast. Maybe it was nobody, maybe it was a threat. She fixed her attention on the rearview mirror, at the same trying to focus on the road. It was hard to tell what type of vehicle was behind her. The lights were bright, almost blinding, and they were approaching fast.

Becoming nervous, she floored it. This wasn't a coincidence; they were definitely after her. The speedometer showed seventy miles per hour. The horsepower in the Bentley kicked in. She tried not to flip off the embankment, going down the hill, keeping control of the car.

The car fishtailed a little, sliding faintly off the road, and the tires screeched, but Kola still had control of the car. She gripped the steering tightly with both hands and accelerated. The vehicle behind her matched her speed. It was catching up.

"I'm scared," Peaches said.

"It's gonna be okay, baby." Kola told her. "Just hang on." She continued traveling at a high speed.

The black SUV, moving erratically, was closing in on her. It made no attempt to slow down. The lights became brighter in her mirror. She could hear the roar of the engine. The road became darker, and her heart was beating out of her chest.

She pushed heavily on the gas. She felt the vehicle move like it was in the Indy 500. Her eyes went back and forth from the rearview mirror to the windshield.

The truck slammed into her rear end at high speed, almost causing her to veer off the road. They jerked inside the car.

Kola hollered.

Peaches started to cry. "I want Papá," she hollered.

It was becoming harder to control the Bentley, with the truck slamming into her purposely, trying to make her stop or crash.

The driver was crazy. He didn't care that there was a child in the car. Kola wasn't used to driving these roads, the other driver was. He continued to crash into her, from the back and the side.

They were approaching a sharp turn on the road. At the speeds both vehicles were traveling, it was inevitable that one or both would flip over and crash.

Peaches was crying. Kola didn't know what to do.

Panic overwhelmed her. Her car continued to skid left and right, becoming difficult to control.

The sharp turn was approaching fast. If she slowed down, the truck had the advantage. If she continued speeding, there was a chance that she and Peaches could both lose their lives.

Another powerful hit from behind almost sent them flying over the embankment, and both Peaches and Kola shrieked from the impact.

Kola couldn't help thinking, *They're gonna kill us.*

The dreaded turn was a few feet away. At seventy-five miles per hour, there was no way she and Peaches were going to survive it.

Another hard hit from behind lifted her back wheels a foot off the ground and sent the Bentley careening into the sharp turn. Terrified, both girls screamed to the top of their lungs. This was it—the end.

"Hold on, Peaches!" Kola screamed frantically.

Death was one way of escaping. Finally, she would be free from Eduardo.

The Bentley went gliding on two wheels, careening out of control, about to crash into a rock wall. From gliding on two wheels, it flipped on its side, and the car went colliding into the rock wall. A loud bang followed. The impact was powerful, and the Bentley was severely damaged.

The truck came to a screeching stop. All four doors opened, and several men stepped out on the pavement. They started to approach the wreckage.

Besides a nasty bruise on her forehead, Kola was alive. She found herself twisted inside the wreckage, but she was alive. Fear suddenly overcame her.

"Oh my God! Peaches!" she screamed out, searching to see if her niece was okay.

"Mama," Peaches cried out.

"It's okay, baby. I'm here." Kola was contorted in her seatbelt, unable to move. She could see men coming her way. She struggled to free herself, but to no avail.

Trapped inside the crashed vehicle, she continued to cry out to Peaches, not knowing what their fate was.

Kola felt the car being flipped over, back on all four wheels, and the doors pried open. She was roughly dragged out of the car. Peaches was still okay, crying, wanting to go home.

In bad shape, Kola fell to her knees. She was shocked to look up and see Eduardo standing over her and glaring at her, his men surrounding her.

"You run away, after I give you everything?" he exclaimed heatedly. "I told you that you will not take my child away from me."

Kola was terrified as she watched one of Eduardo's goons screw on a silencer to the barrel of his gun, while scowling her way. She lowered her head and closed her eyes. She felt she'd let Peaches down. She didn't want to die, but she knew men like Eduardo were rarely merciful.

# TEN

Apple turned the water on, and the shower came to life. She stepped inside the running shower, and Twin followed her. They faced each other, her hands gripping his shoulders, pulling him closer. Twin raised his hands up to Apple's hair and poked his fingers inside her soft, wet hair. He opened his mouth and inserted his tongue in hers. They kissed passionately as the water cascaded on them. Twin lowered his hands to her breasts and felt her softness. They continued kissing, enjoying each other, their lips moving in time with each other.

Apple's hands gracefully moved to below his waist, feeling his naked body. She grabbed his manhood and stroked a huge erection into her hand. He was hard like stone. Her hand continued to slide up and down his cock, her wet hands now completely coating his erection.

She turned away from him, her back now against his chest. Softly, he curved her over into the doggy-style position. Her hands flat against the shower walls, Twin parted her ass cheeks, ready to penetrate her.

Apple didn't care about the incident at the club anymore. The bitch she beat down never came up. She wanted to feel him deep inside of her. She wanted him to care. She wanted to connect with him on so many levels.

In an instant, she felt his large erection penetrate her from behind. He grabbed her hips and thrust. Her fluids coated every inch of him, from his balls to the tip of his dick.

"Oh fuck! Baby, you feel so fuckin' good," he cooed.

His rhythm inside of her was gentle, but fierce. He squeezed her ass and cupped her tits. Her opening closed tightly around him. His body twitched as his hips jerked in and out the tiniest of distances with the throbbing and milking motions of her inner walls.

Her eyes were closed with the waves of pleasure washing over her body. "Fuck me!" she roared.

His thrust became deeper, feeling the euphoria of her fluids engulfing him. "I'm about to come," he announced.

She wanted him to pull out, but Twin was too far gone with the building of an orgasm. He continued to hump away, and she continued to milk his dick and balls as his balls slammed against her butt cheeks.

"I'm coming!" he yelled.

Apple moaned, feeling every bit of him spill inside of her, without any protection.

Inside the bedroom, she comforted him with her whispers and sweet, soft kisses on his face and lips. She gripped him tighter to her. Her womanly instincts wanted to protect him and nurture him, though Twin didn't need much protection at all. She caressed his caramel skin and looked him deeply in his eyes. He had hard and very cold eyes.

With no job, and no income coming in, Apple had to rely on Twin for support, and he did give, though grudgingly. While lying against him, his cell phone went off by the bed. Twin pushed her off his chest and hurried to answer his call.

"Yo, who this?" he answered brusquely.

Apple sighed. Sprawled naked across her bed, she watched Twin walk around her bedroom naked, dick swinging and body looking ripe. She wanted to swallow him whole.

"What the fuck you mean, the count is off? My count is always good," Twin said, looking upset.

Apple propped herself against the headboard, eavesdropping. He paced back and forth in the room with the phone glued to his ear, trying to handle a situation.

"Nah, Mack D be on that bullshit. If it ain't him, it be his fuckin' soldiers. I don't trust any one of those muthafuckas."

Apple removed a cigarette from her pack. She lit it and took a drag. She continued watching Twin conduct business over his cell phone. In her eyes, that was a major mistake. It was always smart to conduct business in person so you could look that person in the eye and read their expressions and body language.

After several minutes, Twin hung up abruptly. Though he was off the phone, he looked troubled.

"Let me get one of those," he said, reaching for a cigarette.

Apple removed one and handed it to him. He placed it between his lips and quickly lit it. He sat at the foot of the bed, his back toward Apple. He inhaled the nicotine and then exhaled.

"Everything okay?" Apple asked.

"Just business. Nothing major," he replied dryly.

"Well, talk to me. Maybe I can help you out."

Twin slowly turned around and looked at her mockingly, almost laughing in her face. "What you know about my world, Sassy? What you know about the game? The streets?"

"I might surprise you."

He chuckled. "You stick to what you know, and I'll stick to what I know."

Twin turned away from her and took another drag from the cancer stick. Apple wanted to get his attention somehow. She wanted to help him, but she didn't want to reveal her past or her true identity to him. He sat down at the foot of the bed and continued to smoke his cigarette, looking pensive.

Apple put out her Newport into the ashtray on the nightstand. "Your first mistake—you talkin' on an open line for too long. Anyone can be listenin'—police, the feds. It's always wise to have a face-to-face with people. And, second, if you have to talk on a cell phone, get you a burner phone. They're almost impossible to trace. Avoid leaving a trail and getting yourself caught up in illegal activities."

Twin turned back around. He wasn't laughing this time or staring at her like she was some dumb bitch. "You always surprise me. There's always something new with you," he said.

"I've been around."

"What? Your last boyfriend was a hustler?"

"You can say so, and I helped him out on a few occasions."

"Oh yeah? Doing what?"

"Whatever needed to be done."

"So you was a ride-or-die chick?"

"I was the *baddest* chick," she said evenly.

Twin smiled. "I can tell you're smart."

"It doesn't pay to be stupid."

"I feel you. So what else you know?"

"I know enough that I ran my own crew for quite some time without any interference from police." Apple felt maybe she said too much.

"You ran your own crew?" Twin said incredulously. "When? And where?"

"I don't care to talk about that. But I had to survive, and I had to learn fast."

They looked at each other. The expression she gave Twin was one of a boss that raised hell in Harlem and got her respect by any means necessary.

"Yeah, there's something more to you, Sassy. You just don't wanna tell. I'm cool wit' that."

Apple lit another cigarette. Twin was facing her way fully, looking like a student ready to raise his hand in his favorite class. Apple took a deep drag of nicotine and exhaled.

Twin was ready to talk.

Twin had been buying his kilos from a guy named Mack D, who had a huge chip on his shoulder. He was virtually extorting everyone in the DMV area. He was a major connect, and someone they didn't want to mess with. He was known to be ruthless, heavily connected, and had over a hundred killers on his payroll. Mack D had reach, power, and men.

Twin's problem with Mack D was that he would rarely be at the exchange when Twin purchased his kilos and would send his lieutenants and soldiers in his place. For some reason, Mack D would always call him back and say that his count was off, and Twin would find himself owing Mack D another ten to twenty grand. Twin's count was never off. Twin felt he was being extorted. Twin's soldiers themselves started to wonder if they were the ones skimming off the money. Or was Mack D simply playing them for a fool?

When dealers in the DMV area went to try and find work from other distributors, Mack D took it personally, and he would war with them, killing the boss and their crews if they didn't play ball. Twin had lost a few friends because of Mack D.

"Nobody's untouchable—he can be got."

"It ain't that easy. The man is like a ghost; he's rarely

seen. He don't stay in one place for too long," Twin explained. "He's too powerful."

Apple felt no one was too powerful. No one was Superman. Apple had gone to war with many powerful men and won. But this was Twin's beef, not exactly hers.

Most of Apple's time was spent with Twin, fucking, smoking, drinking, partying in the same club she was fired from, and living her life one day at a time. Twin was footing the bill for everything, and Apple wanted his rise to the top to continue.

With money tight and her bills piling up, one day Twin told her, "Yo, you gotta get your hands dirty and earn your own keep around me. This dude Mack D got my pockets bleeding. It ain't gonna be any more free rides."

Apple wasn't surprised to hear him say that. He was the cheapest muthafucka she'd ever fucked with.

"Free rides? Fuck what ya momma told you. Pussy ain't free."

"Sassy don't start beefin'. I ain't in no mood."

"What the fuck happened to my new whip and red bottoms? All those promises you made?"

Twin exhaled. "I was gonna give you all that, but like I said I gotta keep comin' out my pocket to that grimy nigga Mack D. Twenty large here, fifty large there. That shit add up."

Apple was tired of hearing him whine. She was used to getting her hands dirty and making her own money.

"What you need me to do?"

"You a ride-or-die bitch, right?"

"You need to pause all that *ride-or-die bitch* shit right now. Ain't no Jedi mind-tricking going down. I make my own decisions. Now, tell me what the fuck you need help with, and I'll let you know if I can rock with you."

"I got a plan to hit this nigga for some work. I need the extra bread," he said.

Apple was listening.

"I know this dude. He doin' okay for himself, maybe a little too okay, and I think it's time for him to start sharing some of his wealth. This nigga got about ten to fifteen ki's in the stash house. He got some cash and guns too, you know what I'm sayin', and I need that."

"I understand. And where do you need me to come in at?"

"Easy—he loves pussy."

"So you pimpin' me now?" she asked, a little attitude in her voice.

"Nah, nah, it ain't even like that, ma. I just need the distraction, and you in a tight dress is one helluva distraction."

Apple remained deadpan, realizing he wanted to use her as bait to catch a nice-size fish.

"Don't worry about anything, Sassy. I got backup for this, and if we do this right, I got ya cut set nice."

"I'm down, but let's do it right."

"I always do it right," Twin said, giving Apple the feeling he'd done this before; perhaps many times over.

Twin and Apple sat in an old, rust-colored '91 Oldsmobile on Patterson Park Avenue in East Baltimore. They inconspicuously watched the row house across the street and five houses down. Flanked by two dilapidated, abandoned row houses, with a lookout standing out front and thugs going in and out, it was definitely a stash house.

Twin's two goons, Thomas and Bulldog, were absent. The police picked up Bulldog in the early morning the day before on a weapons possession, and Thomas was MIA for some reason.

Apple and Twin did their best surveillance of the area. Behind the stash house was an empty lot cluttered with abandoned cars and a few functional ones too. The block wasn't active with too many residents, and was mostly cluttered with empty, decaying row houses and fiends walking up and down the block, searching for their drug dealers.

There were a few cars parked on the block, but it was dark and quiet. One male in a white T-shirt and long cornrows sat on the short steps, smoking a cigarette and lingering by the door of the stash house. He appeared to be the lookout.

Twin couldn't wait to rush inside and take over. He was itching to stick up the stash house. He sat in the car looking too cool, chain-smoking and toying with his pistol.

Apple shared his cigarette. She was cool too. This wasn't anything new to her.

"You ready to do this?" Twin asked Apple.

She nodded. She stepped out of the car wearing a VIP minidress that left nothing to the imagination. She strutted toward the stash house in a pair of six-inch stilettos, looking whorish from head to toe. She was confident she would get the young boy's attention.

Instantly, he looked up and set his eyes on Apple. He never diverted his attention from her. Seeing her coming his way was a treat. He smiled.

"Damn, ma! What you doin' around hurr dressed like that? You lookin' for some company tonight?" he asked.

She chuckled lightly. "What? You gonna be my company tonight?"

"You know it."

"You're cute."

"And you is lookin' good. What's good, tho?" he said in his thick Baltimore accent.

"You," Apple said, flirting with him heavily.

The boy was young, seventeen, and still naïve to certain dangers that existed. A beautiful woman on a known drug block had him slipping and losing focus. A well-experienced hustler would have known something was off. He became excited too quickly. Apple's long legs in the stilettos, a thot outfit, her curvy waist, and nice tits had the boy growing hard inside his jeans.

"What's your name?" Apple asked.

"Out here, they call me Bennie."

"Well, Bennie, I'm Cindy."

"Yeah, you look like a Cindy. You lookin' good tho. I'm sayin', can a nigga get ya number so we can link up?"

"Yeah, that can work."

The boy hurried to snatch his cell phone out of his back pocket, but before he could, he felt the cold steel of a *.9mm* on the back of his head and the chilling words, "Nigga, don't fuckin' move!"

While Apple was distracting Bennie, Twin had crept up behind him in the dark. Suddenly, his smile transformed into a worrying smile.

Apple smirked. She'd done her part too well.

"Yo, I ain't moving," the boy said in a shaky voice.

"This what we gonna do," Twin said. "We gonna go inside nice and calm. Understand?"

The boy nodded.

"How many?" Twin asked.

"Just Loop and me."

Twin was familiar with Loop. He didn't pick this stash house to rob out of the blue. Loop was eighteen, and though he was a newbie in the game, he was coming up fast on the streets, trying to make a name for himself on the East Side. He was also the boss's cousin. Still, he didn't know the ropes too well, and he wasn't too cautious with his product.

Twin gripped the boy by his neck tightly, the gun still held to the back of his head. He had nowhere to run.

"Let's go see Loop then." Twin shoved him forward, making him almost trip up the short stairs leading into the row house.

Bennie was almost in tears and shaking.

Twin was very cautious entering the building. He used Bennie as his shield, just in case. Apple was right behind him with a .45 in her hand. They moved past the dimmed foyer and continued into the building. The sparsely furnished place reeked of weed, letting them know they were in the right place. They could hear music coming from one of the rooms—Jay-Z's and Kanye West's popular song, "Niggas in Paris."

Twin continued to push Bennie along. "What room he's in?"

Bennie pointed to the last room down the hall, a door to their left.

They gaited that way with extreme caution. Anything could be waiting for them behind that door. Twin was already cocked and loaded, a bullet already in the chamber. Apple was ready too.

In front of the door, Twin and Apple took a deep breath. This was it. They didn't plan on turning back.

Twin kicked in the door then pushed Bennie into the room. If there was any gunfire, Bennie would've been the first to get hit. Twin stormed into the room behind the young boy, his gun aimed at Loop, who was on the couch with his pants around his ankles, as he received a blowjob from a young girl. The eighteen-year-old hustler and his female company were startled by the sudden intrusion.

"Oh shit!" Loop hollered.

Loop tried to spring up from the couch and reach for his gun, but it was too far from his reach. He tripped over his jeans and hit the floor face-first.

Twin didn't have to do much struggling with anyone. Loop was already incapacitated.

The young girl, butt naked and wide-eyed with panic, shrieked. Apple quickly ordered her to lie face down on the floor. Bennie too.

Loop was lying on the ground, staring up at the pistol. Twin stood over him, smirking. "Stupid muthafucka!" he said about Loop.

"What you want, man?" Loop shouted. "You know who my cousin is?"

"Yeah, nigga, and I don't give a fuck!"

Loop tried to play hard-core, but he was shaking like a leaf in the wind.

Apple and Twin duct-taped Loop, Bennie, and the girl. Twin asked for their product and money. Lying face down on the floor and restrained with his arms behind him, Loop acted like he didn't want to give it up.

Twin crouched over him, put the gun to the back of his head, and simply said, "I'm gonna count to five, and then guess what? I stop counting and you get dead. So let's make this easy."

Loop didn't respond.

"Cool. Have it your way," Twin said.

He pushed the barrel harder against the back of Loop's skull. "One . . . two . . . three . . . four . . ."

"Ayyite, man, chill. Just chill," Loop cried out. "It's in the stove—everything!"

Twin gestured to Apple to check it out. She walked toward the stove, opened the oven door, and saw nothing. She crouched lower and tapped around until she found a false bottom inside. Once she removed it, she found five kilos of heroin and twenty thousand in cash tucked neatly inside.

"Bingo!" she hollered.

Twin nodded. He was pleased that they'd found it right away. Now, it was time to do what he did best. He pointed his gun at Loop.

Apple intervened, saying, "No, you don't have to kill him."

"What the fuck you talkin' about?"

"They're kids."

Seeing the young girl, naked and full of fear, Apple was reminded of Nichols. For some reason, she was haunted by her sister's memory again.

Twin didn't want to listen. "No witnesses, you understand?"

Hearing this, their captives squirmed and mumbled something incoherent, since their mouths were duct-taped. They continued to fidget on the ground.

"They saw our faces," Twin argued.

"Look at them. They won't talk; they're too scared."

Apple couldn't see herself killing a young girl that reminded her of her little sister. She wanted them to live, but Twin was itching to create a bloodbath. Apple continued to argue with him.

Finally, it seemed like Twin had a change of heart. "Yo, y'all better thank my bitch," he said.

Hearing that, all three looked relieved.

Apple pivoted and headed toward the exit, and Twin turned and followed her, leaving all three bound and gagged.

Twin clutched his .9mm tightly. He suddenly turned back into their direction and started shooting. *Bak! Bak! Bak!* He shot all three in the back of their heads, killing them instantly.

Hearing the gunshots, Apple ran back into the room. "What the fuck did you do?" she exclaimed.

Twin looked at her and said, "This is who I am. We don't leave behind any fuckin' witnesses. I run shit, you understand?"

Apple just stood there, fuming, staring at the dead young girl, and the image flooded her brain with painful memories of Nichols. It wasn't a time to get emotional. There wasn't anything she could do.

"Let's go," Twin said.

Apple took a deep breath and left. Twin had made it clear he wasn't about to compromise himself for anyone.

# ELEVEN

She was still alive, but how, and why?

They'd restrained her with zip ties and thrown a hood over her head, blacking out everything. Beforehand, Eduardo had smacked her around with an open hand just to teach her a lesson, clearly doing more damage to her ego than any bodily harm.

Being in complete darkness, Kola was shuffled out of the compound before dawn came and tossed into the back of an SUV. She could feel many hands on her, escorting her from point A to point B very roughly. She wasn't Eduardo's main bitch any longer. Now, she was some random bitch they could make disappear.

Kola couldn't help but be afraid. She worried about Peaches. What would happen to her? Would Eduardo continue to treat her niece like she was his own? So many worrisome things flooded her head. Everyone was speaking in Spanish. She could barely understand them. She was clueless.

She lay in the fetal position in the back of the SUV, riding in complete darkness. The truck was quiet. She could feel every bump the vehicle hit. Her heart pounded so fast, it sounded like drums banging in a rock concert.

A half hour went by, they were still driving. How far were they taking her? Where were they taking her? Was Eduardo in the truck with them? She didn't know a damn thing. She couldn't move. She couldn't see. The zip ties kept her hands tied behind her. Her body started to cramp, and she started to hurt.

The vehicle came to a stop. Finally. The back lift opened, and Kola felt herself forcefully being removed from the vehicle. When she got on her feet, they pushed her forward, escorting her to some unknown location. They kept her blinded to her whereabouts.

She could hear them speaking in Spanish and could feel their strong paws wrapped around her thin arms. They went left, she went left. She could feel their breaths against her.

*Oh my God! Are they going to rape me, then kill me?* She thought.

She could hear doors opening, and then she felt the chill of a room hit her. Wherever she was, she knew it wasn't going to be a nice, comfortable place.

Finally, they undid her zip ties, but didn't remove her hood. She was pushed into a room so hard, she landed on her side and felt the wind knocked out of her.

The men laughed. She heard a door close afterwards.

"*Quédate aquí*," one of the men said to her.

"What did you say?" Kola exclaimed.

The ground was hard and dirty. Immediately Kola removed the hood from over her face and looked around. She was in a room with a twin bed, no windows, no amenities, and most important, no Peaches.

"Where am I? What is this place?" she screamed.

"*Quédate aquí,*" the man repeated, laughing.

There was a small slot in the door through which they could watch her. She looked around the room. She was screaming her head off. She pounded on the door frantically, but to no avail. She wanted to leave, but it was obvious she wasn't going anywhere.

"I want to talk to Eduardo. Where is he?" she shouted.

The men continued laughing and taunting her.

"*Vamos a violarte,*" another man said to Kola, looking at her with a lecherous grin.

Kola continued to cry out, trapped in the dungeon-style room. She fell to her knees and wanted to die. "Why am I here?"

Finally, they closed the small slot and left her in the room alone.

A week went by, and Kola was still held captive in the hole. They fed her little food and gave her little water. She felt her sanity slipping away. She felt dirty and malnourished. The bugs kept her company. At nights, the cold made her shiver. She did her best to try and console herself. She couldn't cry any more. She thought about her niece twenty-four/seven.

The area was quiet and still. Kola was sleeping on the bed at two in the morning, curled up in the fetal position.

Then, suddenly, everything changed. A deafening noise erupted from outside her cell. Shocked out of her sleep, she jumped up to her feet and looked at the door with fear. She could hear men yelling and shouting. It sounded like an army. They were moving around. She heard doors being kicked in.

*What is going on?* she wondered.

Doors were being knocked down off the hinges with battering rams. Then Kola heard gunfire. Lots of it. There was a lot of commotion, chaos, and screaming. She didn't have a clue what was going on. It sounded like they were at war.

Where was she? Where had Eduardo placed her? *Oh my God I am going to die today!*

Kola figured she was far away from her niece. She stood in the center of the room, looking and feeling helpless. That frantic feeling was sweeping over her.

*Boom!*

It felt like the room shook. Whoever it was, they were now trying to kick down the metal door to her cell.

Kola desperately tried searching for a weapon to defend herself. Not knowing what was going on was more terrifying. Whoever was on the other side of the door, were they there to murder her or help her?

There was another hard bang, more screaming, and more confusion. Defenseless and scared, Kola backed against the wall. There was no window for her to break open and climb out of.

*Boom! Boom! Boom!*

The metal door started to rattle and give way. Kola stared wide-eyed at the door. She clenched her fists. With nothing to protect herself with, she felt like a trapped stag. She was ready to fight and protect herself.

Finally, the door came off the hinges, and a half dozen armed men came storming into the room. They were in heavy riot gear—chest protectors, tactical vests, elbow pads, knee pads, riot helmets, tactical goggles, and machine guns. They were yelling in Spanish.

When they rushed Kola's way, she swung hard and fast, the ghetto coming out of her quickly, her fists connecting with the first man coming her way. It was a nice hit, but she was still outnumbered. She fought them as best as she could, but it was fruitless. They dragged her out the room kicking, punching, and screaming.

It was all happening too fast. Shockingly, as she was roughly being dragged through the perimeter, Kola started to realize something crazy. The entire time, she had been locked in the basement of Eduardo's home—an extremely large compound that was over 35,000 sq. ft. She was downstairs, still on the premises.

Everything around her was in pandemonium. People were running and screaming. Kola heard more gunfire, and then she heard an explosion close by.

"I need to find my niece. I need to know if she's okay!" Kola screamed at them.

Did they understand her? Did they speak English? Kola had no idea. They weren't responding to her at all, but they continued dragging her away, quickly moving her off the property like she was cattle. She was thrown to the ground with other staff members in the house and handcuffed like a criminal.

She didn't see Eduardo anywhere. The men creating the chaos were policemen, or corrupt federals and the National Police of Colombia. It was an army converging onto Eduardo's property like thieves in the night. But they weren't quiet about anything.

With their heavy arsenal, they looked more like the military than police. The entire area was crawling with agents. They were destroying everything.

Kola was ushered outside and thrown into the back of one of the several trucks idling on the property, along with other detainees, mostly the staff, and a few of Eduardo's henchmen.

From her vantage point, Kola could see them escorting Eduardo out in handcuffs. He was going quietly. No struggling. No talking. She scowled. It was all his fault.

But her biggest concern was Peaches.

A feeling of relief came over her when she saw Peaches being escorted out of the home by a male agent. That relief quickly transformed into anger when she noticed that they also had her in handcuffs.

"She's only five!" Kola shouted at the top of her lungs.

No one cared. Law enforcement in Colombia was worse than the criminals.

Everyone watched as the men that stormed onto the estate began looting the place, searching for jewels, cash, or any kind of valuables that weren't already seized by the corrupt government officials. They had seized all of Eduardo's bank accounts, cars, land, business, and properties—a net worth of half a billion American dollars.

Apparently, Eduardo had assassinated the wrong city official, so his reign as a drug kingpin in Colombia was coming to an end. The police were being controlled by an up-and-coming rival cartel that also had a strong influence over many corrupt government officials.

The trucks started to drive off with everyone inside. Kola had no idea where they were about to take her.

Disheartened, she lowered her head, and the tears fell. Once again, she found herself in a scary predicament. And worse, she was separated from Peaches, again.

What now?

# TWELVE

Twin sat at the kitchen table shirtless, smoking a cigarette while cutting up the heroin with talcum powder, making it street-ready. He had the five stolen ki's displayed on the table, along with the cash and the pistol he had killed three people with. He looked unapologetic about their deaths. Rick Ross' "Diced Pineapples" played from the speakers in the other room, and Apple stood by the kitchen window, gazing outside, brooding over the past twenty-four hours.

In the car yesterday, she couldn't help but fume about Twin killing the three kids, but she remained silent. She was used to having blood on her hands; it came with the game. However, that young girl in the row house, caught sucking dick, for some reason, reminded her of Nichols all over again. She tried thinking about the score, not wanting to think about her demons. She was used to being the shot-caller. If she gave an order not to murder someone, then in her past way of life, they would still be alive.

Twin took back the pistol he let Apple borrow for the jux, again displaying his cheapness.

"Yo, we did okay," Twin said, looking Apple's way, the cigarette dangling from his lips. "That little nigga was definitely holding. It was time for him to come up off it anyway."

Apple didn't respond to him. She continued staring out the window.

"Yo, you is definitely a ride-or-die bitch, fo' real. You's built for this. I like the way you handled yourself."

She lit a cigarette and took a drag. It was obvious she was ignoring him.

"Yo, I know you ain't still trippin''bout that shit, Sassy. I did what I had to do. You get caught leaving behind witnesses, they come hunting for you for revenge."

"I understand," she replied dryly.

"So why you acting like that?"

"I'm just thinking."

"What you thinkin' about?"

"Just different shit."

Twin picked up the cash on the table and angrily tossed it at her, saying, "Yo, we got all this fuckin' money to do whatever, and you actin' like a nigga shot down ya moms. Yo, lighten up, 'cuz in B-more, you either kill a nigga, or he gonna kill you. Ain't no hesitation in this shit. You understand?"

Twin took a final pull from his cigarette and doused it in the ashtray. He shrugged and continued his business at the table. He muttered, "Fuck that!"

His cell phone rang, and he quickly answered.

Apple finished off her cigarette and went into the bedroom and sat on her bed. Where was her life going? She started to think about how she grew up poor in Harlem, and then how quickly she advanced in the underworld. She thought about her life in Miami. Memories of her and Kola crept into her mind, along with her mother. Then Peaches.

She lit up another cigarette. She had so much on her mind. Which way should she go, left or right? She stood up, walked to the mirror, and stared at herself for a long time. Her mirror image was beautiful, though scarred. She tried to smile, but she couldn't. She was a warrior. She was meant to do big things.

As she stared at herself, out of the blue, gunshots rang out. The shots came from outside. Apple didn't jump, nor was she concerned. It was East Baltimore—gunshots in the night were common like crackheads drifting about.

She undressed and donned a long T-shirt and panties. She needed to get comfortable. She exited the bedroom and went into the kitchen.

Twin was finished cutting the heroin; it was finally street-ready. "You ready to get this money?" he said, obsession in his voice. He pushed his chair back and stood up from the table. He smiled at Apple. "You know I always gotta show my lady some love." He picked up some cash from the table and handed it to her.

Apple looked at him sideways. There was twenty thousand dollars on the table, and the kilos alone were worth at least sixty to eight thousand dollars alone. It was an insult to her. She refused to take it. She folded her arms across her chest and frowned.

"Yo, Sassy, take the money. You earned it," he said, like he was doing her some favor.

"Really, nigga? Five grand?" she spat.

"What you expect?"

It was a foolish question. She wanted half of the score. She was the only one there for him. His two goons were a no-show. She took the risk, and she helped set everything up. Five thousand was a smack to her face.

Apple smacked the cash out of his hand, and it went flying everywhere.

"What the fuck is your problem?" Twin shouted.

"You, nigga! Seriously? Five grand?"

"Take the money, Sassy."

"No! I deserve more,"

"More?" Twin arched his eyebrow. "How you deserve more?"

"You stand there and ask me that shit, Twin? I'm a partner."

"Partner? Who you partner with? Me? Yo, Sassy, you trippin'—I advise you to scoop the fuckin' money off the floor and be happy."

Apple felt if they both got busted, she would have done equal time.

"Yo, you either take the five, or you don't get anything at all—that's real talk, Sassy. You might as well get that partner shit out of ya head."

"Fuck you, Twin! You're a greedy, selfish bastard! I'm sick of your shit!"

"Bitch or not—don't fuck wit' me, Sassy. I ain't the one—You already know I'll kill for mines."

"Oh, you threatening me now? You ain't the one, huh? Okay." Apple coolly walked out of the kitchen.

Twin thought the argument was over. But he was far from wrong.

Apple walked into the bedroom, opened her closet door, went inside, removed a .380 from the shelf, cocked it back, and calmly went back into the kitchen and aimed the pistol at Twin's head.

"Bitch, you serious?" Twin scoffed, caught completely off guard.

"I'm dead serious."

The two locked eyes. He couldn't believe she had the audacity to pull a gun on him. His gun was still on the table, too far from his reach.

He was ready to call her bluff. "Yo, young girl, you like to wave guns around, but have you actually pulled the trigger? Took a life?"

Apple smirked. The .380 aimed at his head and looking him directly in his eyes without blinking, she growled, "You don't know me."

Twin chuckled, somehow, finding the situation funny. "Obviously, I don't."

She was tired of kissing Twin's ass for money and was ready to find her own crew of killers and get it popping. "Now, I want what is fuckin' owed to me," she said.

"What is owed to you?"

"Plenty."

Twin couldn't argue with a gun in his face. "So, let's talk," he said.

In the end, Apple took her share from the table—two and half ki's and ten grand. It was fair. She had made up her mind. She was back! This would get her jumpstarted in the game. And, already, she was making enemies.

"Get the fuck out!" she told Twin.

He hesitated, scowling.

"Nigga, did you hear me?"

"Yeah, I heard you," Twin replied evenly. "You sure you wanna do this, Sassy?" he said, the gun still aimed at his face. He backed toward the door, with his pistol still on the table. He was fuming from head to toe. But he was paralyzed.

Apple had never been so sure in her life.

She wasn't about to let him leave empty-handed though, she simply wanted what was owed to her. She tossed him the rest of the money and drugs. "I don't want any trouble or beef," she said.

"Oh, it's too late for that."

"I'm not the bitch you think I am," she told him. "Don't come for me, Twin. You'll lose."

Twin looked puzzled.

"My name ain't Sassy."

Twin looked confused by her statement. He left her apartment quietly.

# THIRTEEN

The moment the door shut, Apple didn't waste any time. She locked the door, then ran into the kitchen and dumped the drugs and cash into a black garbage bag. Afterwards, she ran into her bedroom and began packing clothes and anything important she was going to need into a suitcase. She couldn't stay there anymore. It would be stupid.

Where would she go? Maybe a motel, or find a new place. She had ten thousand cash on her and some work to sell. She was okay for now. Twin was a threat; there was no telling what he might do to her. She'd crossed that line, but she wasn't about to allow for him to steal from her what she felt was hers in the first place. She'd earned it.

An hour later, Apple walked out her apartment heavily armed with her luggage and the trash bag. She locked her apartment door but not before turning on the television and radio. If Twin or anyone else came looking for her they would think she was still around, buying her some time. Apple headed toward the street. She threw everything into the trunk of her old car and bounced.

The Motel 6 on West North Avenue was an iconic place if you were a fan of *The Wire*. It was where stickup man Omar Little ambushed Brother Mouzone and shot him in the abdomen.

The dull, run-down room with its stained, frayed carpet came with a queen-size bed, television, and chair, and had a decent-size bathroom with the towel rack falling off the wall. She had seen worse, much worse, especially when she was in Mexico. Besides that, there were no other problems with her room, which was right off Interstate 83.

Apple quickly settled in. She locked her door, closed her blinds, and laid out her guns on the table. She counted the money again—ten thousand. She had the heroin in the bag. In Baltimore, heroin was gold. There were so many users in the city that, with the right people, she could easily sell it off and make a small fortune. But she had to be careful. The wolves were out there, and they would think she was weak. She had a few things working against her, being female and from out of town, and she had no muscle and no connections.

Apple knew she was in a very vulnerable position, but that wasn't going to stop her.

It was late, and she was tired. She went to bed with the deadbolt across the door and her gun in her hand. *One day at a time*, she told herself.

Her biggest concern was running into Twin. Baltimore wasn't New York. It was a small city, only the

East Side and the West Side, with the players, hustlers, killers and wolves cramped into it all.

Twin took a pull from the cigarette with his right hand and steered his Benz with his left through Baltimore's East Side. It was early in the morning, and the sun was fresh in the sky. The drug fiends were already out and about in the warm weather, trying to get out the gate.

Twin couldn't stop thinking about Sassy. He was furious. He wasn't about to let her get away with disrespecting him. No one disrespected him and got away with it. He was ready to show her.

He came back to her block and parked his Benz right outside her building. It hadn't been twenty-four hours yet, and he was already plotting his revenge.

Twin killed the ignition to the car, took one final pull from his cigarette, and flicked it out the window. He picked up his gun from the seat, tucked it into his waistband, and exited the car with a sense of purpose. He marched toward the entrance.

Before he could step inside, a drug addict hurried his way, his eyes sunken in, his clothes filthy, track marks running up and down his arms. The man figured Twin to be a dealer. He had a crumpled ten-dollar bill in his hand and appeared anxious to cop some drugs. "I need one," he said to Twin.

"What?" Twin turned to face him with a hard scowl.

"Give me one," he begged.

The man was too close for Twin's comfort. Twin hated the fiends. They were dirty, nasty, and he didn't feel sorry for them at all, though he got rich off their addiction.

"Yo, get the fuck away from me!" he growled at him.

"I just need one," the man repeated.

The mistake he made was touching Twin; placing his dirty hands where they didn't belong. This angered Twin. The man was contaminating his fresh clothes.

Twin reacted swiftly. He tightened his fist and punched the heroin addict in the face so hard, he knocked him out cold. Then he shouted, "Muthafucka, don't you ever put your dirty hands on me again!" For good measure, he kicked the man while he was down.

He then proceeded into the building to handle unfinished business. He stormed up the stairs and walked briskly to Sassy's apartment. He didn't know if he should kick in the door or shoot the lock out.

*Fuck it!*

He shot the lock out and kicked in the door.

He rushed inside. Immediately, he started searching for Sassy, or whatever her name was. He went into the kitchen. Nothing. Then the living room and her bedroom. The place looked empty. Some of her clothes were gone.

"Fuck!" he shouted.

Twin had to admit, she was a sharp woman. A small part of him admired her street savvy. He walked out of Sassy's apartment with a smile. Then he uttered out, "I'll find you." He walked out the building.

The fiend he punched was still knocked out cold on the sidewalk, the ten-dollar bill still clutched in his hand.

Twin crouched down and snatched it. "Faggot!" Then he got into his Benz and sped off.

Twin wanted to believe that Sassy had to be somewhere in Baltimore. He was determined to find her. He already put out the word that he was looking for her. She would be hard to miss—a beautiful woman with a few minor scars. A woman like her couldn't hide for long.

# FOURTEEN

When arriving at the Buen Pastor women's prison, your only luggage is fear. Kola could feel it in her throat and in the pit of her stomach. It felt like a cold, icy hand had her in its grip. She couldn't believe she went from posh to shit overnight. Why was she in a Colombian women's prison, away from it all—her family, and America? She didn't know if she wanted to throw up or shit in her pants. Prisons outside the States were nothing to play with. Kola had heard the stories. She was from a rough place, but a prison in Colombia was rougher. This place was going to make her time in the Miami jail seem like a vacation.

Kola didn't want to imagine the horrors that awaited her inside. So many horrendous conditions plagued the place, from overcrowding to unsanitary conditions to violence. The first stop was the *jaula*, a pit of evil and perversion where inmates are sorted and assigned a cell block, if they're lucky—two to three people per square meter of urine-and-feces-slick stone floor. Inside, there was overcrowding, lack of hygiene, and absence of care for prison inmates. The male guards looked on at the women with amusement. Kola already knew what they were thinking. Who would stop them?

Kola was thrown into a cell with numerous Colombian women who immediately recognized that she wasn't one of them. The place was dirty, smelly, hot, and sticky, with rodents and bugs crawling around. Clad in grubby garments, and her hair a mess, Kola instantly was ready to fight for her survival.

They quickly gave her the name "*La gringa*," which meant foreigner from a different culture, particularly English-speakers, and especially from the United States.

Kola right away wanted to exert her rights as an American citizen. She wanted a lawyer. She wanted out of the prison. Why was she there in the first place? She didn't understand. She didn't commit a crime. Many women inside were convicted drug traffickers or were about to be tried for a drug crime; others were murderers.

Kola was worried deeply about Peaches. Was she in a harsh and cruel place too? The thought of Peaches being mistreated had Kola crippled with fear and concern. It was hard to think. It was hard to breathe in the place she was in. The foul smell alone was crushing. There weren't enough mattresses, so people were sleeping on the hard concrete or dirt floors in the corridors and bathrooms.

The women were last given soap, toothpaste, toothbrushes, and toilet paper over two months ago. Poor hygiene facilitated the spread of respiratory and skin ailments. Two hundred and fifty women were living in a single corridor with only two bathrooms. Generally, if two toilets worked, three would usually be out of order or blocked. Some inmates were forced to eat on the floor, next to sewers. Water supply was intermittent, and the stench never went away.

For Kola, being American, the conditions were sad to see. Disabled prisoners were sleeping in their own feces. The incontinent prisoners were not provided with adult diapers, and there were no provisions for the prisoners to wash soiled beddings.

The prison only had two doctors and one physiotherapist for over two thousand inmates. And there was one nurse for each prison block. HIV was rampant inside. Terminally ill HIV-positive prisoners weren't receiving any assistance whatsoever. When prisoners managed to get any kind of appointment with the doctor, the most they were ever prescribed was ibuprofen and paracetamol.

Kola tried to make contact with the guards to plead her case to them that she was innocent and didn't belong there. She heard a few speaking English and thought it was her chance to search for help. But the English-speaking guards answered her in Spanish and laughed.

Not speaking or understanding Spanish made Kola feel more alone, and it made her a mark. She wanted to cry, but she kept her tears inside, not wanting to look weak to these women and become prey.

Murder was a weekly occurrence inside. The dirty looks Kola received from other inmates was an indication that they were going to try her very soon. She was outnumbered and scared, but she wasn't going to go out without a fight.

Already, the women inside were talking, knowing who she was, who she was connected with. She heard the name Eduardo spill from the mouths of a few individuals. His name would either protect her or endanger her.

Kola made a sharp shank quickly from a broken toothbrush she found. She planned on protecting herself by any means necessary. There wasn't any way she was going to get stabbed again and left to die like before in the Miami jail.

On her third day, she missed hot showers, American food, and her family. The days were long and slow, affording abundant time for reflection. So far, no one tried to move on her, but she hardly got any sleep trying to stay alert twenty-four/seven. When she did sleep, she was always startled awake from her own nightmare, or an incident happening around her—inmates fighting or arguing, a stabbing, or maybe a murder.

"*La gringa*," the ladies continued to taunt, walking by her slowly, smirking.

Some would say, "Eduardo's whore!"

Their remarks angered Kola, but she felt powerless to do anything about it. She kept her shank on her, concealed, always sharpened, and ready to thrust it into the first bitch who came her way.

On the fourth night, Kola heard a scream. She was curled up in the corner of a concrete room, trying to get comfortable in the sardine environment. It was after midnight, and mostly everyone was asleep. Kola fidgeted next to two overweight ladies with a foul smell.

Three guards walked into the room and picked their victim at once. The young girl was immediately awakened and grabbed up from the floor with brute force. The woman screamed loudly. She was petite, pretty, and wide-eyed with panic.

She screamed in Spanish. *"¡No! ¡No! ¡Ayúdame! ¡Ayúdame!,"* meaning, "No! No! Help me!"

The guards held her tightly by her arms and ripped away her shirt, exposing her tits. The other inmates turned away and pretended like it wasn't happening.

The guards laughed and continued to fondle the scared woman. They dragged her out of the room kicking and screaming.

Kola watched in horror. They took her out into the hallway and raped her there, on the cold hard ground. Kola could hear the guards take turns with the woman through her resonant screams. Kola closed her eyes. It could have been her.

A half-hour later, after they were done raping the girl, they pushed her back inside the room like she was discarded trash. Her clothing was torn, her lips were bleeding, and her eyes were blackened with pain and misery. She'd suffered a horrible ordeal. The girl dropped to her knees and placed herself against the hard, concrete floor in a zombie trance and sobbed all night into the morning.

That night, Kola cried. Many tears fell from her face as she lay in the fetal position, knowing one day she would be next. She yearned for home, the United States. Prisons in Colombia were hell on earth.

She thought about the most insignificant things—her own clothes, opening a refrigerator, watching television, and hearing and speaking English. Inside the prison, only six women spoke fluent English. Kola was the only American.

On her fifth day, Kola sat in the sun in the prison yard. The day was calm, but she still felt the hostility in the air. Not knowing what was next—the apprehensive anticipation of the inevitable happening—was the hardest part.

Every square inch of the place was bustling with inmates. There was no room for her to think. Kola sighed deeply. She was still armed with the shank and watching everyone and everything. No one befriended her.

Then, out of the blue, Kola saw them walk into the yard. Seeing them made her rise to her feet and grip her shank subtly. They looked like trouble. She frowned and waited for the inevitable to happen. She kept her eyes on the two sisters, Maria and Marisol.

When they noticed her, Kola's heart pounded rapidly. She took a deep breath. *Is this it?* she asked herself.

The sisters noticed Kola staring at them from across the yard. One said something to the other, and then they started to approach. Kola readied herself for an attack. She gripped the shank inside her hand, the sharp blade protruding from her fist. She wasn't going to die without a fight.

Kola didn't take her eyes off them. It felt like everyone was watching her. Death felt real close. She thought about Peaches. She prayed her niece would be okay. She knew she had let her down. She wished Apple was alive and standing by her side. The two of them together would have been able to hold it down. Now, she was ready to meet her sister in the afterlife.

Marisol stepped to her first. Kola was ready to thrust the shank deep into her neck and twist it into her flesh. Kola scowled, feeling apprehensive.

When Marisol was close, the first thing out of her mouth was, "Eduardo, he will help us."

*What?* Kola was confused. She was taken aback by Marisol's words. Were they there to attack her or help her? She looked at them intensely.

The sisters spoke little English, so it was hard for Kola to understand them.

Maria repeated what her sister had said, "Eduardo, he help us."

She shook her head, and smiled at Kola.

Was she in the Twilight Zone? A few weeks ago, they were trying to destroy her. Now, it looked like they were the only two friends she had inside. Kola wanted to converse with them. She wanted to know what was going on. She was desperate for information. Where were their children? Why were they locked inside? Why were they becoming so friendly toward her so suddenly?

Just like that, a common thread, Eduardo, replaced the hard feelings and tension that was once pregnant amongst the trio. Eduardo, he could be their savior.

With the help of Brenda, a Colombian native and new ally of the sisters who spoke Spanish and English fluently, Kola was able to converse with the sisters. Marisol and Maria were confident that Eduardo would get them out soon.

Kola wasn't too hopeful. She'd witnessed Eduardo's arrest. She thought he was untouchable in Colombia, thought he owned everyone, from the law, the people, to the government officials. Obviously, she was wrong. Everyone was in the same boat. Kola had overheard a guard speaking English the night everyone was arrested. The man bragged about seizing Eduardo's bank accounts and shutting down all of his operations.

How could he help them? It felt impossible.

When she asked the sisters what got them locked up, the sisters said it was political. Knowing Eduardo was enough for Colombian law to come barging into their home. Plus, they were known drug traffickers. Like Peaches, the sisters' children were taken from them, and they were unaware of the kids' location.

To Kola, it looked like she would spend the rest of her life in a Colombian hellhole. But she didn't want to give up, especially with Peaches still in the country. Kola knew she had to find her own way out, but how?

# FIFTEEN

Twin came to a stop at the row house on E. North Avenue. He lingered behind the wheel for a moment with his gun on his lap, watching the activity. The block was flooded with fiends and hustlers. The money never stopped. The drugs were either shot up or smoked. East Baltimore was a beast—dope and coke twenty-four/seven.

It'd been a week since he'd last seen Sassy. He even went by the club to see if she was stupid enough to show up, but no luck. He made a call on his cell phone to one of his goons.

"Twin, what's good?" Snow answered. He was good at hunting down people and disposing of them for the right price.

"You, my nigga. What you got for me?" Twin asked, not beating around the bush.

"Still ain't no sight of that bitch. You think she still in town?"

"Nigga, what you think I'm paying you for? B-more ain't that big of a place for this bitch to hide. And I know she ain't leave town."

"I'm still on it."

"When you see her, don't kill her. I wanna holla at her first."

"A'ight."

Twin ended the call. He flicked his cigarette out the window and made a second call. A female answered.

"You upstairs, right?" he asked.

"Where else I'm gonna be, Twin? It's my house, right?"

"Bitch, don't get fuckin' cute wit' me. I ain't in the mood for jokes."

She sucked her teeth and replied, "You coming up?"

"In one minute." Twin hung up.

He continued to sit in the car and think about Sassy. He missed politicking with her about Mack D and everything else. He still couldn't believe she'd pulled that stunt on him. No one else dared to pull out a gun on him, but Sassy wasn't the average bitch.

He climbed out his Benz and walked toward the row house. Whoever was in his way and blocking the stairs moved quickly. The entire block knew about Twin's violent and deadly reputation. They didn't want any confrontation with him.

He entered the building and went up to the second floor. He didn't have to knock because his second bitch, Miranda, was already waiting for him at the door in a pair of coochie-cutting shorts and a small T-shirt.

Miranda was dark-skinned with long black hair and stitched together perfectly—thin and petite, but filling out in places that every man desired, and a tight, firm ass and slim waist that curved both up and down to beautiful thighs and breasts.

She wrapped her arms around Twin and hugged him lovingly. "I missed you, baby," she said with a golden smile.

Twin hugged her back halfheartedly. He then removed himself from her arms and walked into the apartment, which was furnished nicely with leather sofas, an expensive area rug in the living room, a giant LED television mounted on the wall, and all the amenities that the projects and the poor were deprived of. Twin made sure the apartment had all the comforts he needed when he came through.

She lived comfortable in the midst of poverty. E. North Avenue was a desolate area, but no one dared to break into Miranda's place.

Twin walked into the kitchen. On the round glass table, Miranda had four kilos of heroin spread out, all the drug paraphernalia nearby. She was preparing his product, making it street-ready; she was his lover and his worker.

Twin lit another cigarette as he inspected the kitchen. He looked Miranda's way and asked, "You got my shit almost ready?"

"Baby, you know I always work hard for you."

"I know you do. That's why I trust you."

Miranda was born and raised in East Baltimore, and both her parents were once drug addicts. Her father was once a known dealer before his addiction to smack. They both were now dead. Her mother overdosed on a lethal batch of heroin, and her father was murdered.

Miranda had been on her own since she was thirteen. She'd started stripping when she was fifteen years old. Every guy wanted her, but Twin took her away from the strip clubs when she was seventeen and put her to work in one of his drug spots. Miranda had a knack for cutting up heroin, making the quality of it superb. She'd learned from her parents and never touched the stuff. Twin found her gifted in the bedroom and in his growing organization.

Miranda, though she could catch a nasty attitude with Twin, was always excited to see him. She was nineteen years old, and already, she had her own car, her own place, and money to burn. Shopping and looking like a diva was her forte. But she only wanted to look nice for Twin. She was in love with him. She was aware he was always fucking around on her, but she still wanted him—flaws and all.

Twin walked to the table and observed the work she was putting into his product. He nodded and smiled. Miranda worked quickly and efficiently. What she could do alone might take three other dealers to do. She enjoyed her work. She always enjoyed her time with Twin.

She went toward Twin and wrapped her arms around his waist. "I missed you, baby," she said to him a second time. "I've been working all morning. I need a break. I need some dick," she said.

"You miss me, huh?"

She nodded. "Mmm-hmm."

Twin planned on having a quick intimate session with Miranda. He needed to release himself. The past week had him stressed out, and besides Sassy, she had the second best pussy.

She rose up his shirt and started to feel Twin's body. They kissed fervently. She moved from his lips to his neck.

Twin placed his hands on Miranda's lower back, and then he slipped one hand down the back of her shorts.

"I want you to suck my dick." He unzipped his jeans and then he placed his hands on her shoulders and forced her down on her knees.

She took his erection into her hand, gently stroked his dick, and didn't hesitate to wrap her full lips around it completely and slide her lips back and forth, making him moan with pleasure.

"Yeah, that's right, baby. Do that shit. Mmmm! Yeah, do that shit."

She worked his dick inside her mouth, licking the mushroom tip and cupping his balls. Miranda was ready to do anything for Twin. For several minutes, being on her knees in the kitchen, she milked his big dick with her mouth and hands, feeling his pre-cum drip on her tongue and urging him to come.

"I love you," she blurted out. She wanted to fuck.

Twin didn't respond. He was too wrapped up in his own pleasures. He wanted to get his nut and leave. He had other places to be.

She stood up and peeled off her T-shirt and pressed her chest against him.

Miranda wanted to kiss him again, but Twin denied her the pleasures. She'd just had her mouth around his dick, and he didn't want to know what his dick tasted like.

He cupped her tits and placed a nipple into his mouth. He pulled her shorts off. He came out of his own clothes too. Then he positioned her by the kitchen sink, curved her body over, and spread her legs.

First, he played with her pussy, stroking it like it was small pet. Miranda purred from his touch between her legs.

Twin rolled the condom back on his dick and took careful aim. He then thrust himself inside of her. The pussy was intense.

Miranda moaned from the penetration. She always gave herself to Twin. However he wanted it, he had it. If he wanted to fuck her raw, she didn't care. Anal, she was down. If he wanted kids, she would've given him "the Brady Bunch."

Twin slammed himself inside of her. While he fucked her, he couldn't stop thinking about Sassy. Every day, she was on his mind.

He gripped Miranda's hips and continued pounding himself inside of her. He closed his eyes and hated that Sassy had his attention.

"Take this pussy," Miranda announced.

Twin's cell phone started to ring. The pussy was feeling too good for him to stop so suddenly. He figured, whoever it was would call back.

"Fuck me!" Miranda cried out.

Twin's cell phone started to ring again. It had to be important. He pulled out the pussy and hurried to answer the call.

"Yo, who this?" he asked sharply.

"It's Snow—good news—I think we might have found her."

Twin lit up. "Oh, word?"

"Yeah."

"Where?"

"Motel 6, by the highway."

"A'ight, I'm there," he said.

Miranda stared at Twin with frustration.

"You where?" she asked, already catching an attitude with him.

"I gotta go."

"You ain't gonna finish fuckin' me?"

"Next time."

"Fuck you, Twin!" she yelled.

"Miranda, don't go there wit' me. This is important business."

"You sure it wasn't some next bitch?"

Twin glared at her. *Bitches and their emotions*, he thought. He wasn't about to argue with her. He had some place to be. He pulled up his pants and fastened them.

Miranda was scowling at him. She couldn't believe he didn't want to finish what they started.

Wearing Timberland boots, sweatpants, and hoodie, and concealing her .380, Apple stepped out of her motel room with a pocket full of work, looking like a butch with more balls than a raging bull. The motel she was staying in was a breeding ground for drug addicts looking to get high, and Apple made sure she took advantage of it. The drugs she had were selling quickly. Her supply was running low. She was making money fast, but she had to be careful about selling drugs on dangerous territory, encroaching on enemy land. There were other dealers out, and many weren't too pleased about her on their turf. But the risk was worth it. Heroin always sold like hot cakes at a lumberjack convention.

She lingered outside in the open corridor outside her room and lit a cigarette. The parking lot below was filled with cars. The fiends were like roaches, scurrying around in different directions. Two nearly naked prostitutes walked back and forth, working the area.

It had been a week. She didn't plan on staying in one location too long. Her mind told her it was time to leave.

Without a strong crew, without any muscle behind her, she was vulnerable to the goons and the rival drug dealers. She was able to handle herself, but she wasn't Superwoman. So every step she made, every decision, it was very cautious. She always slept with her gun in her hand, she kept the deadbolt on the door, and her curtains in the motel room were always closed.

Apple took a few pulls from the Newport. From where she stood, she could see Henry climbing the staircase, coming her way. Henry was a junkie. He had it bad. He copped from Apple night and day. He got his money by panhandling or going out to commit B&Es. He had a toothless smile and bad clothing.

A week at the motel, and Henry became her favorite customer.

"How many you need?" she asked him.

"I want three," Henry said, smiling.

Apple had her hands on three glassine bags. Henry was already handing her the cash. She placed the dope in his hand and took her cash. Meanwhile, her .380 was near her reach. She didn't trust anyone. People, junkies, or teenagers—anyone could be a threat.

After serving Henry, she descended down the stairway and into the parking lot. She walked outside the motel premises and looked both ways. Everything looked okay. Her car was parked around the corner. She didn't want anyone to know what she was driving. The vehicle was unassuming and didn't draw any attention.

Apple walked to the McDonald's up the street. She didn't eat all day, and her stomach was growling, *"Feed me!"* While trekking up the street, she observed every car passing and everything around her, remembering faces and watching her back.

Inside McDonald's, she ordered a Big Mac meal and took a seat near the back of the restaurant, refusing to have her back to the door. The place was relatively empty and quiet. She ate her meal in peace and walked out.

On her way back to the motel, Apple glanced to her

left and she saw him. Immediately, she gripped her pistol when she observed Twin's E-Class racing down North Avenue, toward the motel she was staying in. He didn't see her. He drove right by her. His Benz came to a screeching stop outside the motel.

Apple watched Twin and another stranger jump out the car and rush into the parking lot. She didn't panic. She continued walking, this time placing her hoodie over her head to conceal her face. She looked rugged, like a dyke, which helped out a lot.

Twin and Snow kicked in the motel door and stormed inside. It was the right room, but no one was inside.

"Where is this bitch?" Twin shouted. "Slippery bitch!"

"We'll find her," Snow assured him.

"We better."

Apple couldn't go back there anymore. Fortunately for her, there wasn't anything inside the room. It was empty, no drugs or cash. The most inside the room was a gun or two. Apple had thought ahead—don't ever leave anything valuable inside a cheesy motel room. The cash and the drugs were inside her car parked around the corner, well hidden and out of sight.

Twin was going to be a problem, and Apple knew she had to get to him before he got to her. She had escaped New York, was kicked out of Colombia, and then fled from Miami; there wasn't any way Twin was going to run her out of B-more. Apple was ready to start up her own crew. Baltimore was a nice town to set up in, and with her skills and experience, she could get an operation running in no time. But it was going to take planning, and it was going to take extreme risks. She needed some muscle, and she needed a reliable connect.

The first thing she did was take down Twin's plate number. He and Snow were walking back to the car. Twin was clearly frustrated. He was barking at Snow, who was scratching his head. Twin and Snow climbed back into the Benz and drove away.

Unbeknownst to them, Apple was following right behind them. She was ready to stir up the nest and create her own trouble. Twin had no idea who he was messing with. Apple was a creation from hell. Feeling like she was the devil herself, she was ready to spit hellfire at her foes and burn down anything coming her way.

# SIXTEEN

Kola was going crazy. Ten days in Buen Pastor women's prison felt like ten years. The days were long, hot, and awful, and the people around her were foul. The guards were ravenous perverts preying on the young girls inside. Though she made friends with Marisol and Maria, Kola still felt in jeopardy. She tried to pick up on her Spanish. Brenda was teaching her. It's what ate up most of her day. She regretted not learning to speak Spanish earlier, but her days beforehand were busied with shopping, having sex, going out to the clubs, taking care of her niece, and being Eduardo's trophy piece. She never had time to learn anything new. Now, she had all the time in the world.

Looking at Maria, Kola realized she wasn't pregnant anymore. She looked at Maria, tapped her own stomach and asked, "The baby, what happened?"

Maria put her eyes to the ground, looking saddened and said, "Eduardo."

"Eduardo?" Kola asked.

Tears building in her eyes, Maria looked at Kola. In her best English, she replied, "He got angry. He beat me, and I lost baby."

Kola was shocked to hear it, but at the same time she felt conflicted. She learned that Eduardo had become so angry when the sisters came into his home and disrespected Kola, he beat them so severely that Maria had a miscarriage.

Kola wondered if Eduardo beat on the sisters for disrespecting her or him. For the past weeks, she hadn't felt loved.

Maria was in tears telling her story to Kola.

Kola put their past behind them and did the unthinkable. She consoled Maria in front of everyone, placing her arms around the woman and saying to her in Spanish, "*Lo siento*," meaning, "I'm sorry." She was learning fast.

Kola and the sisters talked about their children regularly. Talking and thinking about their kids made the time go by easier, but it also made Kola's heart heavy. Not being able to speak or see Peaches was daunting. Every night, Kola cried thinking about the horrors Peaches could be going through. She didn't know if the five-year-old was dead or alive, or being prepared for a life in the sex trade.

On the twelfth day, tensions in the prison were high. Kola and the sisters were on extra alert. Eduardo's name was in the papers constantly. He had pissed off a lot of powerful folks, and they wanted him dead and everything connected to his empire destroyed. There was fallout after Eduardo's arrest. Guerrilla forces were mobilizing, with widespread massacre of people who sympathized with the drug lord. Many were calling for his execution, and many were calling for his release. In many villages, Eduardo was well liked. In one northern village, as many as 190 unarmed people were killed, gunned down and butchered like animals.

Kola and the sisters found themselves caught up in the political madness. Eyes were on them, and Kola knew the inevitable was going to happen. The wolves were lurking, and they were becoming restless. Kola was ready. She still had her shank.

She continued learning Spanish, and she had to sleep with one eye open whenever she did sleep, which was rare. She was always on guard, always watching everyone's movement inside, even Maria and Marisol. They were friends now, but things could quickly change. Inside prison, from America to Colombia, there was no such thing as a true friend.

Kola and the other inmates were being escorted into the yard early one morning. Maria and Marisol were nowhere around. Kola was talking to Brenda. It was another hot and humid day. Everywhere Kola turned, a bitch was in her face. There were too many girls in such a little space. She felt uncomfortable. She had her shank tucked within the folds of her labia and walked coolly like everything was okay.

Once outside and under the hot sun, Kola noticed a group of Colombian girls gathered in a circle. They immediately looked her way. Their looks were nothing nice. One pivoted from the group and marched Kola's way. The other four ladies soon followed.

Kola reached between her legs and quickly removed the shank. She was outnumbered, but she didn't care. It was kill or be killed, and today, she didn't want to die.

She gripped the shank tightly, her eyes on the group of girls.

The one coming her way uttered, *"¡Estás muerta, perra!"* and lunged for Kola with an object in her hand.

Kola stepped backwards and then sidestepped the attack.

The girl swung again and missed.

Kola counterattacked. The shank in her hand went slashing across the girl's face, opening flesh.

The woman howled from the pain. Her hands slammed into her face. The other girls stormed Kola's way and surrounded her.

Kola scowled, gripping the blade tightly, blood on the tip. Through her clenched teeth, she said, "First bitch that comes my way, I'll cut their fuckin' throat!" In that frozen second between standoff and fighting, Kola's eyes flicked back and forth, intensely glaring at each girl, but their faces showed no fear or invitational smirk. She was banking on them making a mistake, like their friend had.

They expected it to be five on one. The brawl would be over in a bloody flash, and then they'd go back to their hole.

Again, they charged at her with no fear. Several pairs of hands tried to seize her. Kola staggered backwards, she went slashing away, desperately trying to keep them away, but to no avail. The shank was knocked out of her hand. She went crashing to the floor with two other girls. They started kicking and punching her. Everyone was screaming in Spanish.

"*¡Mata a esa perra!*"

Kola continued to fight, punching the girl on top of her in the face. It was starting to look bleak. If she was going to die, then she would fight to her last breath.

With renewed vigor, she pushed the girl off her and went berserk. She kicked one girl in the shin and tried to quickly get up, but she was knocked back down and overwhelmed by numerous inmates, who wanted to beat her to death.

Then, suddenly, from out of nowhere, Marisol and Maria jumped in the fray. The sisters tore into the women, and abruptly dropped two of Kola's attackers.

That gave Kola time to lift herself up from the floor. She shook herself free from a foe's grasp and punched the woman so hard, a tooth went flying out of her mouth.

Kola and the sisters executed their own savage justice. In no time, the tide had turned.

Maria shuffled to the side and waited in attack. The other woman's agile movement was far too slow, and

Maria made her pay by dropping her on her back and almost breaking her neck.

Kola realized that the sisters got busy with their hands. They were ruthless, hardcore fighters. They saved her life.

The group of women retreated before the guards came to break up the fight. They were badly beaten and bleeding profusely, some having skin hanging off their faces.

Kola was very grateful. She was a little banged up, but she would live. "Thank you."

Maria and Marisol nodded. They didn't have a scratch on them.

Marisol said, *"Fue un placer."*

Behind bars, everything has a price. If you had the money, you received the pleasures. Kola yearned for so many things. After two weeks inside one of the worst places on earth, she was introduced to the cacique, an inmate who governs a row of cells. She ushered Kola and the sisters into her private world. Inside, the three girls saw a giant TV set, a shower, a refrigerator, hot plate, and a double bed. Kola was amazed by what she saw.

Inside hell, there was a little heaven. This inmate was well dressed and smelled good. She spoke English well. She said to Kola, "If you want to sleep here, it'll cost you one million six hundred thousand pesos."

Kola was shocked to hear the price. After eating

stale food, washing up in unclean water, and fighting for her life, she wanted that comfort and luxury. It wasn't a penthouse suite on Park Avenue, but after everything she'd been through, a project apartment in the ghetto was better than her current location.

The problem was, she couldn't afford it. She didn't have any pesos to her name; not even two coins to rub together. Everything had been taken away from her, and what wasn't taken was buried.

But she didn't need the pesos. The whole thing was taken care of. The girls received their own 9-by-9-foot cell. It came with a queen-size bed, Egyptian sheets, hot plates, a refrigerator, fruits and veggies, ductless air conditioning, TV and cable—the whole gamut.

Maria and Marisol were over-the-moon excited.

Kola, not so much. *What's the catch?*

"You see? Eduardo, he come through for us," Marisol said in broken English.

The sisters looked like they'd won the lotto, smiling from ear to ear. They had so much love and faith in Eduardo. They looked at Kola and kept praising Eduardo.

Kola wanted to be hopeful that things would work out in the end, but it was because of him they were incarcerated. It was because of him, Maria lost her unborn child. It was because of him, Peaches was gone.

Eduardo did more harm to her than good. Period!

Kola knew that if a judge didn't release her, she would die trying to get out. If she had to fuck a guard or kill someone to facilitate her escape, then so be it.

# SEVENTEEN

I t was late in the evening, and the temperature was soaring to almost a hundred degrees. But Kola sat cooling in her cell, enjoying a nice meal and some solitude, finally. It was going on three weeks inside the women's prison, and though her conditions inside had improved, she wanted out desperately.

A male guard appeared at her cell, looking stoic. "You're wanted," he said.

"By who?" she asked.

"No questions. Just come."

Kola followed the male guard down the long corridor. She tried not to panic, but it was hard. Women were raped every day by the guards, and no one cared enough to do anything about it.

She walked with the guard casually. She continued to question him, but he wasn't answering her. In the States, she wouldn't be shocked to leave with a guard, but she was in Colombia, where anything was possible. For all she knew, the guard could be leading her to her death.

The guard stopped at a lone room with a black door and looked at Kola. "You go in," he said.

"What's inside?" she asked, looking uncertain.

"You go inside."

"What's inside?" she asked again.

In her mind, there were several guards with rock-hard dicks and just waiting for her to step inside the lions' den. Or rival girls that wanted their revenge.

The guard frowned.

Kola was ready to fight. They weren't about to rape or kill her without a struggle. Her eyebrows narrowed, her eyes flaring up. She clenched her fists. If so, she was ready to flee, but where would she go? The prison was a maze inside.

The guard stepped forward with irritation. He placed his hand around the doorknob and pushed it open. "No problem. You go inside. Man wants to speak with you."

Kola carefully gazed inside the room. No guards with hard dicks, no angry bitches ready to cut open her face.

It was only a suited man seated behind a table, waiting for her to step inside. "Kola, come in," he said. "We need to talk."

Kola walked into the room cautiously. Though it was just one man, she was still on high alert.

It took her a moment, but she recognized him. It was Eduardo's attorney. She didn't know his name, but she had seen him around the house a few times. He was dressed nicely in a black suit. He was Colombian, clean-cut, and very handsome.

Eduardo's attorney sat with his hands folded on the table. His briefcase was on the table too.

Kola took a seat opposite of him at the table, her mind spinning with worry. *Why is he here? Is it about Peaches?* She feared the worst.

"You will be released today," he said.

"What?" She thought it was a joke. Did she hear him correctly? "Please don't lie to me."

"As we speak, your release is being implemented."

"How is that possible?"

"Thank Eduardo."

"I thought he was finished. I saw them arrest him."

"My client has many tricks up his sleeves."

"But they seized his accounts. They took everything from him—"

"Not everything. He still has offshore accounts and money in many places; assets that are untouchable—including you."

"Me?"

"There's a price on your life."

"A price? Why? By who?"

"A few million dollars," the man informed her. "His enemies want you dead."

Kola was taken aback. Why such a high price? Why her? She had no idea what was going on, but she was scared.

"Where's Eduardo?" she demanded to know.

"It is not your place to worry about his affairs or location. Just be thankful you'll be free from here."

"So the government, or courts, whoever's in charge is allowing me to leave here because I'm innocent, right? Eduardo spoke with them and let them know I don't have anything to do with his organization?"

The attorney gave Kola a quizzical look. "If by speaking to them you mean he paid ninety million American dollars for your release, then, yes, Kola. Eduardo spoke with them. Loudly."

Kola was stunned. The adage that something is only worth what someone is willing to pay for it was coming true today. Her heart deepened for Eduardo.

"So where do I go? What about Peaches?"

The attorney didn't have an answer for her.

"What about Marisol and Maria?"

Once again, he didn't have an answer. Instead, he opened his briefcase and removed a cell phone. He started to make a phone call right there.

Kola was sitting on worry and anticipation, the two tearing her apart.

"*Sí, estoy aquí,*" the attorney said into the cell phone. "*Entiendo . . . sí.*" He then handed the phone to Kola. "He wants to speak with you."

She looked at him. She took the cell phone and slowly placed it to her ear.

"You're going to be okay, bella."

"Oh my God!"

Hearing Eduardo's voice made Kola burst into tears. So many thoughts and emotions ran through her mind and body. A few weeks ago she didn't know if he was dead or alive, and a few weeks ago, she didn't know whether this man really loved her. Now, she knew he did. Immediately she forgot everything he'd put her through. She was grateful that he was okay.

"Where are you?" she asked.

"Don't worry about me, Kola. Just know that I'm okay," he answered smoothly.

"Where is Peaches? Is she okay?"

"She's fine, and she'll join you soon."

Tears trickled from Kola's eyes. "Maria and Marisol can't be left inside this place, Eduardo. They have kids—your kids."

"My only concern at the moment is you, and Peaches' safety."

"Will you be released too?"

"Unfortunately for me, I will die in prison," he said.

"Why? What's going on?"

"Too much to say at once. And there isn't too much I can do right now. My only regret in life was that I didn't marry you, Kola. And that we never had any kids together. I wish we did," he said, his voice contrite.

Kola was saddened. "I always felt like the queen of your household, Eduardo. I'm your queen forever. I will always be your wife," she said wholeheartedly.

"I know you are." He was pleased to hear her say that.

Eduardo understood the path he'd chosen, and he understood politics and his situation.

"I will try and rebuild my empire behind these walls, but it will not be easy. Many of my men are dead, and most of my connections disabled. I still have resources, but I need the funds to guarantee my life in prison. For me to stay alive, I have to continue paying off the right people."

"Who are these people? Give me their names." Kola was ready to help him out. The tone in her voice made her sound like she was the ultimate fixer.

Eduardo chuckled at Kola's persistence and loyalty. He had picked the right one to release. She was smart, tenacious, and a pit bull.

He went on to explain his situation to Kola, who listened closely. In order for him to stay alive, and not have the corrupt government open the door of his cell one night and allow the rival cartel to come in and cut his throat, he had to grease palms continually. Which was going to cost him millions each year. He told Kola he was only able to afford her release, and would work on getting Marisol and Maria released too.

"I've made arrangements for you and Peaches to go back to the States," he said.

Kola felt ambivalent. She wanted out of prison, but in America, she was a fugitive. The last thing she wanted was to trade one jail cell for another.

Eduardo told her, "I need a favor from you."

"What is it?"

"I need for you to take Eduardo Jr. and Sophia with you back to America. I need for you to watch over them."

Kola felt reluctant. They weren't her children.

"I will have my attorney give you twenty thousand dollars in cash. You have to leave Colombia immediately.

I've made arrangements. Once you're back on U.S. soil, get you a nice apartment, stay there maybe for a year. It will take me some time to be able to send you more cash. But you need to be patient and cautious. Play everything safe. Kola, you must stay clean, until I can send you some money and support the lifestyle that you deserve."

His voice deepened. "You will be given a cell phone. I want you to keep this cell phone on you at all times. I, or my attorney, will call you. He will make sure the bill is paid at all times."

"I understand."

Eduardo took a deep breath. "This is hard for me to say, but I will say it. I'm not naïve. I know you will eventually find a man, and you'll have sex with him. You will tell me you won't, but as time passes, the inevitable will happen. We all have needs, Kola. I understand. America is a faraway place, and I'll be here, but I will never be a fool. You can fuck a man, but you must not fall in love. You are the only woman to ever capture my heart, so don't break it."

Kola was lost for words. She sat at the table, the cell phone glued to her ear, Eduardo's attorney seated right in front of her, capturing her reaction.

She started to get emotional. She didn't want anyone else. She loved Eduardo. She wanted to be with him. She had fallen head over heels in love with the man. She was willing to forgive him even when he wronged her.

"I promise, you will always have my heart," she said.

Kola would have promised to sell her soul to the devil if it meant getting out and reuniting with Peaches.

"I love you," she said.

"I love you too," he replied.

The tears started to trickle down her face. In her heart, she knew once she was in America, she would never see him again.

Briefly, Kola felt guilty for not mentioning the five million dollars she had buried in a cemetery not too far from the compound. Kola wasn't a fool. She knew rainy days were bound to happen, and it was survival of the fittest out there.

The called ended abruptly. Just like that, Eduardo was gone.

She dried her tears as she handed his attorney the cell phone.

Eduardo was able to negotiate her freedom and his life, but it came with a price. When they told him to choose a girl to release, he immediately picked Kola.

Kola stood up and exited the room.

Right away, she went to see Maria and Marisol. They were lounging in their new cells, living comfortably. They were right about Eduardo coming through with freedom, but it was for her only. She wondered how the sisters would react to the news.

"I spoke to Eduardo," she quickly said to them.

The sisters perked up, ready to hear what Kola had to say.

"¿Que?" Maria asked.

Kola looked cheerless. She locked eyes with both sisters and said, "I'm freed."

"You free?" Marisol said.

Kola nodded.

"And us?" Marisol asked.

Kola kept strong eye contact with the sisters and shook her head. "No."

Maria and Marisol glanced at each other. It was grim news for them both, but they didn't look angry.

Kola expected an outburst from them. Maybe they would attack her through pure jealousy. But they didn't. In fact, they both looked happy for her; no hate or shade.

Kola looked at them dumbfounded.

The sisters realized Eduardo's love for Kola the moment he showed back at their home and assaulted them. In his eyes they saw how much he loved her. A man like Eduardo would have only taken time out to address the situation personally if she meant something to him.

Marisol and Maria were wise, street-smart, and most importantly, they were under his Svengali-like protection.

"He'll get you out soon," she said.

They barely understood her. They were still learning English, and Kola was still learning Spanish. Brenda translated for her.

Maria smiled; Marisol didn't. The sisters knew Kola's statement was untrue. If they were getting out, then they would be leaving with her.

With Brenda translating, Kola said that their kids were leaving for America with her, and she promised she would take care of them. Even if they were against it, they didn't have a choice. It was what Eduardo wanted.

They asked Kola to write and send them pictures, and she promised she would. Then she hugged them both and went on her way.

Kola left the prison before the sun went down. Finally, after three weeks, she was free. A car was idling outside the gate, a black Mercedes with two agents sitting inside. They looked at her with stone-cold gazes and didn't say a word. With just the clothes on her back, she hurried into the vehicle like she was being chased.

When they drove away, she didn't even turn back to look at the prison. Kola sighed with relief, wanting to completely forget about it.

The agents headed straight for the orphanage where Peaches was.

Kola had a dilemma. How was she going to get her five million buried in the cemetery? They were on a tight schedule.

They pulled in front of the orphanage, and there was no need for Kola to go inside. Peaches, along with Eduardo Jr. and Sophia, were already packed and ready for her arrival.

The minute Kola saw her niece, she leaped from the car and ran toward her. Peaches was delighted to see Kola. Kola scooped the little girl into her arms and hugged her so tightly, she almost put her arms through her. She was in tears.

"Mama," Peaches cried out.

"Are you okay? Did anyone hurt you?"

"No. I'm fine."

With Peaches still in her arms, Kola looked down at the other two children, who stood there quietly and innocently. Dressed nicely and looking as cute as buttons, there was no way she could deny them and leave them in the orphanage.

She walked toward them, crouched down and looked at Eduardo Jr. and Sophia. They didn't speak a word of English, so Peaches had to translate for them.

"You're coming with me," she said.

Peaches translated.

The two looked confused and nervous, their eyes cloudy with concern. They were so young.

"We gotta go," Kola said.

Kola took the children with her and went to the Mercedes, where the agents were waiting. She and the children climbed into the backseat, and the car drove away.

Kola needed to collect her money. "I need to make a stop first," she said to the driver.

"No stop. We go to airport," he replied.

"But this is very important."

"No stop. We take you to the airport. We have our instructions."

Kola pouted. She didn't want to leave Colombia without the five million dollars she had buried. It made her sick to her stomach to leave so much money behind, even though she didn't have a clue how she was going to get it into the States.

She had the twenty thousand dollars on her that she was able to bring into the States, concealed in her luggage. The attorney had made sure it was well hidden for it to easily pass through Customs. Everyone had their passports, and everything was legit. Eduardo's attorney had made sure he dotted his *i*'s and crossed his *t*'s.

The driver was adamant—no detours, straight to the airport.

They arrived at Bogota's El Dorado International Airport, Colombia's busiest. Everyone was escorted out of the car and into the airport. Each person was given a one-way ticket to America and clearance through Customs. For the right price to the right people, they didn't have to worry about any harassment from airport security.

"You go," one of the agents said to Kola. "Forget about Eduardo and never come back."

Kola's heart sank. Eduardo would be executed, or he would die in a Colombian jail. He'd sounded positive on the phone, said he and everything was going to be okay, but Kola felt something wasn't right.

The agents nodded at two cops in the terminal, and they quickly guided Kola and the children through security like they had VIP status.

Kola felt ambivalent about leaving the country. She was leaving behind a fortune and Eduardo. But staying could cost her, her life.

They walked through the terminal and boarded the plane. She was almost home. She thought about the money and wondered how will she get back into the country and smuggle the cash out. It was risky, but she was determined to find a way. Somehow.

Kola, Peaches, Eduardo Jr., and Sophia all sat in coach. It was going to be a long flight to New York. Kola sat in the window seat and fixed her eyes on the tarmac. In a moment, the plane was about to take off. She held Peaches' hand and said, "We're almost home."

Peaches smiled.

The plane taxied onto the runway. Kola felt nervous. This was it. She felt the plane climbing into the air, ascending quickly into the sky and clouds. In roughly seven hours, she would be back in America.

# EIGHTEEN

Apple closely followed Twin around for three days, mostly in East Baltimore. He was a very busy boy, with the streets and the ladies. If Twin knew she was following him, it could turn out really bad for them both. For several days, she learned where he kept a few of his stash houses in town, and what bitch he was seeing. He wasn't careful with his movements. He was easy to track and follow. In a way, she thought he was a little too reckless—loose women and lots of drugs was a disastrous combination. Maybe he was just too cocky, thinking no one would come after him.

She smoked her cigarette and thought about her next move. From the end of the block, she observed Twin leaving a row house, the nicest on the block. He was squeezing his crotch, a smile on his face.

Apple shook her head, feeling some kind of way. Though they weren't together, she still had feelings for him. It looked like he wasn't thinking about her, while she was thinking about him. She couldn't judge him, though. She was promiscuous too, with her list of men, but Twin was the man she wanted to be with.

Twin climbed into his Benz and drove off, and Apple followed, remaining three cars behind him.

He drove slowly. It was dusk out, and tonight was the coolest of the week. The temperature had dropped a little, but it was still a comfortable night.

She followed Twin on E. Pratt Street. He then turned left on S. Central Avenue, drove several blocks, and made a left on Lancaster Avenue. This was a different scene from the drugs and poverty of East Baltimore. They were by the harbor, where small sail boats and mini-yachts were docked not far from the streets, the restaurants were nice, and the place was filled with white-collar folks. The real estate started at a hundred thousand or more—no more dilapidated, abandoned row houses, drug dealers on the corners, or fiends scurrying around from block to block.

After Twin parallel-parked on a serene street, Apple stopped her car at the corner and watched him from half a block away. She watched him exit his Mercedes. He was alone and looked comfortable. He headed toward an apartment complex suited with balconies and high-end security.

Apple stepped out of her car, gripping a .45. It would have been easy to take him out, but her plan wasn't to kill him; she wanted to talk to him.

Twin walked toward the building entrance.

The street was brightly lit, and everything felt still.

As Twin neared the corner, two masked men unexpectedly came out of nowhere and stormed at him with their arms outstretched, aiming pistols in his direction.

Twin saw them coming late. He spun around but was helpless. He was wide-eyed. Still, he tried to reach for the pistol in his waistband.

*Bak! Bak! Bak!*

One of the masked men dropped swiftly to the pavement, receiving two bullets to the back of his head.

His partner quickly pivoted. He was glaring at Apple and her smoking .45. Before he could react, she fired several rounds his way. Bullets slammed into his chest and pushed him back, and he dropped dead.

Twin glared at Apple with apprehension.

The gun trained on him, she stepped closer. Her eyes showed chilliness.

"You gonna shoot me next?" he asked.

"I can," she replied coldly.

"What you waiting for? I fuckin' underestimated you, I see."

"You did. But I didn't come here to kill you."

"Then why did you come?"

"To talk."

Twin glanced at the two bodies sprawled on the ground. He turned his attention back to Apple and said, "You picked the perfect time. A .45 is a loud gun. Many of my neighbors heard the shots, and cops will be coming soon."

Apple didn't have much time. Her arm still outstretched with the gun, she was hesitant to leave, but she had to. "You owe me," she said.

"You think I do," Twin replied arrogantly.

She smirked. She slowly backpedaled toward her car, keeping her eyes and gun on Twin. Now he knew she could be anywhere at any time—saving his life, or trying to take it.

Twin watched her retreat. He didn't reach for his gun. He had been caught slipping. She now knew where he lived.

Apple jumped into her old car and sped away, police sirens blaring in the distance.

Twin looked down at the two dead men and wondered who sent them. Could it be payback for the triple homicide he'd committed a few weeks back? Mack D, maybe? His list of enemies was long, but he wasn't going into hiding. He wasn't built like that.

Twin became less angry with Sassy. Seeing her kill two people intrigued him. She took out two gunmen effortlessly. He wanted to know more about her. Maybe it was better having her alive than dead.

Apple had gotten his attention, but she hated that she didn't get the chance to talk to him. She hadn't planned on two men trying to take Twin's life.

She had gotten a room at the Motel 6, off Security Boulevard in Randallstown. The area was quiet, far enough from the East Side, and she could think.

Inside her room, she lay across her bed with her .45 by her pillow. It had two bodies on it. What was her next move? Would Twin still try and come at her, despite her saving his life?

Apple stared up at the ceiling. Her work was dwindling, and she needed to re-up. She had to make moves. Although she'd said she was through with hustling, it was in her blood, in her bones, deep inside her, like her heart beating. It's what she did and knew best.

It had gotten late, and the television was on mute. Apple ended up falling asleep with her clothes on and her gun in hand. She'd conquered New York and dabbled in Miami. Now Baltimore was going to be her reign of supreme. And she planned on having a lot of help.

# NINETEEN

Kola breathed a sigh of relief being back on U.S. soil. She forgot how long it had been—four years, five; it didn't matter. She was home again. The seven-hour flight was tolerable, and the food was decent. She and the kids moved through Customs without a hitch. Security wasn't too concerned with her. Megan Brown was the name on Kola's passport. She had changed her image dramatically years ago; after all, she was wanted by the feds. She answered their questions smoothly and had a poker face with the agents.

The kids helped too. They made her look less suspicious and more like a mother.

She was able to bring in twenty thousand, but she couldn't forget about the five million she'd left behind in Colombia. It was a stinging feeling. She could have done so much with the money.

Kola grabbed a cheap motel room in Queens, not too far from the airport, right off the N. Conduit Avenue. It was clean and quiet and what she and the kids needed at the moment. She paid for a week in advance and planned on moving elsewhere soon.

Settling back in the U.S. was strange. However, hearing English once again being the primary language was a great feeling for Kola. She no longer needed any translators, and the signs weren't scribble-scrabble to her.

Peaches, Eduardo Jr., and Sophia were scared, being in a new country. Colombia was all they knew. America was a big and strange land. New York City was a busy place, moving like a well-oiled machine. JFK Airport was one of the busiest in the world, and the children felt like they were in a maze of wonder. But there was no turning back. No matter how frightened the children were, Kola believed everything was going to work out just fine. It had to.

In the room, the first thing Kola did was feed the kids Chinese food. While they ate and watched cartoons on the tube, she walked out the room, down the hallway, and stepped outside to smoke a cigarette. She wasn't too familiar with Queens, but it was better than Colombia. The only thing she missed there was Eduardo. She wanted to feel his touch again, be held in his arms and feel safe. He was many things—an asshole too—but she loved him.

In Queens, she felt regular. Everything had been stripped away from her. She was used to spending money like water, but now she had to save and conserve. In a city like New York, twenty thousand wouldn't last long.

She gawked at the traffic on the Belt Parkway. *What to do first?* Kola thought. She needed to get something started; an investment or something. She had to make her money somehow. In her mind, there wasn't any time to waste. But she had three kids tagging along with her, and two didn't speak any English at all. What would she do with them? She'd made Eduardo and their mothers a promise. Somehow, she had to take care of them. But how?

Kola finished off her cigarette and flicked it away into the street. She turned and went back into the motel. She walked past the female clerk sitting behind a thick partition in the quiet lobby and put two dollars in the outdated vending machine. Two snacks dropped into the opening—more cheap food for the kids to eat. She wanted to keep them fed and busy, but there wasn't much to keep them busy with.

As Kola entered the room, Peaches leaped off the bed and ran to give her aunt a hug. She was a very affectionate little girl who loved her aunt a lot, believing she was her mother. Kola wasn't rushing to tell her any different.

Eduardo Jr. and Sophia sat at the foot of the bed. They were quiet, looking out of place. They didn't get into much. They were good children.

Kola sighed. "What am I going to do with you two?" she mumbled.

The siblings didn't understand a word on the TV. But Peaches did. She became attached to them, almost a surrogate sister. If they didn't understand, she explained it to them. She was so smart—too smart, and very attentive. She played with the siblings, and they took to her quickly.

If it wasn't for Peaches, the kids would have been really out of place.

"Y'all not hungry?" she asked, noticing the Chinese food on the table was barely touched.

The kids gave her a blank look. Sometimes Kola would forget that they didn't understand her. Peaches had to ask them in Spanish. They shook their heads no. They weren't used to eating Chinese food.

"Y'all need to eat something," she said.

In Spanish, Sophia cried out, "I want my mommy."

Kola had no idea where to turn first. Who could she call? Who was still alive? Who could she trust? Why did Eduardo thrust her into such a daunting task?

Harlem had probably changed a lot since she left. Who would be the new players in the game? Did her name still ring out? Would they remember her?

Kola remembered that she and Apple had left Harlem, and the country, for a reason. So many people had died the year she left—Cross, Chico, Denise, Guy Tony, and so on. They'd left behind a bloody mess, and she remembered running to Eduardo for help. What he did to her that day made her feel violated, but she needed him. He was their knight in shining armor. She hadn't planned on coming back to the U.S., and definitely not with three kids.

⚜

Kola and the kids climbed out of the gypsy cab on Northern Boulevard. It was a chilly and cloudy day, meaning the winter was approaching soon. Kola had to get her act together. The first thing she needed was her own transportation; public transportation wasn't cutting it for her. She took ten thousand to spend on a decent car. It wasn't part of her budget, but it was getting cold; a car would be suitable in the city.

The used car dealership on Northern Boulevard looked reasonable to Kola. The lot had a display of a few midgrade cars, different models, different years, the price and other information about the vehicle written on the windshield in chalk.

Immediately, a dealer approached her. He was a handsome white male in his late twenties, clean-shaven and dressed in black slacks and a white button-down shirt. He was eager to make a sale, but he wasn't too pushy.

He complimented the children, saying, "Cute kids."

Kola responded with a dry "Thanks."

He told her his name was Jonathan.

"So, what can I help you with? What kind of car are you interested in?" His voice was smooth. He had strong eye contact and a winning smile. He was a pro at this.

"Something nice and cheap," Kola replied.

Kola set her eyes on a silver sedan, four doors, not a dent or scratch on it, marked for $15,000. Too rich for her blood.

"Well, you came to the right place. We take care of our people here, and our prices are always right, and our cars top-of-the-line," he said proudly.

Kola looked at him. *I'll be the judge of that.* Her eyes shifted from the sedan to a black Toyota, the interior was black and clean.

"I see you set your eyes on the Toyota," Jonathan said. "Nice choice."

The price tag on the windshield for the four-door vehicle was $9,000.

"It's a two thousand, and a V6."

Kola interrupted his sales pitch. "How many miles?"

"Um, roughly, a hundred and sixty thousand."

"Too many miles. Don't want it breaking down on me."

"This baby right here," he said, tapping the hood, "She's good to go."

Kola wasn't interested in the car anymore. She pivoted, he followed. She slowly walked through the lot with the kids in tow. They had everything, but she wanted the right car for the right price.

Jonathan continued to try and butter her up. "I'll give you a good deal, because of the kids—I love kids—and you're cute."

Kola didn't smile or entertain his flirting. She was there for one thing only, driving home in something reliable.

"How much are you willing to spend?"

"Enough."

He chuckled. "Okay."

It was a thwarting feeling for Kola, being in a used-car lot, trying to negotiate for a cheap car when she was used to driving a hundred thousand or better—exotic, sleek and fast. Whether New York, Miami, or Colombia, she drove in nothing but the best. She would easily walk into a top-notch dealership, pick whatever she liked, drop cash money, sign a few papers, and ride out the same day.

She walked toward a grey four-door Mazda.

Jonathan was pitching it to her immediately. He smiled. "Now this car, it's definitely you. It's a two thousand six, five-speed manual. Can you drive stick?"

"I can."

"Then you're good to go. I can have you taking off in no time. Zoom! Up in the air, like *The Jetsons*." He pretended to be a plane with his arms spread out like wings and flying around his customers lightheartedly. His energy was contagious. He even made the kids laugh, and the siblings didn't understand him. But his personality was very affable.

Kola didn't want to pay $8,500. "How many miles?"

"Roughly, I say sixty-five thousand."

It was fitting, so far. The price was a concern.

"Oh-oh! I can see that look on your face—Houston, we have a problem," he joked.

"We do."

"Is it the price?"

"It is."

Jonathan slapped his hands together and said, "Okay, it's time for me to make some magic happen." He did a quick magic trick and made a quarter suddenly appear behind Peaches' right ear.

She laughed and smiled. She was impressed. So were Eduardo Jr. and Sophia. He was good with kids. He gave her the coin.

"You see that?" he said. "I'm already saving you cash."

"Cute," Kola replied nonchalantly. "Now, let's talk about the price."

"Okay, here's what I can do for you. Because I really, really like you and your kids, I'll drop it down to eight thousand."

Kola gave her reply by threatening to turn away and go somewhere else.

Before she could take two steps in the opposite direction, he exclaimed, "Okay, okay, you're killing me here. I should have you arrested for murder. But the lowest I can go is seven thousand eight."

Kola thought about it. She locked eyes with him and said, "Okay, I can afford that."

"You better. You're so cute, I might help you pay for the car."

Kola was ready to take him up on his offer. They went into the office to go over paperwork. After an hour, she was handed the keys and his phone number, and she was driving out the lot with her brand-new used car.

Next, it was finding a new place to live. She couldn't stay a day longer in the motel, which was costing her close to five hundred dollars a week. Everywhere she went, the kids went too.

She found a nice one-bedroom studio apartment in Harlem, her old stomping grounds. Being back in Harlem, she started to feel a little nostalgic. Everywhere she went in her old neighborhood, she was flooded with memories—some good, some bad, and some really ugly.

The studio apartment was $900 a month, and she gave the landlord six months' rent in advance. On the west side of town, on tree-lined 148th Street, the studio had hardwood floors and new appliances. It was small, yet comfortable. It was nothing the children were used to in Colombia, but they had to adapt somehow.

After a week in her new place, Kola bought a bed, a pull-out sofa, and a small table, and she stocked the fridge with plenty of food. Money was dwindling fast. She was down to five thousand dollars. It cost to take care of three kids. She had to think of school, health, and everything else.

Every night, Sophia mostly, would cry herself to sleep, missing her mommy. Eduardo Jr. had his moments too. Kola and Peaches did their best to make them feel at home, but sometimes their best was not enough.

Kola did everything under the name Megan Brown. She did her best to keep a low profile. Her hair and clothes were different, and she carried an accent. She felt like a whole new woman. Kola couldn't afford to get caught up, arrested, and sentenced. What she and her sister had left behind—the bloodshed, the destruction, and violence— lingered in the community, and there were still some people around that didn't forget.

After two weeks in the country, everything was going fine. However, the siblings were becoming difficult to deal with every day. They started to whine more. It was frustrating having Peaches interpret everything back and forth. And they were picky; they didn't want to eat anything. Kola literally had to force-feed them, so they wouldn't starve to death.

Kola sat on the side of the tub, smoking a cigarette, and stared at the bathroom wall. The kids were in the other room, watching cartoons. The door was shut. She needed some alone-time. She took another pull then exhaled, remaining pensive.

Out of the blue, she heard a cell phone ringing. She ran out of the bathroom and looked around for it. It wasn't her Galaxy on the bed. It was another cell phone. Then she realized Eduardo could be calling. The phone ringing was the one given to her in Colombia. Kola rushed up to remember where she'd put it. She scurried around the bedroom, searching for the ring. She'd left the phone in her traveling bag. She hurriedly opened it, grabbed the phone, and immediately pressed the button to answer.

"Hello!" she exclaimed into the phone, excited to hear his voice.

"Hello, bella," Eduardo's smooth voice said.

"Eduardo! Oh my God! I've been so worried about you. What's going on?" Kola asked in one breath.

"Everything's fine."

Kola felt he was lying to her, trying to protect her. His voice brought tears to her eyes. Her heart started to beat faster.

"I see you landed safely in the U.S."

"I did. We went through Customs without any problems. I did and said what you told me to do."

"That's good."

"I miss you."

"I miss you too. How are the kids?"

"They're fine."

"Are they adjusting to life there well?"

Kola took a deep breath. "They're trying, Eduardo. Everything is so different over here."

"I know. I understand. But I know you're strong. I know you will look after them and protect them."

"I will."

"I can't talk long. I just wanted to call and make sure you and the kids are okay."

"I know."

Kola wanted to ask him a million and one questions, but their time on the phone was limited. He told her he'd call once a week. She was hoping he kept his word. When he hung up, she sobbed on her bed. How could she go on? She missed him greatly.

# TWENTY

Apple sat nursing a clear drink at the end of the long bar, her eyes on the six-foot thug with the lean body, narrow face, and tattoos. He sat four barstools away from her. All it took was a simple smile tossed his way, and right away she had his attention. He flashed teeth filled with silver and gold. She held his gaze. Her eyes smiled. He downed his drink and continued looking.

The old-fashioned bar in Park Heights wasn't crowded. It was an early-evening weekday; only the stragglers and hardcore drunks swamped the bar during happy hour. The atmosphere inside was serene, though it was a rough neighborhood. Alicia Keys' "Un-Thinkable" was playing from a corner jukebox, while a lone middle-aged bartender served drinks and talked to the few customers inside.

Apple downed her clear drink and ordered another one. She looked delectable in a pair of tight blue jeans, a tight shirt, and high heels. In her purse, she concealed a

.9mm. She kept a cool attitude sitting at the bar, minding her business, looking like she didn't have a care in the world.

Finally, the man mustered up enough courage to remove himself from the barstool and approach her.

Apple kept cool, her eyes on him. His smile was crooked, his thick, black beard intimidating. He definitely was a player in the streets.

He came close and hovered over her like an alien spacecraft invading new territory. His smell was musty—cigarettes, alcohol, and cheap cologne.

"Didn't ya muther teach you dat it was impolite ta stare at a nigga?" he said, his vernacular bordering on illiterate.

"My mother didn't teach me many things," Apple quipped back.

"Oh, she didn't, huh? Why not?"

"Because I never listened."

He smiled. His gold grill shined brightly in the dimmed bar. He casually moved closer, taking up too much of Apple's personal space, trying to mack. Apple already knew he was an idiot. But he could be useful.

"What ya name?"

"Karen."

"I like dat name."

"I'm glad you do."

"And what's yours?" she asked.

"Goliath."

"Like the Bible?"

"Who?"

*He is stupid. He doesn't even know where his own name comes from.*

"Can I buy ya a drink?" He pulled out a wad of cash, trying to impress her.

"I didn't plan on staying long."

"Where ya go to?"

"Someplace quiet, where I can think," she said.

"What ya need ta think about?"

"Stuff."

"Oh, stuff, huh?"

"Yeah, stuff," she said, trying to hold in her laughter.

Apple was toying with him. There wasn't much promise in him. He had choppy conversation and low intelligence. He would always be a "do boy," or muscle in the streets. But he was somebody not to fuck with. She knew him, but he had no idea who she was.

"You wanna come?" she asked, teasing him.

"I thought ya never ask, ma."

Apple giggled. She removed herself from the bar.

Goliath placed a twenty-dollar tip on the countertop and followed her to the door.

"My car or yours?" he asked.

"Yours."

Apple followed him to a champagne-colored Crown Vic parked up the street. She observed the bulge underneath Goliath's shirt and jacket.

When he got near the car, he deactivated the alarm, and the doors opened. Apple slid into the passenger seat.

Goliath plopped behind the steering wheel and quickly lit up a blunt.

"You smoke, ma?"

"No, you enjoy."

Goliath enjoyed the blunt for a moment. He took a few strong pulls while lingering behind the wheel.

Apple watched him closely. What he had on was nice, typical for his character—a gold big-faced watch, a diamond pinky ring, a gaudy grill, and gold chains.

Apple was ready to make moves. "You wanna go park somewhere more private and quiet?"

"Yeah." He nodded. "I like da way ya think, ma."

"I'm glad you do."

Without saying anything graphic, Apple hinted that things could get sexual between them. Goliath started the car and drove a few blocks north and parked somewhere in a back alley. It was dusk out, so traffic in the area was thin, giving Apple all the privacy she needed.

Goliath killed the ignition and finished off his blunt.

Apple placed her hand against his crotch.

He grinned. "Dis must be my lucky day or my birthday. Either way, I like it."

"It must be."

She started to undo his jeans, which he'd pulled down to his ankles, exposing his flaccid black dick. She wrapped her hand around his cock and started to stroke it, creating a hard-on. She jerked him off for a minute.

Goliath moaned from her touch, closing his eyes and leaning back in his seat. He didn't notice her free hand slip into her purse. She didn't miss a beat jerking him off while grabbing her pistol.

"Oh yeah! Do dat shit. Ooooh, so good."

"You like that?"

"I like that."

"I bet you do."

"Suck my dick," Goliath blurted out.

"It's coming, baby. It's coming."

Swiftly, she pressed the cold barrel of the .9mm against his nut sack and squeezed his penis.

Goliath was quickly taken aback. He looked at the gun and Apple wide-eyed with shock. "What the fuck is this?" he shouted.

"You move and I'll have nut juice all over your front seats," Apple said with a hard frown.

"Baby, just chill out and let's keep cool, okay?"

"Not okay."

"What do you want?"

"First, take off that watch, your ring, and slowly remove the cash out your pocket," she told him.

"Ya robbin' me now?"

"It's a start," she replied, smirking. She dug the gun into his genitals.

Sweat started to drip from Goliath's brow.

"You even twitch wrong, and you'll regret it. I can get really surgical with this gun, give you and unwanted circumcision."

"Please don't. Not my dick," he begged.

"Everything, into the bag."

Very slowly, Goliath removed his watch, his diamond ring, and the wad of cash from his pocket. He placed everything into her purse.

"We good?" he asked nervously.

"No, we're not good. We need to have a quick talk."

"About what?"

"Your friend, Twin."

"What ya need ta know?"

"Let's start with locations and drop-offs, and then I want you to call him."

Goliath didn't have a choice. He started to sing like a canary.

Ten minutes later, Apple had all the information she needed. After her counsel, Twin now went through disposable phones like he did his women, and was a hard man to reach. She wouldn't have been surprised if he'd changed location after the incident with the gunmen.

For good measure, she pistol-whipped Goliath in the car, knocking him unconscious, before fleeing the scene.

Twin couldn't get enough of the VIP treatment inside the clubs. He and his crew popped bottles and swallowed ecstasy pills. He had a lot on his mind. Baltimore was becoming a little too cramped, and he needed to escape. This time he was in DC, enjoying the limelight at Club Chocolate in the nation's capital.

The club boasted five distinctive floors, each with its

own event options, state-of-the-art lighting and sound systems, and projection screens for large-scale video productions.

Twin sat comfortably in VIP, flanked by his peoples, over a dozen bottles of Cristal and Moët on ice. His Rolex sparkled for his audience, and he fondled and flirted with the loosely dressed women eager to snatch the ballers' and hustlers' attention.

The VIP level of Chocolate offered the perfect setting for a regal experience. Long walls wired with color kinetic lighting allowed a spectrum of lighting options. Inviting pewter-colored suede couches lined the rich green leather panels, and the exquisite mahogany wood bar, paneling, and flooring, along with modern metallic accents, highlighted the richness of the place.

The energy inside the club was electrifying. The celebrities came out in droves. Who's who in the DMV area was partying like it was New Year's Eve 1999. Twin pulled a bottle of Cristal from the ice bucket and popped it open. He then poured some of the gold champagne on a few hoochies, who were practically wearing nothing at all. Everyone, including the girls, laughed it off.

While Twin was partying like a rock star, Apple entered the club looking scandalous in a slinky halter dress with a plunging neckline, low back, decorative hardware, and necktie closure. She caught heavy attention but ignored it with a stone face. She moved through the crowded floor with a drink in her hand. She was on a serious mission, not there to party.

The dance floor was packed, and the bar was crowded with people. It took four bartenders to serve the crowd. DC's nightlife was a lot different from Baltimore's. There were a lot more players and shot-callers in the nation's capital. The music was mostly go-go, and it was a fashion show from wall to wall.

Apple wasn't interested in VIP. She noticed Twin partying hard like he was somebody important; mingling and flirting with the hoochies. She felt some kind of way about it. She downed her drink and stepped out of sight from it all. Patience was all she needed.

Three hours later, Twin exited the club with a voluptuous woman under his arm. She looked eager to go back to his DC place and please him to the fullest.

Twin was extra lively, joking and laughing. He stood outside the club, smoking a cigarette, waiting for the valet to bring his car around. He wasn't shy about fondling his newfound beauty in public.

"Yeah, yeah, we gonna have some fun tonight," he said, squeezing her round, succulent ass.

"You gonna be good?" the woman asked.

"Nah. I like being bad."

She laughed.

The valet pulled his E-Class to the front and stepped out. Twin gave the young boy a fifty-dollar tip. The kid was very pleased. He kept the door open for Twin to slide inside.

Twin drove to his condo in Woodley Park, an affluent community in Northwest DC. No one knew about his place in DC. He didn't trust anyone, and he felt secure in Woodley Park. Security and police were rife night and day, though he would never call them for help at all.

He parked his car and walked toward his condo with the girl under his arm. They continued to laugh and flirt. She was ready to unzip his pants, pull out his dick, and suck it before they even stepped inside the condo. She knew he was a baller and hoped that if she fucked him good, he would drop a few hundreds her way in the morning.

Twin unlocked the front door and pushed his big-titty bimbo inside the apartment. He cut on the lights. He pulled out his pistol and left it on the glass coffee table. He had no need for it right now. His weapon of choice tonight was his dick.

"Ooooh, you have a really nice place!" she said, looking around and twirling.

She took in the open kitchen with the breakfast bar and stainless-steel appliances, beamed ceiling, parquet floor, wall molding in both the living room and bedroom, and the balcony.

"Yeah, I know I do," Twin said. "But I ain't bring you here to like my place. You supposed to like me." He wrapped his arms around her waist and pulled her closer.

"Oh, and I do like you. You're cute."

"I'm cute, huh? Well, show me how much you really like me," he said.

"Let's do this in the bedroom."

"Ain't no problem with that. I like to get comfortable."

Twin took her by the hand and guided her to his bedroom. He pushed open the door, and the minute he clicked on the lights, he found himself face to face with the barrel of a .9mm.

Apple was seated in a chair, looking casual, her gun aimed at his chest. At that range she couldn't miss even if she had her eyes closed.

"What the fuck!" Twin shouted.

The woman screamed.

"Hey, baby."

"How the fuck did you find me?"

Apple chuckled. "It was easy."

Twin stood frozen at gunpoint. The girl he was with was panicking. She hid herself behind Twin, begging not to die. Her screaming started to travel, upsetting Apple.

"Tell that bitch to shut up and leave." Apple wanted to shoot his date on principle. She hated that Twin was about to fuck her. She still liked Twin a lot, and it was hard to see him fooling around with other women who weren't on her level.

"Yo, leave," Twin told the girl.

She didn't hesitate. She spun around and ran toward the front door like a track star.

"I thought you had better taste than that, Twin. You disappoint me."

"Yo, you is a fuckin' trip, Sassy, or whatever your fuckin' name is. How did you find me?"

"Like I said before, I have my ways."

"Obviously, you do. What do you want?"

"I want us to have a nice, long talk. Last time, we were rudely interrupted."

"I heard what you did to my man Goliath. Was that fuckin' necessary?"

"It was, and I enjoyed that. He's a fuckin' idiot. Stupid muthafucka didn't even recognize who I was. Are all your men so stupid?"

"They listen, they kill, and they respect me—that's all I need."

"You truly believe that?"

"What do you want from me? You think I owe you a favor from the other night? That's it?"

"I saved your life. I could have killed you."

"But you didn't."

Apple stood up, the gun still trained on him. This was the second time she had the drop on him. "I just want us to talk," she said.

"I have no choice but to listen, right? You the one with the gun."

She looked at him and lowered the gun. "I don't want to be a threat. I feel, you and me, we can work better together than against each other."

"I'm listening."

"Have a seat."

"In my own bedroom?"

"I'm being nice."

"So am I," he countered.

Apple and Twin took a seat, she in the chair, he on the bed. She remained cautious around him. Though she had the upper hand, she still had to remain careful. Twin was a devious muthafucka.

"I wanna make some money," she started.

"You're doin' fine by robbing my niggas."

"No, I mean some real money. You need me, and I need you."

"Why should I trust you? You burned me before."

Apple stood up. Twin kept his eyes on her.

She reached into her pockets and pulled out a wad of cash. She tossed it on the bed. "That's what I owe you—five thousand."

Twin picked up the money. There was nothing sweeter than that nice green cash in his hands. "And you think this makes us square?" he said.

"There's more."

"And what's that?"

"Me."

Apple placed the gun in the chair, leaving herself vulnerable, taking a huge chance. She was used to taking risks, and most times, it paid off.

Twin hooked his eyes on her. She was still beautiful to him, and he did miss her.

She started to undress slowly.

Twin didn't say a word. He looked into her eyes and saw a woman so much different than he expected. There was something about her that threw him off, but he loved her in a strange way. She was skillful, bold, and smart. How could he go wrong with rekindling his relationship with her? He saw more perks than disadvantages.

Apple approached slowly. She was butt-naked. She allowed Twin's hands to touch her, roam her body. Whatever he wanted to do with her, she didn't care.

"I missed you," she confessed.

Twin took a deep breath. His hands cupped her ass cheeks. "I missed you too."

Apple's naked frame straddled him on the bed. They kissed fervently. She started to undress him. Twin didn't fight back.

Twin gazed into Apple's eyes. He said, "Sassy, what the fuck is your real name?"

Apple hesitated with her answer. She fought with telling him or not.

Twin was waiting for the truth. He looked at her intently.

She exhaled and said to him, "It's Apple."

"Apple? Really?"

"Really."

"I like that."

But that was all she was going to tell him. She wanted her past to stay her past.

Twin didn't ask any more questions.

That night, they fucked their brains out. It seemed like all was forgiven.

# TWENTY-ONE

Kola had settled into Harlem, but every day was a struggle. Her cash was about to run out. She was desperate to do something. She needed a hustle. Eduardo Jr. and Sophia were becoming a headache, always crying, and expensive to keep. The siblings were getting on her last nerves. With money sparse and their apartment too cramped to house four people, Kola decided to make a brash decision.

She pulled up to the Lincoln Projects on 132nd Street. *Home sweet home—Not!*

It was early afternoon, so the neighborhood kids were in school, but the siblings weren't. It was difficult to place two foreign, non English-speaking kids into public school and not raise suspicion. She couldn't babysit them all day. She needed to free up her time somehow.

Kola and the kids poured out her new Mazda and walked into the projects. It'd been a long time since she'd stepped foot on the premises. She didn't want to stay long.

She came to conduct small business, hoping the person was still around.

Kola shuffled the kids into the project building. They moved through the bleak lobby and stepped into the elevator, which smelled like urine. The kids kept close to her, clinging to her legs.

They stepped onto the fifth floor into the narrow hallway. Knocking on apartment B5, Kola sighed deeply and looked down at Eduardo Jr. and Sophia. She hoped she was making the right decision. She'd made a promise, but that promise was becoming too hard to keep.

The faded brown door opened, and an elderly woman with a cigarette dangling from her mouth and aging skin appeared. Clad in a blue housecoat, her gray hair in curlers, she took a long pull from her cigarette. She gawked at Kola. "What the fuck you want?"

"You don't remember me, G-ma?" Kola said.

"Am I fuckin' supposed to?"

G-ma eyed Kola up and down, frowning like an old bat. She puffed out smoke and coughed. She was in her sixties and cursed like a sailor and smoked like a chimney. She wore too much makeup and could easily scare small children with her appearance. In fact, all three of the kids were hiding behind Kola.

"I'm Kola. You remember Denise's daughter?"

"Denise? Ain't she dead?"

"She is, but that's irrelevant right now."

"Oh, I fuckin' know you. You're that twin. I thought you was dead too," G-ma said snappily. "Then it must have been your other twin sister."

G-ma stood for grandma or gangster, depending on who you asked. She had a tart tongue. Her apartment was always crowded with people, her grandchildren and other people's children, and there was always heavy smoking and drinking.

"What do you want, chile?" G-ma said. "A bitch is busy."

"Can we talk?"

G-ma looked reluctant. She was ready to go back inside and get back to her card game and finish her drink on the table. She never let a good drink go to waste.

"Come inside. Hurry up, chile. I don't want my fuckin' neighbors knowing my fuckin' business." She pushed Kola and the children into the roach-infested place and shut the door.

Peaches, Eduardo Jr., and Sophia clung to Kola's legs tightly. They didn't want to go anywhere without her.

The place was unclean—cluttered with everything you could think of—smelly, and hot. Kids ran around unattended. A few teenagers were smoking weed openly in the living room, and the young girls were dressed like they were about to turn tricks.

G-ma's place was the party place where a young kid could bring a willing girl for a good time if his or her parents were home, or they couldn't afford a motel. Pay G-ma the right price, and her bedroom was your bedroom, for an hour or two. She was about her money.

"Hurry up and talk, chile," G-ma spat. "Time is

fuckin' money, and money is fuckin' time."

"Look, I need a favor. I need you to take these two kids in for me."

G-ma looked down at Eduardo Jr. and Sophia. She stared at them like they were a product Kola was trying to sell.

"Them your kids?"

"No, they're not mines. But I promised someone I would look after them. I can't afford to keep that promise right now."

"Well, you know a bitch ain't watching no fuckin' kids for free, baby. You gotta pay like the rest."

"I know. I'm able to give you three hundred a month."

"That sounds fair. How long they stayin'?"

"I don't know yet."

"Well, they got clothes, food, toys?"

"Not much."

"Well, with all these damn fuckin' kids running around this fuckin' place, it will be easy to find them something to play with."

"One other thing, G-ma."

"What's that?"

"They don't speak any English."

"You serious?"

"Yes."

"Where these two rug-rats from anyway?"

"Colombia."

"Colombia? And they here because?"

"It's a long story."

"Never mind. As long as my money is right, I don't need to know." G-ma held out the palm of her hand. She expected payment right away. "And my three hundred."

Kola sighed. It was more money, money she couldn't shell out, but she had to. G-ma didn't do the I'll-pay-you-later plan. She reached into her pockets and put three hundred-dollar bills into her hand.

Once G-ma had her money, it was all good. She was ready to welcome the two children into her home.

Kola was ready to depart from them. She couldn't spend another night with the brats in that small studio apartment. Also, she didn't have any money to support them, and the money Eduardo had promised her wasn't coming anytime soon. She needed to do something.

When Kola tried to leave with Peaches, Eduardo Jr. and Sophia tried to leave with her. The arrangement had already been made. Kola hurried out the door, while G-ma stared at the two little kids and then finally ushered them into a back room.

They started to cry and whine. "*¡Queremos ir demasiado! Queremos ir demasiado!*"

Kola lingered in the hallway for a moment. She could still hear them crying out. She took a deep breath. When she heard G-ma scream, "Be quiet," it was her cue to leave.

Peaches was gazing up at her, looking confused. "Why aren't Eduardo and Sophia coming with us?" she asked sadly.

Kola didn't know what to say to her niece. Peaches had grown attached to them. She took Peaches' hand into hers and walked away. She didn't want to give her any explanation. Maybe, she would come back and get them, if the money came from Eduardo. Maybe.

The lights abruptly shut off at 6:05 p.m., and Kola and Peaches found themselves in the dark. Her light bill was three weeks past due. The refrigerator was almost empty, and all they had was a few articles of clothes she managed to buy. Kola couldn't even afford to put gas in her car. And she didn't have a job.

It was dark and getting cold outside. Winter was right around the corner. Without lights and heat, they would freeze. Peaches started to become scared.

Kola took her niece into her arms and hugged her. "It's going to be okay, Peaches. I'm going to take care of everything."

Desperate times meant doing desperate things. Kola wasn't about to let her niece starve and freeze to death. Her plan was to leave Peaches asleep, and then she would head out to hustle. Although she had made a promise to Eduardo to keep it clean, a lot of promises were made and broken between them. Kola figured, What's one more?

It started off slow, her stealing and scheming. With the holidays approaching, many shoppers were out and about, worrying about deals and merchandise. Learning from when she was young, she would pickpocket if an unfortunate someone was caught slipping, or snatch up unattended wallets and purses.

It was easy for Kola, a quick bump into a passing stranger, a subtle and swift movement of the hand, and that person was quickly relieved of their wallets, watch, necklace, or anything valuable on them. She hadn't pickpocketed since she was fifteen. She used to run with a group of girls that mastered thievery. They called themselves "sporty thieves." At fifteen, Kola made stealing and shoplifting quite lucrative.

Sometimes she would score fifty bucks, sometimes five hundred. Every little bit helped. But whatever the amount; it just wasn't enough to take care of her and Peaches properly. It felt like pennies.

Kola would walk around the city looking normal, keeping sharp from one scheme to the next. Anyone was a target in her eyes—male, female, black, white, it didn't matter.

It was risky pickpocketing and shoplifting, but that didn't stop Kola. They had to eat. The city was more conducive. The white-collar folks most times weren't too protective of their valuables. They moved with a sense of urgency, scurrying to work, maybe an important meeting, brunch with a client. Becoming a victim of a theft was the last thing on their minds. With cops and security cameras everywhere, many white people felt secure and protected in the city.

This grind was taking its toll on Kola. Every day felt like war; it was survival of the fittest. Most nights, it was fast food—Chinese food, McDonald's, pizza from Domino's,—and then maybe something cheap from the supermarket. This was not the way she felt she nor Peaches should live.

The cell phone rang. It wasn't her pre-paid, but the other phone, meaning Eduardo was calling. Usually, she couldn't wait to hear his voice, but since she didn't have his children, she didn't know what to say to him.

Immediately, Kola began making excuses for why the kids couldn't come to the phone—they were outside playing, maybe sleeping, or they were at a new friend's place in the building.

Before he hung up, he said to Kola, "Next time I call, I better speak to them, no excuses."

It had been a month since Kola left Eduardo and Sophia at G-ma's place. If Eduardo didn't call asking for them, then she didn't give them a second thought. She already had enough problems to deal with.

Kola and Peaches stepped off the elevator and onto the 5th floor. She could hear loud music blaring from G-ma's apartment. She was there to drop off the $300 she owed. She knocked. The door was unlocked.

Kola walked in, with Peaches right behind her, into a heavy cloud of weed smoke coming from the six men lounging, drinking 40s, playing Xbox, and rolling up blunts.

She noticed the guns on the table, and the drugs. One police raid into the apartment and they had enough evidence to incarcerate everyone.

When they noticed Kola, they stopped what they were doing and gawked at her.

"Hey, Kola," Doc said. "We heard about what happened to Apple down in Miami. I'm sorry to hear 'bout that. She was gangsta, fo' real."

Hearing Apple's name put Kola in a sour mood. She never wanted to talk about her sister's murder. But everyone knew, so there was no hiding it. The streets talked, from Miami to New York.

"Where's G-ma?"

"She in the bedroom. You want me to go get her?"

"Yeah. Where the kids?"

"What kids you looking for? You know we be having a little school running around here," Doc joked dryly.

"The ones that don't speak any English."

"Oh, those two . . . I guess they around here too; they all look alike to me."

Kola went into the kitchen and looked in the fridge. It was empty. The cupboards too. There was nothing to eat in the entire place.

G-ma walked into the kitchen clad in her usual housecoat. She didn't care for any pleasantries. "You got my fuckin' money?"

"Hello to you too," Kola replied dryly. "What did they

eat today?"

"Chinese food."

Reluctantly, Kola handed over the three hundred dollars over to G-ma, who took the cash and stuffed it into her bra.

The three-bedroom apartment was overcrowded with nine adults and six kids. And between all of them they didn't have two nickels to rub together.

Peaches clung to her aunt as she traveled through the apartment toward the bedroom. The entire place reeked either of weed and funk.

Kola walked into the messy bedroom, filled with young teens and kids. A teenage girl and an adult male were asleep on the top bunk bed, and from the smell of the room, Kola knew they'd just finished having sex, probably right in front of the children. Three sloppy-looking kids were lying around on the floor watching adult cartoons.

She found Sophia and Eduardo Jr. in the corner, near the window, their heads down, looking traumatized. The moment the siblings noticed Kola and Peaches in the room, they quickly jumped up and ran to her and hugged her, screaming, "¡Titi! ¡Titi!"

They were excited to see her and Peaches, who'd missed them a lot.

Kola looked at their faces. Both of them had bruises, old and new. She held Sophia by her chin gently, lifting her face upwards, inspecting her angelic face that had been obviously assaulted. She was only four years old. Eduardo

Jr.'s pants were soiled from pee. Seeing them looking like third-world kids broke Kola's heart.

Kola turned and stormed out of the bedroom.

G-ma was seated in the kitchen, talking to one of her girlfriends, when Kola barged in.

"How the fuck can you mistreat them like that? They're fuckin' babies!"

"First off, you don't fuckin' come in my muthafuckin' house and scream on me—Bitch, is you fuckin' crazy? And, second, you knew exactly what the fuck you was getting when you dropped their non-English-speaking asses here!"

"You're wrong!" Kola screamed back.

"Bitch, this isn't the Waldorf Astoria. And if you cared so much for those fuckin' brats, you should have fuckin' taken care of them yourself! Bitch, you could take them fuckin kids and leave!"

"I will!" Kola was in her face. She didn't care who she was, or if that bitch was her elder. She had to stop herself from beating down a grandmother. But she was real tempted. G-ma's mouth was really greasy. "I want my money back."

"Money back? Bitch, we don't give refunds here! What goes into my bra fuckin' stays in my bra. The only way you get money back is on my fuckin' deathbed."

Kola shouted, "Maybe I need to make that happen then!" She suddenly grabbed the old woman by her housecoat and slammed her into the fridge. She wanted to knock the dentures out of her mouth.

When G-ma started to scream, the dudes in the living room came rushing into the kitchen and tried to pull Kola off G-ma.

"Yo, Kola, chill out!" G-ma's grandson shouted. "You lost ya mind!"

"Do y'all fuckin' know who kids those are?"

Glaring at Kola and fixing her housecoat, G-ma yelled, "Get this fuckin' bitch outta my fuckin' house!"

"You know who their daddy is? One phone call and he'll have everyone in here DEAD."

The young men knew she ran with some heavy hitters and powerful men back in her heyday, and how foul and deadly the twin sisters got down. The hood had blamed the twins for their mother's and sister's murders, amongst others.

"G-ma, just give the damn money back. It ain't worth it," her grandson Pop said.

With more persuading from her grandsons and others to give the money back, G-ma reluctantly reached into her bra and gave Kola her money back. She frowned. "Take your bad luck ass and them brats and get the fuck outta my place!"

"Gladly!"

Kola grabbed the children and left. She scooped Sophia into her arms and told her, "Everything is gonna be okay." She knew they didn't understand her, but her look and smile made them smile.

She took the children back to her small apartment. She fed them and then bathed them. Then she put them all in the sofa bed. All three slept together peacefully, snuggled closely together.

For a moment, she watched them sleep. She now planned on keeping her promise.

Kola slept on the floor. Now, she was starting to feel like a mom, their protector. No harm was about to come to any of these kids ever again.

Whenever Eduardo called, Kola would ask him for money. Once again, he continued to tell her that she needed to be patient, and in the interim, should get a job.

*A job? Where?*

Kola was tired of having her hand out. She came out her mother's womb hustling. She had to realize Eduardo was going to do life in a Colombian prison, or they were going to execute him. He was almost three thousand miles away. How much help could she expect from him? She needed to hold him down, not the other way around.

It was time to start doing her. The hood nicknamed her Coca Kola for a reason.

# TWENTY-TWO

Twin took the pussy from the back, slamming his erection into Apple, who was bent over doggy-style, her face pushed into the bed, the dick making her moan. Apple's breath became ragged, feeling Twin's throbbing dick in her soaked pussy. Twin thrust hard, gripping her hips, sinking his big dick into her. She clamped her eyes shut and whimpered in surrender as Twin fucked her in his queen-size bed.

They'd found a passionate rhythm with each other. Twin was on the edge of coming. The way she backed her ass against him brought him on the verge of release.

Apple gripped the headboard while Twin continued to plunge hard into her. "Fuck me, baby! Fuck me harder!" she hollered. "I want to feel you come!"

Moments later, Twin's body became hard as steel, and he drove his dick deep as he exploded into her.

Twin had gotten over his anger issues with Apple, and they became a couple. The plan was to get money and take over the city. The trips back and forth from DC to Baltimore became more frequent. They also hit cities like Philadelphia and Richmond. She had his back, and he had hers.

Apple started to put together her own crew in the city, and she ran it with an iron fist. She had Phillips, a mean white boy from south Boston who stood six three and could kill like the best of them. He was a veteran, good with explosives, and had a knack for disposing of bodies. She'd met him through bartending at the club. He liked her, but she didn't like him. Yet their conversation was deep. He stood out in Baltimore as a tall white boy, but no one fucked with him.

Then there was Dino, young and violent. East Baltimore had always been his home. He was nineteen and eager to please Apple in anyway. He respected her. They lived in the same building. Apple treated him with respect when everybody else thought he was a bum—stupid and inept. Both his parents were drug addicts, and he was born a crack baby. Dino was an introvert, but when upset, his temper was fierce. Apple saw something in his eyes she could take advantage of.

Next in her crew was Muppet, a man she'd met while working in the club. Muppet was a short man from the East Side with a baby face, but what he lacked in height, he made up for with a pugnacious attitude and a deadly temper. Apple witnessed Muppet get into a few fights inside the club while she was working, and no matter how big or large the man was, Muppet showed no fear or intimidation. He was able to hold his own, and no one was going to punk him. While working, she'd started having casual talks with him, and over time, the two grew on each other.

This was Apple's crew. They looked like the gang who couldn't shoot right, but they were already taking Baltimore's streets by storm.

A man was shot eight times in his car on E. Madison Street. They said it was Apple's crew. Two bodies found with their throats cut in an abandoned row house on N. Glover Street were linked to Apple. A man shot in the head on Jefferson Street—a bitch named Apple green-lighted the hit.

Apple hit the streets hard, selling kilos by the dozens and bumping heads with East Side rivals. She was in a new city with the same ol' tricks. It was like she couldn't help herself. She'd quickly forgotten that she was supposed to be a dead woman, and keeping a very low profile.

With Twin out of town and money coming in like train smoke, Apple decided to celebrate. She and her crew went to party at the same club she was fired from. Now, it would be her turn to sit in VIP and pop bottles.

Apple hit the club hard like a boss bitch. Some of her former co-workers envied her. Flanked by her boys, she felt heavily protected. Each one would kill for her. "Mama's boys," she liked to call them.

Phillips was the hound dog both on the streets and in the clubs. Not only did he chase kills, he chased pussy just the same. Muppet was the same, lurking in the clubs, looking for either pussy or drama to get into. Dino, the quietest of them all, sat near Apple stoically. He refused to drink or smoke. He was always on alert, watching and waiting for anyone to do the unthinkable. Dino was Apple's watchdog. Armed and dangerous, his bite was louder and more vicious than his bark.

While Twin was in DC, Apple held down the fort in Baltimore. Bottles of Cristal and Dom Perignon champagne sat in front of her in ice buckets. Once again, she felt like gold, and life was good. The streets were going to respect her, no matter what.

Apple was in VIP, partying and flirting with a few men, but she didn't dare take it any further. Twin had his goons everywhere in the city, and the last thing she needed was another confrontation with him. She couldn't wait to wrap herself in his arms again and feel him inside of her. They fucked like rabbits and couldn't get enough of each other.

"I see ya big time now and forgettin' about a nigga," Apple heard a familiar voice say to her.

She turned and saw Pug, his baldhead glistening, standing right there in front of her with his own rough crew. They locked eyes, and he seemed very displeased.

"Look what the fuckin' cat dragged in—a dick-less bitch that couldn't hold down the fort for at least a minute." The liquor was fueling Apple's reckless mouth.

"You think you can talk to me like that, bitch?" Pug frowned at Apple with a murderous rage.

Apple continued to laugh and mock him. "Nigga, you is a nobody. You never was a somebody. Who you? Bitch-ass nigga! I fucked with you because I was bored, nigga!"

Pug was seething. Not only was Apple ridiculing him in public, but her crew was encroaching on his territory, and two of his men had been gunned down.

"Bitch, you think you protected with ya boy Twin," Pug growled. "Don't sleep on me, bitch!"

Dino stood up, and so did the others in Apple's crew, fire burning in their eyes as they glared at Pug and his men. Before a violent confrontation ensued, security intervened and escorted Pug and his men out of the club, but the tension was thick in the air.

Later that night, Apple and her crew exited the club. She was feeling tipsy and horny, and it made her miss Twin dearly. But he was in DC and wouldn't be back in B-more for a day or two.

Flanked by her goons, Apple walked to the Range Rover parked halfway down the block from the club. It was a clear, cool night, and the streets were thick with people exiting different locations and walking to their cars. She laughed with her men as she smoked her cigarette.

Out of the blue, the sound of gunfire erupted, and everyone in the area scattered for cover.

Apple hit the pavement, taking cover behind a car, as the car windows shattered around her, with bullets puncturing the door and her men taking to the pavement. She was unaware of where the shots were coming from.

Guns came out, and her crew was ready to shoot back. But just as quickly as the shooting started, it ended, but not before the screeching of tires.

Apple slowly stood up, dusting herself off. She'd scraped her knee and ruined her dress.

"You okay?" Phillips asked her.

"I'm fine." Apple was furious.

It had to be Pug. She knew it was him, and she planned on hunting him down and cutting his balls off.

This was nothing new to Apple. She'd escaped death plenty of times, but each time, she felt her nine lives were rapidly counting down.

# TWENTY-THREE

One picture turned into two, then three, and four, and before she knew it, Kola was about to have herself a small collection of albums of herself and the kids. She sent a lot of them to Eduardo and the siblings' mothers in Colombia. She didn't know if they would receive her package or not, but at least she tried.

The package contained many pictures of her and the kids, either in the park or in the city, and in the apartment, or just in their rooms. In each picture, Eduardo Jr., Sophia, and Peaches were smiling and laughing, looking like they were having a great time in America, but things weren't going so great. They were poor and struggling. Kola would write letters to Eduardo, Maria, and Marisol. She badly wanted to keep her promises.

Each day it got colder and colder in Harlem. The warms days were fading, and the nights sometimes were brutal without any heat. They had to sleep in their clothes and underneath a ton of blankets to keep warm.

Kola thought about going into boosting again. It'd paid off when she was younger, but the risk wasn't worth the low reward. She couldn't take the chance of getting knocked. Times had changed. Security had upgraded, and now there were stiffer laws for people caught boosting. Pickpocketing in the city was also not cutting it anymore. The winter weather meant heavier clothing and people didn't linger outside in the cold. They kept snuggled in their winter coats and moved with a sense of urgency to get out of the cold.

Kola hadn't lived like this since she was young and staying with her mother. She vowed that she would never be poor again. It felt like she'd gone back on her word.

Kola got use to leaving the kids home alone. Not for long hours, just long enough for her to have some alone time. On those days, Kola found herself sniffing around in her old neighborhood. Lincoln Projects was a breeding ground for crime and trouble. The old players were no longer on the corners or controlling the market. New faces had taken over. People moved on, were killed, incarcerated, or just got tired of the game. Only a few stayed around.

She found herself walking down Fifth Avenue, the November cold nipping at her face. The one thing she did miss about Colombia was the year-round warm weather. Everything else in that country, they could keep—besides the five million she still yearned for.

Wrapped up in her long winter coat, she walked into the local bodega with fifteen dollars to her name. She wanted a pack of Newport and a few lotto tickets. She only bought cigarettes. It was the only thing she could afford. She needed the nicotine to relax.

After stepping out of the store, Kola quickly lit up, took a long, deep pull, and exhaled. She sighed heavily. Fifth Avenue was busy like always. She gazed at the towering projects across the street, and so many thoughts flooded her mind. The things she could have done differently.

Nichols flooded her memory, making her feel nostalgic. It had been so many years since her murder, but still, when she thought about it, it always felt so fresh.

Kola took a few more pulls from the cancer stick and flicked it away. She loitered in front of the bodega, braving the cold weather. It was thirty-five degrees and windy. The sky was gray and gloomy, just like her life.

A long time ago, she felt like the queen of Harlem. She had anything she wanted or needed in a heartbeat. She used to drown herself in twisted pleasures. She ran strip clubs and controlled a stable of hot young women who men from all over came to see. Her parties were unmatched, and the connections she made were unparalleled. Did she miss it? Heck, yes!

It was hard to think about her past, when now, she didn't have much. She was tempted to sell her car for some quick cash, but traveling with three kids in the New York cold was excruciating.

A burgundy Chrysler, windows tinted and rims chromed, came to a stop right in front of her, blaring rap music.

Kola admired the car.

The driver's door opened, and the driver stepped out in a red leather jacket, his fresh Timbs touching the pavement, his jeans sagging, a red bandanna protruding from his back pocket. He approached the bodega.

Kola looked at his long cornrows and recognized him immediately. She hollered his way, "Khalifa."

He turned and looked at her. Instantly, the corners of his mouth turned upwards, and he hollered back, "Oh shit! Co-ca Kola!"

Kola smiled. "Khalifa, what's good?"

The two embraced. He was the first person she was glad to see.

"Yo, what you doin' back in Harlem?"

"It's a long story."

"It's been a minute, luv. I heard you was like in Mexico or somethin'."

"Colombia."

"Damn! You went way out there. You always was on that other shit, fucking with them major niggas. But you lookin' good, Kola," he said, admiring her from head to toe. "You still ain't change."

"Thanks. And I see you out here still doing your thing."

"Shit, you know the game don't stop for no one. I gotta keep on grindin', or a nigga ain't gonna eat. You feel me?"

"Tell me about it."

"So what you doin'? You back in the game?"

Kola told him, "I need to do something."

"Oh, word? Yo, you got a cigarette?"

She pulled out her pack and gave him two cigarettes.

Khalifa lit one. "But, fo' real, it's good to see you again."

"The same here."

"Yo, I heard about your twin. I'm sorry. Apple was good peoples."

"We had our differences, but I miss her."

"I miss her too. It ain't the same out here. Shit done changed, Kola, fo' real."

"I see that."

Khalifa took another pull from the cigarette. Quickly, he inspected his surroundings. He was always on alert. He came up in the dope game, and his reputation was strong, but he still had enemies. He had his pistol in his waist, and it was always cocked and ready to bust.

"So where you at now?" he asked.

"Over on the West Side, on a Hundred and Forty-Eighth Street."

"How long you been back in town?"

"Almost two months."

"Yo, it's good to see you back."

"It's good to be back." Kola couldn't hesitate anymore. She looked at Khalifa and said, "I need a favor from you."

"Yo, what you need? You tryin' to get back in?"

"Nah, but I do need something else."

Khalifa took another pull. "I'm listening."

"I need work."

"What kind of work?"

Kola asked, "Who's promoting the hottest clubs in the city right now?"

"You mean like partying or underground?"

"Something underground . . . the strip clubs?"

Khalifa smiled. "Oh, you tryin' to get back into that, huh? Yeah, you always did your thing with them clubs, got shit poppin'. But, yo, Skinny Stan is still doin' his thing, ya know."

"Skinny Stan?" she replied, looking surprised.

"Yeah, he still hustlin' that part of the game. He gettin' that money."

"Back then, he made a lot of that because of me."

"Yeah, we ain't forget. You was definitely the HBIC."

"Yes, I was," Kola said, reminiscing.

"But you tryin' to link up wit' the nigga?"

"Khalifa, I'm tryin' to do something."

"Yo, I wish you would get back into this game, hook me up wit' that Colombian connect. I know you fuckin' wit' them cartels hard body. You was the shit, girl—niggas ain't forget. Right now, I'm working for this real dick-nigga, fo' real, Kola."

"Who?"

"Nigga name Mack D."

"I never heard of him."

She thought she knew everybody who was somebody in Harlem, but she realized she had been gone for some time now.

"He a foul dude, yo. We miss real muthafuckas in the

game like you, Cross, and Mike."

Kola wasn't ready throw herself into that lifestyle again. A few things haunted her. She had been through a lot, and it was risky for her right now. Though she was well known in Harlem, times had changed, and she had to take care of her niece and two others. If she only had herself to think of like back in the day then she would start slinging coke again. No hesitation. However she had three little ones to "mom," and if she got knocked then it would be over. Peaches and the rest of dem babies would be raised up in the State's custody. Kola would never allow that to happen.

Khalifa and Kola talked for a moment. He updated her on current conditions in Harlem, and then he gave her Skinny Stan's phone number. He hugged her good-bye.

Kola watched Khalifa climb back into his car and drive away. She lit another cigarette before she walked to her car. Having Skinny Stan's number, she couldn't wait to call and catch up.

Skinny Stan stepped out of his BMW and looked at Kola like he had seen a ghost. They met in the parking lot of Diamond's, an elite strip club in the Meatpacking District in New York.

"Well, damn!" Skinny Stan said excitedly. "Look who is back in town."

He stood five feet ten and weighed 180 pounds. He was indeed slim, with a unique look, having a pointy nose, baldhead, and thin face. His most "attractive" feature was that he knew how to pour on the charm to get women to fall in love with him.

Clad in a pea coat and wingtip shoes, Skinny Stan hugged Kola and kissed her on the cheek.

"It's good to see you, Skinny Stan," Kola said.

"Same here. What brings you back into Harlem?"

"It's a long story."

"Well, I'm glad you're back. We missed you."

"I missed y'all too. But I need work, Skinny Stan."

Skinny Stan always was soft- and well-spoken. He was like the Count of Monte Cristo—intriguing, sometimes articulate, but also street. Skinny Stan knew the best of both worlds. He'd learned from the best—Kola.

"Work? You tryin' to get back into the business?"

"I just need to do something."

Kola stood in front of Skinny Stan looking marvelous. She didn't want to look like a broke-down bitch in front of him, so she glammed up in high heels and makeup.

"You still look great, Kola. You always did."

"Thanks."

"I'm glad you called. Well, I know the owner to this club. He's pretty cool. He's reasonable. You sure you want to get into this? I mean, back in the days, you was that bitch. I just can't imagine you on the opposite end of this business."

"Things changed, Stan."

"I understand."

Kola followed Skinny Stan into the building. It was empty, and the lights were on. It was mid-afternoon, so the party hadn't started yet. Kola walked past a raised platform as a stage. It was shaped like a capital T with a pole. The stage had chairs all around it and an additional platform to put drinks on. The bar, long and stocked with every drink possible, was on the opposite end of the room.

Skinny Stan went to a backroom and knocked.

"Come in!" someone shouted.

Skinny Stan opened the door and walked in, and Kola followed him.

Inside the office was Steve, an aging white man nicely clad in a three-piece suit with a cigar in his mouth. He was seated behind a large desk, busy on his laptop. He had salt-and-pepper hair and a grayish goatee and looked very distinguished.

"Steve, I want you to meet a very good friend of mines, Kola," Skinny Stan said.

Steve glanced up and gave Kola a fleeting look. If he was attracted to her, she couldn't tell. "She here for a job?" he asked, eyes on his computer screen.

"Yes."

He didn't say anything else at first. The laptop screen had his attention.

Kola stood in the office, feeling awkward. This was never her—begging for a job—but at the moment, her hands were tied.

Steve lifted his eyes again. This time he looked at Kola a little bit longer. "You're pretty," he said.

"Thank you."

"Listen, if Skinny Stan recommends you, then I'll hire you. Three things, though"—He reclined in his high-back leather chair, took another puff from his cigar—"First, I don't allow drugs in my club. You use or sell, you pay the price. Second, you pay the house ten percent of your earnings, and third, no sex in my club. If you want to fuck someone, you take that business off my premises. I run a legit business here. I can't afford to get shut down. Do you understand me?"

Kola nodded.

"Okay. Now that we have that cleared up. You start tonight," he said, not giving her a choice.

"Thank you," Kola said, looking deadpan.

"We're done."

Skinny Stan and Kola left the office. Once again, Skinny Stan asked her, "You sure you want to do this?"

Kola nodded. She didn't have a choice. She had to keep her nose clean and stay out of trouble. She didn't forget about the shit storm she'd left behind and the feds coming after her. She just wanted to dance and take care of herself and the three kids. She had to start bringing her own food to the table.

# TWENTY-FOUR

The loaded clip with the hollow tips slid into the Glock 19. The hammer was cocked back, and the safety off. The gun was in Twin's hand, and he was ready to hunt down Pug and blow his fuckin' head off. He'd heard about the incident at the club and was furious. He'd never liked Pug. The moment he saw him at Apple's place a few months back, he wanted to put a bullet in his head. Now, he was excited that Pug had rekindled the beef. He had his reason—Pug and his goons had tried to kill his girlfriend.

It was a chilly Saturday night, and the East Side was bustling. The money and the drugs never stopped. As long as the planet kept spinning, the East Side was going to be the East Side—a dangerous, rowdy, and deadly place. Twin was ready to add to its murder rate.

The Range Rover was crammed with killers, including Apple, who sat shotgun while Twin drove. Phillips and Dino were in the backseat. Everyone was heavily armed. Twin was itching to find Pug.

Apple took a few pulls of the burning weed and passed it along. Her eyes were low, and her heart was cold as the winter months. For a moment, it felt good to be back to her old self. She did miss being bad Apple.

They intentionally drove around Baltimore into rival territory. The vehicle was quiet, the air thick with weed. Twin always went with the motto do onto others before they do onto you. And he was ready to do onto them.

Phillips took a pull from the weed. The high made him feel invisible. He toyed with the .50-cal. Desert Eagle like it was a water gun. It was his favorite gun. He could put down a charging elephant with it, and what it did to men, especially up close, was odious.

Bloodshed had become a regular in Baltimore. People were scared to leave their homes. The East Side especially was starting to look and feel like Baghdad, with gunshots ringing out day and night, and police trying to take control over the heavy crime plaguing their city. Drug crews ruled their streets, killers felt like they were gods, and drug fiends walked around like they were lost in paradise.

Pug was trying to establish himself on the East Side. He was known to have a stash house on E. Chase Street and Bond, and another spot on N. Gay Street. He lingered in front of the row house with three of his men. His right-hand man, Marko, was behind the wheel of an idling Escalade, patiently waiting on him.

Pug had an important meeting to go to, but at the moment, he was briefly holding court with his crew on the street. Everyone was focused on Pug, as they gathered around him like he was the president giving his State of the Union speech.

Apple spotted the group from a block away. She was sure it was them. She was ready to implement her plan and put Pug out of commission permanently. They drove around to the next block, where Dino got out. Twin drove on, shrewdly circling the block.

Dino crossed the littered lot, throwing the hood over his head to conceal his face. He walked with his head down and his gun in his hand but out of sight. He could see Pug and his men in the near distance.

Twin circled the block once again, without Pug noticing. Apple cocked back the Glock. With Dino on the other end, near Chase and Bond, and Twin and Apple on the opposite, coming from Broadway, they had Pug and his crew trapped on Chase. It didn't matter which way they ran; they were going to run into bullets.

Twin cut the headlights off and approached slowly. They were about to do it LA-style at first, but Apple wanted to get close enough to Pug to shoot him dead with him looking at her. She wanted to see the look on his face.

Pug said to his men, "Yo, ya make sure you get at dat nigga Light. I ain't playin' wit' him. It's been a week now."

The gun nodded. "I'm on it, Pug."

Pug took a drag from the Newport in his hand. "Y'all faggots, get on ya job. Hold it down."

As the group was about to disperse, Pug noticed the dark figure coming his way coolly. He couldn't see who it was because of the hoodie covering the man's head, but Pug's gut feeling told him the man walking his way was trying to not be noticed.

Pug's right-hand neared the pistol tucked in his waistband. For a moment, he thought he had the advantage. He was ready to shoot the nigga down the minute he leaped his way.

*Bam! Bam! Bam! Bam!*

*Boom! Boom! Boom!*

Deafening bursts of gunfire came from the opposite direction, and two of Pug's men immediately went down, bullets ripping through their flesh.

The rest tried to take action, including Marko.

Suddenly, Dino opened fire, shattering the glass of the Escalade. He caught Marko in the head as he was about to exit the truck to return gunfire. Marko's head exploded, spilling his brains and flesh on the street, and he hit the pavement face-first, sliding into the front wheel.

Pug found himself in the middle of chaos, inundated by a hail of bullets, making it impossible for him to aim. "Fuck!" he screamed.

Apple and Twin were like the Terminator, storming forward, guns blazing, knocking everything down like bowling pins.

Pug didn't even see it coming. Dino hit him from behind, and the back of his head splattered with blood.

Apple and Twin, for good measure, pumped a few more bullets into Pug's body as he slumped to the ground.

"Bitch-ass nigga!" Twin said.

"Oh shit!" Phillips looked shocked.

Everyone turned to see what spooked him. The man was cool as ice, so this had to be something major.

They noticed the backdoor of the Escalade was open. Apple went to check it out, and she was taken aback. She'd thought Pug was alone, just him and his men. His eight-year-old daughter was lying dead in the backseat of the Escalade with a hole in the head.

Apple was speechless and shocked. How could she have known?

"Fuck it! We need to go!" Twin said.

The little girl reminded Apple of Nichols. She didn't know Pug had a daughter.

"Apple, we ain't got time to feel sorry," Twin said. "We gotta fuckin' go!"

Phillips slowly pulled Apple away by her arm. "C'mon, there's nothing we can do for her."

Apple came to her senses and left the scene.

The Range Rover drove from the crime scene in haste. Apple kept quiet. She was many things, but the one thing she didn't want to be was a child-killer.

The shooting on E. Chase Street in East Baltimore flooded the news.

The anchorwoman reported live on the scene, *"An eight-year-old girl was shot and killed in East Baltimore, Friday night after two groups of people opened fire on each other during a drug conflict, which left six dead, including the young girl's father."*

Apple and Twin watched from the living room of their home that they shared together on the outskirts of the city.

*"It's a story we seem to be hearing too often here—another young child killed in the crossfire of gang violence in East Baltimore. The gunfight happened sometime around eight o'clock Friday night. One neighbor said, 'It sounded like a war on the street.' The police don't have any suspects right now, but the investigation is ongoing."*

"Turn it off!" Apple shouted, saddened by the news. She sat back on the sofa.

Twin obliged, and the flat-screen went black.

"Yo, it wasn't your fault, Apple," Twin said. "We ain't know."

They didn't know which bullet killed the little girl, but it was state-wide news. The mayor was talking about the incident, which was now a federal case.

"We need to lay low for a minute," Twin suggested. "Chill out. Maybe stay apart from one another."

Apple looked at Twin with a raised eyebrow. "Apart?"

"This shooting ain't gonna blow over no time soon. We fucked up. I'm gonna shoot up North for a week or two."

"Where?"

"It's better if you don't know."

"But why can't I come with you?"

"If we're separate, I feel we're better. I mean, they can't trace us back to the shooting. The Range, we set that shit on fire far from here, and everyone else is dead. Every last one of the guns involved, we dismantle and toss into the water. And your peoples ain't gonna talk, right?"

"They won't."

"A'ight. So we go somewhere, we cool our heads and wait for this shit to die down and come back and continue on wit' business."

Apple wanted to be with Twin, but she thought he was right. Maybe they needed to go somewhere else and think for a moment. She decided to head back to New York for a week or two. It was risky going back home, but she didn't have anywhere else to bounce too. She felt it would be the last place anyone would look for her. Besides, she was already considered dead.

# TWENTY-FIVE

Kola tucked the kids into the bed and kissed them good night. Every day she was trying to make it better for them and herself. The babysitter was in the living room waiting for her to leave so she could do her job. Kola somewhat trusted the nineteen-year-old college student, who was helping raise her little sisters.

Kola walked out the bathroom. It was time for work. The babysitter, Samira, who lived on the floor below, was standing in the living room with her schoolbooks in her hand. She was always studying. She was dressed conservatively, but looked a little frumpy with her bushy ponytail, weight, and thick glasses.

"Is everything okay?" Samira asked.

"Yes. They're fed and sleepy, so they shouldn't be a problem for you tonight."

"Okay."

"I shouldn't be too late tonight. The club is slow on Wednesdays."

"Okay."

Kola paid Samira twenty-five dollars a night. She was the cheapest and the best. She didn't have a social life. Her life was school, work, and home, and babysitting gave her time to study.

Kola grabbed her coat and belongings. She went out the door, ready to dance and show off her body—another night, another dollar. It'd been three weeks since she'd started. She turned heads, being the new girl in town.

Kola wasn't a stranger to the strip clubs and the lifestyle. She knew how to work the crowd and wasn't shy about taking her clothes off. Her body was to die for. The way she twerked, tweaked, moved her hips, and worked the pole made her a crowd favorite. She knew how to flirt and was able to hold a conversation with anyone and make them feel like the world revolved around them.

The minute Kola had walked in on her first night, she was sure about herself. The only thing she was thinking about was making that money.

Through the weeks, she'd established a steady clientele of generous tippers. They would stuff tens and twenties into her G-string. They yearned to fuck her, but it would be only business. It was only lap dances and peep shows. The club didn't allow any sexual solicitations at all.

Night after night, she started making money. Three hundred on one night, five hundred the next, and on a good night, she would make close to a thousand dollars. On a bad night, she would make a hundred dollars or less. But it was legit income.

A few years earlier, she got into promoting and running the business because there was a lot of money in it. She loved the money, power, and respect it garnered. She'd made a name for herself. Being on the other end of the business wasn't so bad. She took her clothes off to feed three kids.

Tonight, the club was packed for a Wednesday night. The manager was promoting an event with the girls—baby-oiled strippers boxing each other in G-strings and pasties. The winner would receive five hundred dollars.

Kola didn't volunteer for the event. She had no desire to fight for extra cash. She simply wanted to make her money dancing and flirting with her customers.

While she was changing in the locker room, a few of the strippers started to talk about the boxing event. She sat away from the other girls.

The talk in the locker room went from strippers boxing to a man named Mack D.

"Yo, I heard Mack D is supposed to come through tonight," Brandy said.

A naked, big-booty girl named Spice said, "You know Steve and him are tight. They like brothers. And he's the real owner of this club."

Another girl said, "Girl, if Mack D comes through tonight, I swear I would probably suck his dick right there on stage."

Everyone laughed except for Kola.

"Yo, he control these niggas out here," another stripper said. "That's what I be hearin'."

Kola already knew that Mack D was a boss nigga based on what Khalifa had told her. She felt that if these bitches had a boss courting them, they probably wouldn't know what to do with power and dick like that. *Fuck it up, most likely.*

Mack D sounded like the kind of man Kola needed and wanted to get with, though she had pledged her loyalty to Eduardo. She was used to being a boss, or dating the boss. She knew how to talk to them, how to sex them, and how to hold them down.

In her stripper attire, Kola walked into the dimmed club, music blaring. The men were crowded around the stage and the bar.

Diamond Star was giving them one hell of a show while the boxing ring was being set up on the opposite side of the club. She worked the pole with enchantment.

Kola started to work her charm inside the room, smiling, touching, and conversing with her regular customers. She made a hundred dollars in half an hour. The sexy off-the-shoulder garter dress with the attached stockings garnered much attention from the boys inside. Sipping on Cîroc to ease her mood, she didn't plan on staying long.

※

Glistening in baby oil, her long legs stretched out in stilettos, Kola gripped the pole, lifted herself toward the ceiling, and came twirling down like a Cirque du Soleil act, showing her upper body strength. She wrapped herself around the pole again like a snake and continued to execute a variety of complex positions, becoming a contortionist suspended above the stage. She had them all hypnotized by her freaky performance.

She then moved with precision to the smooth R&B beat, her booty bouncing, her tits shaking. What little she had on came off, and the money came raining down on her like a blizzard.

Dancing on her knees, cupping her tits, Kola saw what looked like a familiar face, but it wasn't him. He favored Cross a lot. He sat with his friends, and each had a wad of cash in their hands.

The man had low waves and bright caramel skin. He had a really nice body that showed underneath the shirt he wore. He tossed twenties and fifties her way like it was pennies into a fountain. It was obvious that he was attracted to her.

When Kola came close, he couldn't pass up the chance to say, "Yo, you are beautiful. What's ya name?"

Kola told him, "Goddess."

"Goddess—Yo, I like that!" He held her wrist gently, not allowing her to rush off anywhere else so soon. His hold was firm, indicating he wanted her undivided attention.

They locked eyes. He was cute, but Kola wasn't interested. She needed to continue to get her money.

"I can change your world, beautiful."

"Sure you can," she replied dryly. "But I'm not interested."

Kola pulled herself from his grasp and went back to work. Before she was too far away, she heard him say, "My name is Twin."

She didn't give Twin a second thought. It was back to entertaining.

He sat in the same seat most of the night and watched Kola. She was the only girl he tipped heavily.

The nude boxing match was about to begin. Two curvy, dark-skinned young girls climbed into the small ring with boxing gloves on, and the bell sounded.

The men cheered and gawked over the music.

The boxing match was a hit. A stripper named Starfish won.

Kola made what she could and decided to call it a night. She got dressed and was ready to go home to be with the children.

The minute she stepped out of the locker room, Twin was waiting nearby. As she walked past, he jumped forward and took a hold of her hand.

"Hey, Sexy," he said, staring at her. "My Goddess. Damn! Let me take you out."

"Take me out." Kola looked at Twin like he was crazy and laughed. "I don't date men from the club." She walked off.

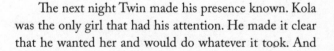

The next night Twin made his presence known. Kola was the only girl that had his attention. He made it clear that he wanted her and would do whatever it took. And like the night before, Kola took his cash but ignored his flirting.

Twin was a thug and a killer, but he was also a businessman. And when he saw something that he liked, he didn't hesitate to go after it.

For two weeks straight, Twin frequented the strip club, doing whatever it took to grab Kola's full attention. He bought her drinks and continued to tip her. It felt like he was paying her a salary with the money he tossed her way.

Kola started to think he was a stalker. A few times she was tempted to call security on him, but his tips made her decide against it.

"Have a drink with me," Twin said.

"Why?"

"Why not? I won't bite. Believe me, I'm a really nice guy. And one drink won't do any harm, right?"

She thought about it, and it didn't do any harm.

They sat at the bar. Kola ordered her usual Cîroc, and Twin got himself the same.

Twin said to her, "I can file my tax return and put you as a write-off, with the money I gave you."

It was funny to Kola.

Then he said, "Tell me about yourself."

"Why you wanna know about me?"

"Because I'll tell you everything about me. Promise."

"You first," Kola said.

"I was raised to believe ladies first."

She shot back sharply, "I wasn't."

Twin smiled. His teeth were white like snow, and the way the corner of his lips curled up when he smiled, he seemed almost innocent enough. But his eyes told a different story.

She thought he was a low-level thug with not much to say, but he surprised her. His speech was intelligent, he was humorous and, at the same time, compassionate with his words. They talked for a half hour, and he continued to tip her—a twenty into her G-string, a ten-dollar bill placed in her hand—and drinks were still on him.

Kola kept her drinking moderate. She wasn't the one to get pissy drunk and make herself an easy mark for a cheap fuck. She'd seen girls have sex with a guy for free because of too much liquor, when regularly, they would charge him an arm and a leg for some good punani.

Their conversation turned serious when speaking about death. Twin had brought it up, mentioning Marcus, his little brother that he'd lost five years earlier to gun violence. Maybe speaking with Kola allowed him to open up, something he rarely did with anyone.

"He was killed a few years ago—shot by a stray bullet that wasn't even meant for him. He was just in the wrong place at the wrong time."

"I'm sorry to hear about your loss."

"It was a long time ago."

"I know, but death can always feel fresh in your heart when you were really close with the person."

Twin looked at her, almost amazed by her words. She was right. Every time he thought about his little brother, it put him in a sour mood. But he would quickly snap out of it.

Kola mentioned the death of her little sister a few years back. They had something in common, and it got them to talking more. Before she knew it, she spent the night with Twin, conversing about everything under the sun—movies, the streets, books, and even sex.

The one thing Kola didn't say or share with him was her past or anything more about her family. At the moment, it was forbidden territory.

By the end of the night, Kola came off with eight hundred dollars.

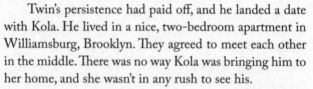

Twin's persistence had paid off, and he landed a date with Kola. He lived in a nice, two-bedroom apartment in Williamsburg, Brooklyn. They agreed to meet each other in the middle. There was no way Kola was bringing him to her home, and she wasn't in any rush to see his.

They met at the strip club in downtown Manhattan. Kola drove and parked her car. Twin hadn't arrived yet, so she sat and waited for him in her car, dressed to kill.

It would be her first date in years. For over five years, Eduardo was the only man in her life, and the only man she loved. It felt awkward waiting in her car to see another man.

Kola decided to go with a pair of Seven jeans with pink stitching to match her snug V-neck sweater that suggested she'd soon show off the goods in the next "hot body" contest.

Twin was fifteen minutes late. He asked her out, not the other way around, and she didn't appreciate his tardiness. Kola was ready to pull off, when Twin came rushing to the window and tapped on it.

She rolled down the window.

"I'm so sorry for being late—traffic was a bitch coming into the city. I know it isn't an excuse to have you waiting in the cold, but I promise, I'll never be late again. You're too beautiful."

Kola looked at him deadpan. "Just don't let it happen again."

"My car or yours?"

"Yours. I wanna save gas."

He laughed. "No doubt."

Kola climbed out of her car and walked to Twin's idling 650i coupe, gleaming with perfection. She slid into the passenger seat and crossed her legs.

Twin got behind the wheel. The smile on his face indicated he'd never been so happy.

"I hope you have someplace special to go," Kola said. "I don't like my time being wasted."

"Believe me, gorgeous, I arranged an entire special evening for you and me," he said confidently.

Kola was ready to be impressed. If she wasn't, then she wasn't going to be shy in letting him know.

First, it was dinner at Buddakan. Twin spared no expense. Whatever Kola wanted, she was able to order.

After dinner, the two went into Times Square and got lost among the thousands of tourists on the streets. They went to a movie at one of the theaters in the area and then walked around the brightly lit area.

They spent three hours in Times Square actually enjoying each other's company. There wasn't a boring moment with him. He was energetic and sparkling with conversation. He was romantic—the perfect gentleman, or pretending to be. Either way, it piqued her interest.

After Times Square, he whisked her away to Central Park, where he indulged Kola in a horse and carriage ride through the park on a cold night beneath a full moon.

While in the carriage, with Kola in his arms, he whispered in her ear, "Are you impressed?"

She was, but she didn't want to tell him that. She tried to hold back her smile, but it was hard with Twin. She didn't expect it to be like this. It had been a long time since she'd been wined and dined by a man.

"You're doing okay," she replied nonchalantly.

Twin could only smile.

After the carriage ride, Kola knew it was time to go home. They drove back to the Meatpacking District, and Twin continued to amuse her. She laughed and laughed.

"So, when can I see you again, besides at the club?"

"I don't know," she replied. "Maybe sometime soon."

"Soon, like tomorrow?"

She chuckled.

Twin was up close and personal, ready for a good-night kiss.

They chatted lightly, and then Kola said good-bye. On her way home, she smiled, thinking about Twin. Could it be that she really liked him?

# TWENTY-SIX

As they got to know each other better, Kola had a set of strict rules that Twin needed to follow and respect. He couldn't meet her kids nor come upstairs, which he totally respected. Twin loved her vibes, her look, and everything about her. She told him about Eduardo in Colombia. She informed him that he was doing life in prison, and that he would always come first. If he couldn't accept it, then he was free to leave. No matter what, she would always take Eduardo's calls, and if Twin so happened to be around, then he needed to keep his mouth shut while she was on the phone.

Reluctantly, Twin agreed to all of her terms. He could have been with any woman he wanted, but he wanted to be with Kola. After two weeks together, it felt like they were together years. She was smarter than any woman he knew.

Twin was a top-level player in the drug game, running his own crew and moving serious weight across state lines.

He had his share of kills, but only when his hand was forced. Despite his history of violent crimes, he was good-natured toward his friends, and had a passion for animals. He kept his life private, and didn't trust too many people. The only man to ride or die with him was his right-hand man Jigga.

Twin and Jigga grew up together and were like brothers. Jigga was a no-nonsense player in the streets. He was strictly business, making money and making moves. He didn't talk much. Both he and Twin dropped out of school in the sixth grade and started dealing drugs on the corners for a mid-level player. Eventually they became primary soldiers in the criminal organization. And Jigga became responsible for driving and picking up money. Together, they grew strong in the game, made connections, established a clientele, and became a force to be reckoned with.

What Twin also loved about Kola was her knowledge of the drug game. When she started helping him with his business, giving him advice in the drug game, he wasn't too prideful to listen. He didn't know what to make of it, but it made her his dream girl.

Kola lay naked on the huge queen-size bed in the middle of his bedroom, relaxing and listening to smooth R&B. Twin's naked body was glowing and defined in the moonlight from the open floor-to-ceiling curtains. Near the bed was an ice bucket with a bottle of champagne chilling in it.

Twin was built from head to toe, his muscles ripping, his dick long, thick, and looking luscious. Kola approached him. He popped an ice cube from the bucket into his mouth, leaned over her, and pressed his lips against hers. He buckled and contorted at the sudden blend of sensations—the warmth of her mouth, the cold of the ice.

They continued to kiss passionately. She slid her hand down his chest, brushing her hand against his erection. She enjoyed how rigid and tense his body became. His face hardened for a moment and then softened to a smile as she drew away, leaving the ice cube to melt on his tongue.

"I fuckin' want you so much," he announced. His voice was like a low growl into her ear.

Kola wanted him too.

They both paused and waited. She waited for his anxiety to build before wrapping her hand around his hard, thick, black dick. She started to stroke him up and down. Twin was breathing deeply now, recovering from one sensation and preparing for the next, his body taut and close to ejaculation from her cherished touch alone. Kola could tell.

Their eyes met and held, and the energy between them was undeniable.

As things got hot and heavy with Twin, Kola thought about Eduardo. Feeling, licking, and groping on Twin, the twinge of guilt wanted to make her break away and collect herself. Could she really go through with this? Eduardo had given her the okay, knowing she was a woman with needs, but it'd been a moment since she'd had sex.

He squirmed. "I want you!"

Twin pushed inside her in one long stroke, pressing firmly against her G-spot. Kola felt his breath coming faster, her own gasps mingling with his. They built a rhythm together, as she met him, thrust for thrust. He crushed between her thighs, sucking nipples and feeling every bit of her warm moistness. Their movement combined and set a pace that kept them both at the edge of their own climax.

With Twin thrusting inside of her, Kola managed to forget about Eduardo.

Finally, Twin gave into his own climax, gripping Kola's body as it was firmly pressed up against him. He held her tightly against him, driving his last thrust into her as he moaned into her neck.

Twin was truly a sweetheart, and Kola had opened up her heart to him. She still had many questions about him, though, but didn't pry too much into his life. She wanted to ask him why they called him Twin. She assumed it was because he was a Gemini, which would explain the tattoo of the zodiac sign on his forearm.

Twin pulled up to Diamond's strip club and parked. He and Jigga stepped out of his 650i coupe. It was a cold night, and both men were wearing leather jackets, Timberland boots, and jeans. Both men looked like they could be extras for a G-Unit video. The Meatpacking District was supposed to be a safe zone, but Jigga carried his gun everywhere.

Twin couldn't stop talking about Kola, but the one problem he had was Eduardo. Though the man was incarcerated way off in a foreign country, Twin still felt like he was a threat. He wanted Kola all for himself. The sex was amazing. She was amazing.

It was a Sunday night, and the club was active with patrons and dancers. They walked inside to blaring rap music and half-naked girls. Twin didn't care for the girls, though they were beautiful and sexy. He only wanted to find Kola. He hated that she was still dancing in the club. Now that they were together, it burned him to have other men staring at his woman and lusting over her.

"What you drinkin'?" Jigga asked.

"Cîroc."

"Ayyite." Jigga went toward the bar.

Twin searched for Kola through the thick crowd. It was hard finding her in the dimness and smoke, but he was relentless. When he finally located Kola, she was with someone, a client supposedly. Though it was her job, he hated to see her dance on other men.

But there was Kola, her ass perfectly contoured to the man's pelvis in the back of the club, allowing her to control a well-perfected and prolonged sexual tease. As the DJ flooded the room with hip-hop beats, there was a push and pull between them, like erotic foreplay. She knew how to dance.

Twin gawked at their movement, uneasy with what he was seeing. He approached with his eyes on them.

The man with Kola appeared to be in his comfort zone. He gripped her thighs and touched her butt and cupped her tits. He was a little too fresh with her body, pulling her hips into his, moving his mouth over the damp skin along her neck. Most likely, he wanted a little something extra.

Twin watched the man turn Kola around and put his hands on her bare thighs, sliding them along the hem of her skimpy outfit as he leaned into her.

Then it happened suddenly. Twin grabbed the gentleman by his shoulder and spun him around, and he punched him, sending him stumbling backwards.

The man reacted with his own punches, and a scuffle ensued. Jigga quickly jumped into the fight, aiding Twin at full throttle. Security intervened and broke up the melee.

Kola said, "Twin, what is your fuckin' problem?"

"He's my fuckin' problem!" Twin shouted. "I want you to quit this shit!"

Twin thought about their arrangement. After two months together, he still hadn't met her kids and had to remain quiet whenever Eduardo called. And he still hadn't seen her place. Twin wanted to know everything about her. There were still unanswered questions. He wanted to be her main man, to take care of all her needs and those of her kids.

# TWENTY-SEVEN

New York, New York—the Big Apple, the city of dreams. Apple was home again. It was the concrete jungle, a city of the haves and have-nots, with misery and commerce jumbled together. It was cold like the Antarctic, but Apple was warm and cozy in her hotel room. She stood by the window and peered out at the city, puffing on a Newport.

She wanted to forget about the shooting in Baltimore. The media was all over it, not letting it die down. A week or two out of Baltimore would do her some good. Police still didn't have any suspects, and Apple didn't want to worry about it. It was a tragedy that eight-year-old Michelle Butler had been killed, but it was an accident.

From twenty stories up, near Times Square, the city felt quiet to her, but it was still bright. Times Square was colorful and bright like Disneyland. Lingering by the window, she thought about Twin. She missed him so much. A week without him was just too long.

She decided to call him. His cell phone rang several times, but there was no answer. She called again and got the same results. She didn't want to worry about him, since he could take care of himself. What she did worry about was his fidelity. He was in DC alone with millions of bitches—now that truly worried her.

To get her mind right, she was tempted to take a trip up to Harlem to see her old neighborhood, which would have been a huge risk. But New York wasn't the town to remain inside a hotel room. It was a city where there was always something to do.

Dressed in tight jeans, a cashmere sweater, knee-high Prada boots, and her fitted Montclair jacket, Apple stepped out of the hotel lobby into the cold air and a very busy and loud city. She quickly hailed a yellow cab and climbed into the backseat. The distinct odor of stale cigarette smoke from previous passengers wafted up her nose.

"Where to?" the driver asked.

"Anywhere."

"I'm going to need a specific location."

Apple sighed. Harlem was out of the question, and Brooklyn was never a safe place, so the city was the only place left. She wanted to hit the club, get a drink, and mingle with the right crowd.

"Take me downtown . . . anywhere."

The driver nodded and drove off.

Apple sat back and gazed out the window, a .22 in her clutch. She rode in silence, taking in the city like she was a tourist. Through the heat, the cold, the rain or snow, New York was always alive with people and traffic.

She ended up at Greenwich Village, also known as "the Village," a pulsating area with lounges, restaurants, and bohemians. She paid the driver and climbed out of the cab. Her first destination was a quaint lounge nestled on a city block. The patrons inside were a mixture of straight and gay. She ordered a drink and took in the place.

Ten minutes later, she decided it wasn't the place for her. She walked out, climbed into another cab, and headed toward SoHo, with a lengthy catalog of places to choose from. She went into places like the Gold Bar then Noca on West Broadway, and The Anchor on Spring Street.

While partying, Apple overheard some folks talking about a new strip club named Diamonds in the Meatpacking District. From what she heard, it was the place to be.

Apple climbed into a yellow taxicab again and gave the driver her location, which wasn't too far away.

She got out the cab and looked at Diamonds, with its wide entrance and a few people lingering outside. The club already looked interesting to her.

As she headed toward the place, she noticed a few people looking at her, but she paid it no mind. Men always looked her way. She was shocked that they easily let her inside without paying any cover charge.

When she walked inside, she heard one of the bouncers say, "Goddess, I thought you was already inside."

Apple, having no idea what he was talking about, ignored him. She went into the strip club, and immediately, all eyes were on her. She pushed her way toward the bar and ordered a Grey Goose and Sprite.

"You changin' up today, Goddess?" the female bartender asked.

"Excuse me?"

"Not your usual Cîroc?"

Apple asked her with a slight attitude, "Do you know me?"

The bartender smiled. "Okay, no fuss about it. I'll get your Grey Goose." She turned and went to make the drink.

Apple felt like she was in *The Twilight Zone*. Why were they calling her Goddess and acting like they knew her? After receiving her drink, she turned and looked at the petite, topless dancer with blonde hair working the pole on stage.

The girls walked around the sizable club working for their tips and entertaining the fellows.

Apple thought about Kola. This was definitely her atmosphere. Her sister would have been running this place. It was a proud thought about Kola, one that made Apple feel a little sentimental. It'd been a long time since she'd seen her sister. *I wonder what the fuck she got going on in Colombia. Did I make a mistake leaving her alone with Eduardo?*

Out of the blue, she felt someone tap her ass lightly and say, "Damn! You change fast."

Apple turned around and glared at the man. He was smiling like he had won the lotto. He was cute, exactly her type, but she didn't like how he felt her up. Her body was off-limits, never mind they were in a strip club, and he needed to understand that.

Apple was ready to put him in check, when suddenly, a commotion broke out on the opposite end of the crowded club. She turned and saw security running toward the skirmish. *Not even ten minutes in the place and there is already a problem.*

She heard someone shout, "He's my fuckin' problem! I want you to quit this shit!"

The sea of people between her and the conflict made it almost impossible to see what was going on and the faces involved. It wasn't her business, though. She had her own troubles to worry about. The only thing she could see was several beefy bouncers escorting two patrons outside of the club—Apple didn't see the faces of Twin and Jigga. A stripper rushing toward the locker room looking highly upset caught Apple's eye. She saw a glimpse of the stripper, though the crowd obstructed most of her view, and something inside of her made her quiver.

Apple desperately tried to get a better look at the stripper hurrying toward the back room, but to no avail. Apple left right after finishing her drink. Unbeknownst to her, she was just a room away from reuniting with her sister, Kola.

The next night Apple took another taxi tour. Her old neighborhood was calling, so she took a cab into Harlem. She wanted to ride around the old neighborhood and see what had changed.

The cab turned right onto 135th Street. Apple eyed Lincoln Projects, where she was raised. Looking at her old building, she immediately started to feel reflective about everything that had happened in her past. She rode by the spot where they'd found her little sister's body. She thought about her deceased mother, Denise, and then she thought about Kola. She started to feel emotional and alone.

She took a deep breath and continued to sightsee into her past.

The cab circled the project a few times. The corners changed, as did some of the people. The kids back then had now grown up. Some of the storefronts on Fifth Avenue had also changed.

Apple witnessed two uniformed cops execute a stop-and-frisk. She shook her head. NYPD was still a pain in the ass, harassing young black men for no reason at all. Her hatred for cops was embroidered into her soul like a stitching. When her sister had died, they didn't do anything to really try and solve her murder. Apple felt that the detectives on the case didn't feel any empathy for a young, black girl.

Apple turned her head away from the stop-and-frisk. It wasn't her business.

She also toured 125th Street, which was pretty much the same—people, traffic, numerous stores, The Apollo, and street vendors selling everything from bootleg DVDs to books and socks.

She rode up Amsterdam Avenue and took her time looking around. Harlem would always be a part of her, no matter how long she was away. It would always be home.

As she rode in the backseat, her thoughts and memory continued to linger. Kola and Peaches were the only family she had left. She'd give anything to see her daughter again, simply hold her, and say how much she loved her.

Whenever she saw a woman with kids, her gaze would remain on them. A family was something she didn't have, and probably never would. Every mother and child sent Apple into a tear-jerking mood tonight.

The cab turned onto 148th Street in Harlem, a quiet tree-lined block. Ahead of them, Apple noticed a young woman in the distance climbing out of a grey Mazda and walking with three kids into a building. She looked hard from a distance and an indescribable feeling swept over her. The woman walked and moved like her sister, but she brushed it off, since Kola was in Colombia with Eduardo. And why would she be with three kids going into a mundane-looking building?

By the time Apple was close enough to get a better look, the woman and the kids were already inside the building.

"Stop!" Apple told the driver.

The cab stopped in the middle of the street. Apple stepped out of the car and looked at the entrance to the building. She was tempted to go inside and see for herself. She loitered in the middle of the street, looking at the building.

A car honked behind her, snapping her abruptly from her thinking.

Once again, she brushed it off and climbed back into the cab. *I'm seeing things*, she thought to herself. "Go," she told the driver.

# TWENTY-EIGHT

Twin was delighted to finally meet Kola's kids, though they weren't actually her kids. He fell in love with all three of them, and they with him. He made them laugh, and he didn't come to Kola's place empty-handed. He came with gifts for the kids.

"Santa Claus," Peaches said about Twin. "Mama, he's funny."

The girls received pricey dolls, teddy bears, and clothes. Eduardo Jr. received a few action figures, a basketball, though he liked soccer, and all three got their own Nintendo 3DS. Kola had never seen the kids so happy in America.

"Hey, baby, you know I couldn't forget about you," Twin said, smiling heavily.

"Oh, you didn't?"

"You know you always come first."

Twin had to make up for the incident he'd caused on her job at the club. He'd apologized repeatedly and was willing to do whatever it took for her to forgive him. He was paying her rent and all of her expenses. He'd encouraged Kola to quit stripping, and after persistent complaining and begging, Kola relented and stopped dancing. Twin promised to take care of her, and so far, he was keeping his promise.

While the kids were playing with their gifts, Kola and Twin sat at the kitchen table just a few feet away. Twin closed the door and removed a jewelry case from his leather jacket. He opened the box and revealed a 3-caret diamond necklace that cost close to $10,000.

"Only the best for the best." He smiled.

Kola couldn't believe it. It was beautiful.

He removed the necklace from its case and clamped it around her slim neck. She went over to the mirror and looked at it. It was definitely magnificent.

The longer Kola stared at the necklace, the sadder she became.

Twin noticed her reaction. "What's wrong, baby?" he asked with concern.

Kola took a deep breath. "Nothing."

"You sure?"

She nodded. "I love the gift." The necklace reminded her of the time Eduardo did the same thing. It was the same moment, but a different guy this time.

"I know it was you the moment I saw it."

"Thank you."

Twin leaned into her, and their lips locked fervently.

"There's more," Twin said.

"More what?"

He sat Kola down on her bed and looked at her. "Yo, I want you to move in with me."

"Move in?"

"Yeah, baby. I want you in my life twenty-four/seven, and the kids. They're getting older, right? Your apartment is too small for the four of you. Let me make things more comfortable for y'all. I live alone. I know it's more than enough for y'all. And later, we can find something bigger. But I want you in my life, baby, and I don't want to have it any other way."

Kola looked at him, gazing into his eyes and seeing the gravity in them. He was definitely serious.

"Look, if you need time to think about it, then do it. I gotta make a run out of town for a few days, take care of some business."

"What kind of business?"

"You know I always been honest with you—I gotta meet with a connect, Mack D; we got business together."

"Mack D?"

"Yeah. You know the nigga?"

"No. I just heard his name mentioned in the locker room a few times from the other girls. They say he's some big shot, a very dangerous dude."

"And I'm a dangerous muthafucka too. You know I can handle myself. But shit is drying up out there, baby. I need to get my hands on some quality work. I need to make some serious moves."

"Be careful, baby."

"I will."

The two kissed again. Kola didn't want him to leave, but she understood. She was ready to move in with him, but she decided to tell him the good news after he came back from his trip.

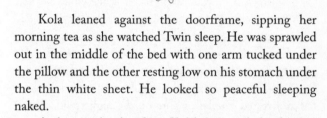

Kola leaned against the doorframe, sipping her morning tea as she watched Twin sleep. He was sprawled out in the middle of the bed with one arm tucked under the pillow and the other resting low on his stomach under the thin white sheet. He looked so peaceful sleeping naked.

A slow smile played on Kola's lips, and she felt her body react to the man in the bed. Finally, she felt happy. Twin was doing everything right.

Kola had moved into his apartment three weeks earlier. His place was just right—three bedrooms with hardwood floors throughout and a formal dining room with sweeping views east and north from his private terrace—perfect for those spring, summer, and fall nights. The spacious foyer with two large coat closets led to the 29-ft. living room with large windows and access to the terrace.

Twin was home for the week. He was busy with the street life, but he was still making time for her and the kids. He was constantly out of town, but their love was going stronger. Every day without him Kola missed him deeply. Most importantly, she trusted him.

Watching Twin sleep, she thought about a future with him. She wondered where they'd be ten years from now. She had to believe it would get better. Twin had made her so many promises, and she wanted to believe him. He showered her and the kids with love and respect. He was faithful and honest and went out of his way to please her. Just like Eduardo, Twin would give her stacks of cash to shop with while he was away. And just like when she was with Eduardo, Kola was stashing for a rainy day. She made a vow to never allow herself or the kids to go hungry again.

Today, she wanted to do something special for him. He had done so much. Twin was leaving again for Baltimore the following morning. So while the kids were fed and rested, she left a note on the nightstand: Watch the kids, ran out for a minute, I'll be back.

She jumped into his 650i coupe and drove into the city. She wound up in the Diamond District on 47th Street and 5th Avenue. She went into one of the jewelry stores and took her time searching for the right piece of jewelry for him. It took her fifteen minutes to find it, but there it was—an old school rose gold rope chain with a rose gold and diamond cross necklace. Twin was going to love it.

After leaving the Diamond District, Kola drove to St. Patrick's Cathedral Catholic church on 5th avenue to have the cross blessed, to keep her man safe. Then it was off to Toys"R"Us, where she grabbed some Lego sets, learning games, and a few dolls for the girls.

Kola took everything out of the trunk of her car and struggled toward the lobby entrance, trying not to drop anything. It didn't work out too well; one of the bags went crashing to the ground. She decided to leave two bags in the car and come back for them.

Unlocking the door to Twin's beamer, she heard the faint sound of a cell phone chime somewhere inside the car. It sounded like a text alert. She searched for the phone and found it in the console. She wasn't aware that her man had two cell phones. When she'd left the bedroom early in the morning, his cell phone was on the nightstand.

"Sneaky muthafucka," she uttered to herself.

She quickly checked the text that came in. The message read: *tomorrow night, meet me @ Carmine's in B-more harbor to celebrate our 1yr anniversary. 8pm sharp... love u.*

*Anniversary!*

A wave of emotion swept over Kola. She was shocked that Twin had such duplicity in him. No, she was fucking furious. But a man was going to be a man, right? She thought Twin was different—that he was the one—but he was just like Eduardo. He had a whole other life in another city.

It didn't end with that text. Kola went through his whole phone, and there were more bitches and more texts and phone calls dialed and received.

Kola snatched the bags out of the car and continued into the building and into her apartment. The kids were in the living room watching cartoons on the flat-screen. They jumped up and went to hug her, each one excited to see her home. She smiled at them, but inside, her heart had exploded into a million pieces. It felt like shards of glass cutting into her from the inside.

She went into the bedroom. Twin was finally awake and in the shower. She closed the bedroom door and sat at the foot of the bed. She stared pointlessly at the wall and fought back the tears about to escape.

She took a deep breath and held it in. *I'm not gonna allow it. I'm not*, she told herself. She took another deep breath and kept the anger and tears inside.

Twin emerged from the shower with a towel wrapped around his waist. "Hey, beautiful," he said with a smile.

He wanted to give her a kiss on the lips, but she shied away from him.

"Everything okay, baby?"

"Yeah, I'm okay," she said dryly. She didn't want to let on that she'd read all of his text messages from his bat phone, and seen who'd called and who he was calling. It took every ounce of control not to rise up and bash his fucking head in.

In fact, she had a better idea. She went ahead and had a family day with the kids and Twin.

The following morning, Twin packed a small bag and left for Baltimore.

Unbeknownst to him, Kola had a bag packed too. Baltimore was only three and a half hours away, so she got dolled up like a superstar and piled the kids into the Jeep Cherokee Twin had purchased for her and headed to B-more to give Twin the surprise of his life.

# TWENTY-NINE

Kola searched for Carmine's in Baltimore via Google. Through the wonder of GPS, she was able to put in the restaurant's address, and she was off.

She arrived at the restaurant late that night, around 9:30 p.m. The kids were sleeping in the backseat. At first, she drove around the harbor looking for Twin's car, but she didn't see it parked anywhere. Maybe it was in the garage. Or, maybe, he actually stood the bitch up. It was a fleeting thought, though.

She called his cell phone, but it went directly to voice mail. She decided to park across the street from the restaurant and wait. It was hard to keep cool knowing the man she loved was having an affair with a bitch out of state; driving three hours for some pussy.

So, she sat and waited, feeling trepidation and anger at the same time. She glanced back at Peaches, Eduardo Jr., and Sophia sleeping against each other underneath a blanket. She had the car idling and the heat on, trying to keep them warm. It was a shame they had to travel with her. They should have been sleeping in a warm bed.

Kola continued to sit and wait, every minute going by fueling her rage even more. She'd quit stripping because of him and gave up her own place to move in with him. She gave him her heart, and he used it, like Cross and Eduardo did before him.

The doors to Carmine's opened up at 10:25 p.m., and Twin came walking out with an entourage behind him, all of them laughing. Her eyes narrowed in on him. He peered around the place cautiously, while everyone else was oblivious. There was something extra serious about him.

Kola's heart started to beat fast. She wasn't about to drive three hours and simply watch him. Hell no! She jumped out of the car and stormed toward Twin and his entourage.

"You sonofabitch!" she screamed out, catching everyone's attention.

Twin turned and looked at her with nonchalance. And then his eyes widened. It looked like he had seen a ghost. "What?" he shot back.

"So this how you fuckin' do me, nigga? This is your fuckin' business in Baltimore?" Kola yelled. "You cheatin'-ass muthafucka! You nasty-ass whore!"

Twin looked around perplexed. "Yo, this a fuckin' joke, right?"

"Nigga, *you* are the fuckin' joke!"

Twin looked like he was in a daze. His minor entourage looked confused too.

Kola slapped the shit out of him.

"You crazy fuckin' bitch! What the fuck is wrong wit' you?"

Kola pulled out her pistol and aimed it at him. Part of his entourage swiftly went ducking for cover, while the others just stood there frozen.

"Yo, just put the gun away, and let's talk about this," he said coolly. He kept looking back over his shoulder, baffled.

"Fuck talkin'!"

Kola felt betrayed on so many levels. She thought that if she killed him, maybe she would get off for temporary insanity. She glared at Twin, tears trickling from her eyes.

The kids had woken up and exited the car. Now they were in the street staring at Kola holding a gun on Twin. They began screaming and crying, scared to death.

"Kola? Oh my God! Kola! Kola!" someone screamed.

Too much was going on in a short span of time.

Kola turned around toward the direction of the person screaming, and when she saw who it was, she turned white with shock. No, it couldn't be true. It couldn't be her. "Apple," she said faintly. She lowered the gun, her eyes on her twin sister. How was she alive? She had buried her next to her family. Apple? Why wasn't she dead? Was she real? She is real. Why hadn't she contacted her in all this time?

A series of questions flooded Kola's mind about the past until the present came rushing back.

*Is she also fucking Twin?*

At the moment, it didn't matter. The two embraced strongly, merging into one body.

"I thought you were dead! I thought you were dead!" Kola chanted. "Oh my God! I thought you were dead!"

Apple said, "I thought you were in Colombia!"

For a long moment, they hugged each other; not believing this was for real.

Twin couldn't believe his eyes. There were two of them.

The sisters' reunion became even more emotional when Apple pulled away from Kola and noticed the three kids standing behind her. She took one look at Peaches and knew she was her daughter.

Apple went over to her daughter, smiling widely. She couldn't take her eyes off her. "Peaches," she said in disbelief. She looked at Kola and she nodded. It seemed so unreal. It was the first time she had seen her daughter since giving birth to her five years earlier.

Apple dropped to her knees and pulled Peaches into her arms and hugged her tight. She cried like a baby. "How did you find her? Oh my God! How did you find her?"

"It wasn't easy," Kola said.

Apple kissed her cheeks and forehead.

Peaches looked confused, probably wondering why she had two mamas.

Apple didn't want to let Peaches go, afraid that she would disappear from her grasp and never be found again.

Kola looked at Twin and Apple. She wanted an explanation. The reunion was great, but there was Twin's infidelity.

If Twin didn't see it with his own eyes, then he wouldn't believe it. Sassy/Apple, she was a twin. He had a surprise of his own.

Kola wanted an explanation.

Twin smiled. He made a phone call and said, "Yo, it's me. You need to come down to the harbor right away. Yeah, it's important." He hung up and said, "Your explanation is on its way."

Fifteen minutes later, a cocaine-colored Lexus pulled up and parked. Who stepped out next took the sisters by surprise.

"No way," Kola uttered.

Twin was a twin too. There were two of them, Jamel and Kamel. Jamel was older by two minutes. He was dating Apple, and Kamel was dating Kola. No one could believe twin brothers actually hooked up with twin sisters in different states. It was unbelievable.

Come to find out, Jamel had left his cell phone in Kamel's beamer after their last meeting, and Apple had texted him. The mishap was all squared away.

They quickly got acquainted with each other.

That night, Apple and Kola got a nice hotel room for them and the children, without the men, to catch up. They had a lot to talk about.

Apple wanted to sleep in the same bed with her daughter. She wasn't about to let Peaches out of her sight. She just wanted to hold her close and look at her cute little face.

# THIRTY

In their hotel room, Apple and Kola talked about everything. Each wanted to know what was going on with each other. Kola wanted to know how Apple was alive. What happened in Miami? Who did she bury? And Apple wanted to know what happened in Colombia, how Kola got to America and where was Eduardo.

Apple explained that she, Cartier, and Citi had faked their deaths after paying off a coroner. Their war with the Gonzales Cartel was getting too hot. They liquidated their assets and put everything they owned into a storage facility on the outskirts of the city to make a clean getaway. Only, Citi double-crossed them both, running off with the money.

"You sure Cartier didn't have anything to do with it?" Kola asked.

Apple shook her head. "Nah. She was just as shocked as I was. Come on now, how long we've known Cartier? She's good peoples."

Kola agreed. "You know you can't let this shit go. This Citi bitch violated you and needs to be taught a lesson."

"Six feet deep," Apple replied. "I swear on Nichols' grave that I'ma find that bitch and put her six feet deep."

Kola listened attentively.

Apple then talked about her time in Baltimore, keeping a low profile, getting two jobs, changing her identity. She also gave details about how she met Jamel, or Twin.

It was Kola's turn to tell Apple about the mistreatment in Colombia, the constant affairs Eduardo was having with other women, being locked up in a women's prison and the harsh treatment, and the reason she had Eduardo Jr. and Sophia. She didn't hold back any punches. She even talked about the five million dollars she'd left behind in Colombia.

"Five million?" Apple said, incredulous.

"Yes, five million dollars."

"Do you have any plans on how to get it?"

"So far, not one."

They'd had their differences in the past, but now they felt closer than ever.

The sisters finished off a bottle of champagne and shared a cigarette in the adjacent hotel room.

Apple said. "We both went through a lot, I see."

"I know." Kola looked into her sister's eyes. "Whatever our differences were in the past, our constant bickering and warring with each other. I want to dead that. We're older now and we're all we got. When I thought you were dead, it killed me. We have to promise to never allow anything or anyone to come between us."

Apple agreed. "I love you, Kola. And I've made mistakes with you"—Apple looked down toward the floor—"and Nichols. I want to make it up to you and prove that I've changed. I'm different now. I see things differently, and I can never be anything but grateful to you for all you've done for Peaches."

Kola smiled. She felt whole again.

Apple continued. "And what are the odds of us dating identical twins?"

"Crazy! I didn't know what was going on. I thought Kamel was cheating on me, so I packed our shit, drove down here to whup a bitch ass."

Apple laughed. "I feel you. I probably would've done the same thing."

"We both fell in love again, huh?"

"I guess we did." Apple downed her drink. She then stood up and peered into the next room where the kids were sleeping on the same bed. They all looked like angels.

"I thought I would never see her again," Apple said softly with the gaze of a happy mother looking on her child. She then turned to Kola and said, "Thank you."

Kola smiled.

"How did you find her?"

"Long story."

"I want to hear it," Apple said.

Kola told her sister about the money and the manpower Eduardo applied everywhere to help find

Peaches. He didn't spare any expense locating the little girl.

Apple continuing gazing at her sleeping daughter, and she wanted to lie in the bed next to her child, like she'd done last night.

She and Kola continued to converse.

"About these twins, I thought it was hard to tell us apart, but damn it, how can we tell which one is which?"

"Well, I'm not calling my man Twin anymore. I'm gonna start calling him by his real name—Kamel."

"You know what, I agree with you, sis, and I'm gonna start calling Twin, Jamel. Referring to them by their birth names can make it much easier on us."

"Cheers to that," Kola said, raising her hand, and they both clinked glasses.

Their week together in the hotel became awkward. It was taking some time for Peaches to warm up to Apple, who was upset to hear her call Kola mama. They beefed about that, and Kola realized that Apple hadn't changed at all. Her being upset wasn't reasonable. Kola felt that all that grateful talk went out the window. Kola couldn't understand why Apple had to harp on "names or titles." Big deal that Peaches called her mama, especially when everyone thought her real mother was dead. Apple couldn't understand why Kola had Peaches calling her mama instead of aunty from the gate. But then Peaches started to warm up to Apple, slowly.

Apple wanted to be with her daughter, and Kola understood. Apple was always competitive with Kola and wanted to win Peaches' heart away from her sister. She decided to move to New York from Baltimore to establish a stronger relationship with Peaches.

"I just need to be closer to my daughter, Jamel. You need to understand that." Apple said.

"What about what we got goin' on in B-more—what we started in this city?"

"My daughter is more important."

"I thought I was important too!"

"You are, but I haven't seen my little girl in five years, since she was born."

"Then move her here with you!"

Apple shook her head. "She's through been too much. I can't uproot her from all she's known until she can trust me and love me on her own."

Jamel smirked. "Then let her come through on the weekends until y'all get tight."

"You know what, Jamel—I'll be damn if I let any nigga drive a wedge between her and me. Do you fuckin' understand? This is my kid!"

"Yeah, I understand." Jamel looked at Apple like she'd lost her mind. "I gave you a second chance, thought we were a team, and you do this to me?"

"It's for my daughter, and you need to understand that. And I'm not leaving you; I'm still here, Jamel. It's us. It will always be us."

"You know, I liked it better when you called me Twin."

"Well, that was yesterday."

"Shit changing now, since you got your sister and your daughter back into your life, huh?"

Apple continued to pack her things into her suitcase.

Twin continued to gripe. "Kola the one putting ideas in your head for you to move back to New York with her, right?"

"Leave my sister out of this, Jamel. This is my choice."

"I want you here, ma." He began to pout. He hated not having his way. All his tantrum was really about was control and ego. Truthfully, with Apple farther out of town, it would leave room for him to continue his whoring. Maybe now he could fuck with this bitch named Jazz that worked at the bar where Apple used to bartend.

"Well, I can't stay. This is important to me, and you need to understand that."

Jamel helplessly watched as Apple prepared for a move to New York.

"You know, instead of complaining, why you don't move to New York with us? Your brother is already up there. It won't hurt."

"Me and my brother are two different people. We twins, but he ain't me, and I ain't him."

Apple looked at her man with uncertainty. She didn't want to argue with him about something frivolous. She was with family again. It was a dream coming true, and no dick was going to fuck that up.

They all were fortunate enough to get a second chance, and in life she knew that was rare.

Jamel had started to despise Kola. They had bumped heads on a variety of things. He was always starting with her, being petty and emotional because he was jealous of his brother. He also resented her because he wanted to fuck her and knew she was off limits. Although Apple was beautiful, the faint scar on her face that used to give Apple character, now made her appear imperfect. Now Jamel felt Apple was a 9 ½ and Kola was the perfect 10.

Kola felt Jamel was borderline psychotic and superficial and wasn't right for her sister. She hated him. He was nothing like Kamel. She wasn't shy about expressing her feelings to Apple, who resented her for speaking out. But in the back of Apple's mind, she knew her sister was right. There was something about Jamel that was dubious. There was something about Kamel, when the twins were together, that stood out. If they were horses in a race, Kamel would cross that finish line first. He was the thoroughbred of the two—the one investors wanted to breed—and Kola had his heart.

Kamel went out of town a few days for business, leaving Kola alone with the kids. Apple decided to take them to the movies. She wanted to spend some quality time with them.

With Apple taking the kids to the movies, Kola had some time for herself. Missing her man, she walked around the apartment in one of his T-shirts that was scented with his cologne. His apartment felt still without him and the children around. He was expected to be back sometime the following day. Kola couldn't wait to see, feel, and fuck her man again.

She was grateful that Kamel was nothing like his brother. Even though they both were drug dealers and gangsters, Kamel was the nicer one—more caring and understanding.

Kola ran some bath water. She grabbed a bottle of champagne and a long-stemmed glass and set the bathroom up with a few scented candles. Her plan was to listen to some R&B, submerge herself into the tub and enjoy some Moët.

Before she could get naked and enjoy the soothing water in the bathroom, there was a knock at the door. She wasn't expecting any company.

"Always something," she said, tying her white robe together. She put on a pair of slippers and went to see who was knocking. She looked through the peephole and smiled.

It was Kamel. He was back early.

She quickly opened the door and didn't question why he was home a day early and knocking on his own door. *Maybe, he forgot his keys.*

"Baby, you're back early," she said, throwing her arms around her man.

"Hey, baby. Missed you."

They kissed passionately.

Kamel stepped inside the apartment, his arms still wrapped around Kola. Gazing at her with warmth and longing, his eyes showed absolute hunger.

"Where's everyone?"

"My sister took them to a movie, so you came back just in time, baby. We have the entire place to ourselves."

"Ooooh, I like the sound of that."

"I knew you would."

Kamel started to stroke her body as his brown eyes continued to gaze deep into hers. As she held his stare, she put his finger into her mouth, sucking it.

"Baby, let me see what you workin' wit' under that robe."

"Damn, baby! You act like you never saw it before."

"I can never get tired of lookin' at that body. That's why I love you."

Kola smiled. She untied her robe, revealing to him her naked flesh.

He ran his hand over her breasts, caressing each hardening nipple. Then he stroked a hand up and down her leg, making her yearn for him to place something special in between them. He picked her up into his arms and carried her into the bedroom.

"I had a bath running," she said.

"Well, the bath can wait. I want a piece of my beauty.

I got in mind to get something else wet someplace different."

She laughed.

Kamel looked at Kola like he wanted to eat her. Inside the bedroom, he said in his husky voice, "Now take it off."

She did.

"Now turn around. Give me a twirl."

She did, showing off her magnificent figure to Kamel. He couldn't control himself any longer. He joined her on the bed. She ran his hand over his crotch, wanting to unzip him.

They kissed again. Their tongues entwined, fighting a glorious war of dominance. She felt his fingers on her and then inside of her.

Kamel quickly shed his clothing.

His fingers gently stroked the side of her neck, caressing her. She wanted him so much. He lay down next to her and she was so wet. Kamel placed his mouth and lips around her breasts and kissed them. She felt his strong fingers stroking her back and around to the front.

He caressed her gently between her thighs. "I wanna fuck you," he growled into her ear.

Kola was quivering all over, trembling with lust and desire. "I got a treat for you first," she said. She shifted into a comfortable position, eager to take Kamel's hard dick into her mouth.

First, she stroked his dick, slowly moving her hand up and down, being more deliberate with each stroke. Then she placed her lips around his dick. She licked his hard length from his nut sack to his tip.

"Oh shit!"

"You like that?"

"Baby, you know I do."

Kola tightened her lips and kissed and sucked his scrumptious dick, lubricating it with her full, wet lips, sliding them up and down.

Kamel sat back and enjoyed the show. He unclenched and clenched his fist as Kola increased her rhythm. She could feel his pre-come on her tongue. She felt him stiffen and quiver as her tongue licked around his mushroom tip, his dick pulsating in her hand.

"You're wonderful, ma."

For a moment, Kola wondered where the 'ma' had come from. Usually, he called her 'beautiful,' but she didn't give it a second thought. She continued to suck his dick.

"I wanna fuck you, baby."

"Your wish is my command."

Kola spread her legs, and Kamel climbed on top of her. He roughly penetrated her, slamming his dick into her at full throttle. Usually, he was gentler and more passionate with his strokes inside of her, but the dick still felt good. Kamel then pulled out of Kola and flipped her over and fucked her from the back, doggy style. He thrust hard, sinking his cock deep into her, until he came inside of her.

Kola clamped her arms around him. "Damn! That was different."

"I know." He smiled.

Kamel stood up and started to get dressed. Usually, he liked to cuddle and would nestle himself against Kola. The way he looked at her this time made her feel like a piece of meat. She couldn't put her finger on it, but something had changed about him. Everything was right about him, from the tattoo to the dick, but she had a strange feeling.

What she was unaware of was that Kamel and Jamel had purposely tattooed the same images on their bodies, so that if one ever caught a case, bringing in the identical twin with the same marking could cause enough reasonable doubt.

"I gotta make a run."

"Run? You just got home, baby. Where are you going now?"

"I got business to take care of." He threw on his jacket and headed for the front door.

Kola tried to follow behind him, but he was moving too swiftly. Something wasn't right. She knew it. She called out, "Kamel!"

When the door closed, Kola feared she'd done the unthinkable. *No, I didn't,* she thought, trying not to panic.

"No, I didn't," she repeated.

Her worst nightmare came true when Kamel arrived home the next day, using his keys to enter the apartment and he didn't have any recollection about the previous day.

Kola wanted to throw up. She'd fucked Jamel. How could she have been so stupid? How could she not know it wasn't him?

"Hey, beautiful. You missed me?" Kamel asked, placing a loving and sweet kiss on her lips.

"I did."

Now Kola was torn on whether or not to tell Kamel. She decided not to. She felt that if she told him, he would probably murder his brother.

But that didn't bother her as much as what would happen between her and Apple when it got out that she accidentally fucked Jamel. Once it got out, she was sure that her now mended relationship with her sister, with both of them trying to put the past behind them, would suddenly come to an end. Apple would blame her for everything.

# THIRTY-ONE

With Apple now in New York, she and Kola began to build lives that didn't include them being directly in the drug game. Apple couldn't afford to leave her child an orphan. After so many years away from her, she wasn't trying to lose Peaches again.

Kola started to see growth in her sister as a mother. She convinced Kamel to put in her share on a five-bedroom apartment that she and Apple wanted to buy in lower Manhattan. Apple had her own cash to invest. Kamel gave Kola the cash without any problem at all. This apartment would only be for them and the kids, which Kamel understood and respected.

Eduardo Jr. and Sophia were learning English very well, and Kola had improved her Spanish. Even Apple was willing to learn Spanish.

*"De nada,"* Peaches said, trying to teach her mother and aunt Spanish.

*"De nada,"* the sisters repeated.

"You know what that means?"

"Please tell, Peaches," they both said.

"It means you're welcome, like don't mention it. And *fue un placer* means it was a pleasure. And *con gusto* means with pleasure."

"My baby is so smart," Apple proudly announced.

"She is."

~

After a year, everyone started to settle into their own lives. The kids were growing up. And Apple and Kola wanted to start their own business. They were still dating the twins, and Kola continued to keep her secret that she'd fucked Jamel by accident.

Apple and Kola loved their new apartment in downtown Manhattan—five bedrooms and four and a half bathrooms in a pricey neighborhood. An elegant foyer opened to the spacious living room, formal dining room, and windowed modern kitchen with concrete countertops. The sweep of space provided for gracious living and entertainment for everyone. The hallway led to the private bedroom quarters, comprised of split bedrooms, including the master bedroom with en suite marble bath, and a second renovated bathroom.

Together, Apple and Kola were content with their living arrangement. Sometimes they would talk about their past, and sometimes they wouldn't, depending on what was brought up, especially when it came to Nichols. But their rekindled relationship was making them stronger.

For the kids, they were making things work and doing things right. Eduardo still called, but picking up for his calls once week became once a month and the letters and photos from Kola to Eduardo, Maria and Marisol had slowed down tremendously. When Kola did pick up for Eduardo she tried to fake her feelings and make him feel loved and wanted and missed, but it was hard. Eduardo felt her slipping away, and he would beef about it. From her end of the line, Kola would be rolling her eyes. How quickly she forgot all the wonderful things Eduardo had done for her—the opulent lifestyle, maids, mansions, unlimited funds, getting her niece back, and most importantly paying a huge ransom for her release.

Eduardo was still locked up in a Colombian prison. He was becoming her past, as her feelings for him shifted to a younger man. Kola found her own way to survive and make it happen, and it came to the point where she wasn't expecting anything from him. She believed that his empire had crumbled, that his power had faded.

Besides, she was in love with Kamel, and she wanted to be with him. He was there for her and her kids. She didn't want to lose him.

But then, one day, out the blue, there was a knock at the door. Everyone was in the kitchen enjoying lunch. The sisters weren't expecting company.

Kola removed herself from the kitchen and went to answer the door. When she looked through the peephole, she saw a man in a black suit with a briefcase. She had no idea who he was.

"What do you want?"

"I'm looking for a Kola," the man said.

"Speaking."

"I have something for you," the man said, "from Eduardo."

Kola became flustered. *Eduardo?* She took a deep breath and slowly opened the door. She invited the stranger inside.

By now, Apple entered the room and kept her eyes on the stranger. She had her pistol on her, just in case it wasn't a pleasant visit. She was ready to pump holes into the man if he tried anything funny.

"I have something for you, from Eduardo," he repeated.

It had been over a year. Kola didn't expect anything from him at all. She had given up hope.

The man took a seat on the couch and placed the briefcase on their glass coffee table. "You have a nice home," he said.

"Thank you."

Apple chimed, "Why are you here?"

The stranger didn't answer her question. He leaned forward and unlatched the briefcase to reveal the contents inside. It was money, lots of it. Apple and Kola were taken aback.

Kola asked the man, "How much?"

"Six hundred thousand dollars."

"How? I thought Eduardo was—how could he afford this?"

"My client has very reasonable means, and as you Americans say, 'it's not over until it's over.' Well, it's not over. And my client always keeps his promises."

Kola went to the briefcase. It was still hard to believe Eduardo actually came through for her after so many months went by, and their phone conversations were becoming sparser. Eduardo never ceased to amaze Kola. She'd done as he asked, and now he was doing exactly what he'd promised to do. Though Kamel was supporting her, it was always great to have more money coming in.

One thing worried Kola. How did Eduardo find out where she lived so quickly? They'd just moved in, and she didn't share her new address with anyone. It meant Eduardo still had unlimited power and could reach her even from a prison cell in Colombia.

Apple looked at Kola and the stranger talking. She kept quiet. She had her own secret to keep. In a way, she was impressed, but also jealous. She wanted to tell Kola that she'd fucked Eduardo, mostly to get back at her for taking Cross from her. She still harbored some resentment, but now that they were moving on with their lives in a positive way, she fought to hold it in.

# THIRTY-TWO

Jamel hurried into the building with blood on his sneakers and a smoking gun in his hand. He frowned as he rushed into the apartment he was sharing with Kamel in New York.

He had fired the first shot. His temper got the best of him, and two men were dead, their bodies sprawled out in the middle of a cold Brooklyn Street. One of the men killed was Mack D's nineteen-year-old son, and the other was a trusted lieutenant.

Jamel knocked frantically on the apartment door, his breathing heavy. He was a mess with sweat, blood, and a torn shirt. His eyes were wild and crazed. He felt he did what needed to be done. They couldn't go on forever doing business with a selfish tyrant like Mack D. Something had to be done. He refused to continued being shaken down by that man.

Kamel was on the sofa smoking a cigarette and on the phone with Kola. He heard the banging at his door and stood up. Picking up his pistol from the table, he said to Kola, "Beautiful, let me call you right back. Somebody knocking at my door."

"Okay."

Kamel approached the door carefully and looked through the peephole to see who it was. It was Jamel, looking crazy. He opened the door, and Jamel came flying into the place like he was escaping from hell.

"I fucked up, Kamel," he said.

Kamel took in his brother's appearance and instantly knew something terrible went down. "What the fuck did you do?" he asked, worried.

"I fucked up. I was tryin' to make it better for us, get us to the top."

Kamel exclaimed loudly, "What the fuck did you do?"

"I just murdered Mack D's son and his lieutenant."

"You did what?" Kamel yelled, grabbing Kamel by his shirt collar and slamming him against the living room wall.

"I did it for us, so we can get ahead. I tried to go after Mack D. I thought it was him, but it was his son."

"You fuckin' idiot!"

"Nigga, at least I had the balls to try something!" Jamel said heatedly. "I ain't just about to sit around and continue being used and played by that muthafucka! Everybody wants him gone. I just had the heart to try and make it happen."

"You killed us, man. You fucking killed us."

"Nigga, he bleeds just like everyone else. Who the fuck is Mack D?"

Kamel, looking despondent, took a few steps away from his brother. The last thing he wanted was a bloody war.

Jamel and Kamel never did business together, but they both bought kilos from Mack D. The second time Kamel went to cop, Mack D claimed the count was short five large. They both were being played and extorted by the man and his goons. The twins wanted their respect, especially Jamel, who was the hothead. They talked about going after Mack D, but Kamel was against it, knowing the bloodshed it would create. Going to war with Mack D and his army, he felt, would be a losing battle. But Jamel wasn't trying to hear him. He had a grand vision of taking over everything and wearing the crown.

"I thought it was him, so I made a move. It wasn't. I fucked up, but we can turn this into our favor, Kamel. We can show the streets how we're built," Jamel reasoned.

Kamel took a seat on the couch and refused to look at his twin brother.

Jamel walked over and said, "Yo, this nigga ain't a fuckin' god. Yo, he can get got, and we can be the ones to get him, and you know what? The world is ours."

Kamel didn't want to listen to his brother. He was always thinking about the future and knew with every action, there was always a reaction. With the death of Mack D's son, the streets from New York to the South were about to run red.

Kamel stood up while his brother continued talking, trying to explain. He went into his bedroom and closed the door behind him, knowing, most likely, it was the beginning of the end.

As Kamel predicted, Mack D wasn't going to take the death of his son lying down. A week later, four men were brutally gunned down in cold blood in Brooklyn in retaliation for his son's death. The twins had a high contract on their heads, and everyone was going underground. Week after week, shootings and killings happened on both sides.

Jamel was like a general in charge, leading his troops into war, promising victory and riches once Mack D was dead.

The sudden war didn't just affect those in the game, but families and civilians too. One night, Apple, Kola, and the kids were arriving home from seeing a movie. Unbeknownst to them, they had been followed from the movie theater. As they were walking into the building, a black minivan sped their way, the doors slid back, and gunfire erupted from the vehicle, sending bullets flying everywhere.

After the smoke cleared, everyone was okay. No one, thank God, had been hit. But Apple and Kola were furious.

Kola immediately called Kamel, and he rushed over with Jamel. Kola constantly worried about Kamel. She loved him so much. Everything around them went from utopia to dystopia. Things were too dangerous for anyone to breathe easily, no matter where they were.

It got so bad in New York and Baltimore, Kola was tempted to reach out for help from Eduardo. She figured he was the only force strong enough to match Mack D's strength. She had seen his handiwork, and it wasn't pretty.

Kola knew it was risky. If Eduardo found out that she got involved in a war in the States for the man she was in love with, he would surely have Kamel murdered, and probably her too. And if he found out that his kids were affected by this war, there wouldn't be any "probably." Kola and Kamel would be dead.

She discussed this with Kamel.

"I'm a fuckin' man, Kola," he said. "And I don't need another man fighting my battles. I can handle my own business. I can take care of us and the kids."

Kamel also felt a little jealous about Eduardo. He suspected that Kola still loved him to some extent. For her to go to another man to handle his beef had him feeling insecure and less than a man.

He now wanted to lock down Kola to not only prove to himself, but to Eduardo as well that she loved Kamel and *only* him. Kamel proposed to Kola, presenting her a 7 caret flawless emerald cut diamond set in platinum engagement ring with a price tag of $50,000.

"Will you marry me?" he asked, down on one knee and looking up at her.

"Yes!"

Kola knew they could never make their engagement official, but for now, Kamel was satisfied.

# EPILOGUE

With the bloodshed, the violence, and the chaos, Apple and Kola decided to have a day out with the kids. They all went to the amusement park in Coney Island to have a good time, enjoy the rides, the games, the boardwalk, and the beach. The park was crowded on a gentle spring day.

The children were laughing and eager to try every ride in the park, even the fast, dizzying ones, and eat all the cotton candy they could. It was a day the sisters needed together. With everything going on, they wanted to get away from it all for several hours.

Peaches was wide-eyed at the large stuffed teddy bears presented by the carnival games as an inducement to try your luck at a game of chance or skill. She slipped her hand free from Apple's and ran off into the crowd toward the colorful, eye-catching balloons a man was giving away.

"Peaches!" Apple called out after her.

The man said to Peaches, "You want one of these little ones?"

Peaches nodded.

He placed the string to the balloon into Peaches' hand, and she smiled.

"Give it back, Peaches," Apple said, hurrying to take her daughter's hand again.

The stranger took Peaches' hand into his and walked toward the sisters. He looked Dominican, late forties, dark skin, soft, curly salt-and-pepper hair, and was dressed nicely in a suit.

He seemed harmless from afar, but the sisters came from a world of danger and deception, where they learned to trust no one, no matter what they looked like.

Kola was on her cell phone. She took a call from Eduardo, who always seemed to have wrong timing.

Apple trained her eyes on the man now holding her daughter's hand and walking their way. "Oh my God!" she said under her breath, noticing his gun subtly aimed at Peaches. He didn't create any chaos as he moved in her direction with coolness and a smile.

Kola was oblivious to what was going on at first. But then she noticed the trouble too and suddenly became speechless while on the phone with Eduardo.

The crowd in the park, and around the sisters, was unaware of what was going on. They didn't see the gun, so they didn't feel threatened. Everything went on as normal.

The sisters soon realized thugs, their guns discreetly hidden from the unsuspecting public, surrounded them.

One gunman composedly walked up to the sisters, who were now glaring at the threat, and said to them, "Ladies, I think y'all should formally meet my boss—Mack D."

Mack D continued to casually walk their way. He took his time, strolling and breathing in the beach air while holding Peaches' hand with no concerns or worries at all.

Apple kept her eyes on her daughter, ready to protect her.

Kola was trying to think on her feet. She could still hear Eduardo on the phone. What should she do? Scream to him for help? But how could he help her at this particular moment from Colombia?

Eduardo said, "So my wife is engaged to a dead man?"

Kola was taken aback. She couldn't speak. She couldn't even process the threat on Kamel's life when hers was now in danger.

As Mack D continued to approach with Peaches, the sisters finally got a good look at the perpetrator very closely, and they were in awe. It couldn't be. After all this time, it was him.

Apple spoke first, simply saying, "Daddy?"